RANDOM
HOUSE
LARGE
PRINT

THE THIRD GATE

THE THIRD GATE

· A NOVEL ·

LINCOLN CHILD

R A N D O M   H O U S E
L A R G E   P R I N T

Copyright © 2012 by Lincoln Child

All rights reserved.
Published in the United States of America by
Random House Large Print in association with
Doubleday, New York.
Distributed by Random House, Inc., New York.

Cover design and illustration by Will Staehle

The excerpt on page 45 is from **The White Nile** by Alan Moorehead, published by HarperCollins Publishers, Inc.

The Library of Congress has established a Cataloging-in-Publication record for this title.

ISBN: 978-0-7393-7835-9

www.randomhouse.com/largeprint

FIRST LARGE PRINT EDITION

Printed in the United States of America

10 9 8 7 6 5 4 3 2 1

This Large Print edition published in accord with the standards of the N.A.V.H.

To Luchie

THE THIRD GATE

PROLOGUE

The doctor helped himself to a cup of coffee in the break room, reached for the cylinder of powdered creamer on a nearby counter, thought better of it, then poured in some soy milk from the battered lab refrigerator instead. Stirring the coffee with a plastic swizzle, he walked across the pale linoleum floor to a cluster of identical heavy-sided chairs. The usual sounds filtered through the door: the rattling of wheelchairs and gurneys, bleats and beeps of instrumentation, the drone of the hospital intercom.

A third-year resident named Deguello had sprawled his lanky limbs across two of the threadbare chairs. **Typical,** thought the doctor—a resident's ability to fall asleep instantly, vertical or horizontal, in no matter how uncomfortable a position. As the doctor settled into a chair beside him, the resident stopped his faint snoring and opened one eye.

"Hey, Doc," he murmured. "What time is it?"

The doctor glanced up at the industrial clock, set over the line of lockers along the far wall. "Ten forty-five."

"God," Deguello groaned. "That means I've only been asleep ten minutes."

"At least you've managed some," the doctor said, sipping his coffee. "It's a quiet night."

Deguello closed the eye again. "Two myocardial infarctions. An open-skull fracture. An emergency C-section. Two gunshot victims, one critical. A third-degree burn case. A knife wound with renal penetration. One simple and one compound fracture. An old gent who stroked out on the gurney. Oxycodone OD. Meth OD. Amphetamine OD. And those were all in"—he paused—"the last ninety minutes."

The doctor took another sip of coffee. "Like I said—quiet night. But look on the bright side. You could still be doing grand rounds at Mass General."

The resident was quiet for a moment. "I still don't understand, Doc," he mumbled. "Why do you do this? Sacrifice yourself on the ER altar every other Friday. I mean, I've got no choice. But you're a big-time anesthesiologist."

The doctor drained his cup, tossed it in the trash. "A little less curiosity in the presence of your betters, please." He pushed himself to his feet. "Back into the trenches."

Out in the hallway, the doctor glanced around at the relative calm. He started toward the operations desk on the far side of the ER when he suddenly noticed an increased bustle of activity. The head nurse came jogging up. "Car accident," she told him. "One victim, arriving momentarily. I've set aside Trauma Two."

The doctor immediately turned toward the indicated bay. As he did so, the trauma doors buzzed open again and a paramedic team wheeled in a stretcher, followed by two police officers. Instantly, the doctor could see this was serious: the urgency of their actions, their expressions, the blood on their coats and faces, all telegraphed desperation.

"Female, thirtysomething!" one of the paramedics bawled out. "Unresponsive!"

Immediately, the doctor waved them in and turned to a waiting intern. "Get a suture cart." The intern nodded and jogged away.

"And call Deguello and Corbin!" he called after him.

The paramedics were already wheeling the stretcher into Trauma Two and positioning it beside the table. "On me," said a nurse as they circled the body. "Careful with that neck collar. One, two, **three**!" The patient was lifted onto the table, the stretcher pushed away. The doctor got a glimpse of pale white skin; cinnamon hair; a blouse, once white, now soaked with blood. More blood made a drip trail on the floor, leading back toward the trauma area.

Something alarming, like a cold electric current, began to tingle in the back of his brain.

"She was T-boned by a drunk driver," one of the paramedics said in his ear. "Coded once on the way in."

Interns piled in, followed by Deguello. "You got a type?" the doctor asked.

The paramedic nodded. "O negative."

People were busy now, attaching monitors, hanging new IV lines, trundling in crash carts. The doctor turned toward an intern. "Get the blood bank, call for three units." He thought of the spatter trail across the linoleum. "No, make it four."

"O2's full," called out one nurse as Corbin hurried in.

Deguello came around to the head of the table, peered down at the motionless victim. "Looks cyanotic."

"Get a blood gas in here," the doctor rapped. His attention was fixed on the woman's abdomen, now bared but slick with blood. Quickly, he peeled back the temporary dressing. A dreadful open wound, hastily sutured by the paramedics, was bleeding copiously. He turned toward a nurse and pointed to the area. She swabbed it and he looked again.

"Massive abdominal trauma," he said. "Possible supine subpulmonary pneumothorax. We're going to need a pericardial tap." He turned toward the paramedic. "What the hell caused this? What about the air bag?"

"Slid beneath it," the man said. "Dashboard snapped in two like a twig and she got hung up on it. They had to come in from the top with the Jaws. Awful scene, man, her Porsche was totally flattened by that drunk bastard's SUV."

Porsche. The cold little current in his head tingled more sharply. He straightened up, trying to get a view of the head, but Deguello was in his way. "Significant blunt trauma," Deguello said. "We're gonna need a head CT."

"BP's down to eighty over thirty-five," said a nurse. "Pulse ox is seventy-nine."

"Maintain compression!" Deguello ordered.

The exsanguination was too great, the shock too severe: they had a minute, maybe two at most, to save her. Another nurse came in, hanging blood packs on the IV rack. "That's not going to do it," the doctor said. "We're gonna need a large-bore IV—she's bleeding out too fast."

"One milligram epi," Corbin told an intern.

The nurse turned to the suture cart, grabbed a larger needle, pulled the woman's limp hand forward to insert it. As she did so, the doctor's gaze fell upon the hand: slim, very pale. The hand bore a single ring: a platinum wedding band inlaid with a beautiful star sapphire, whiskey colored against a field of black. Sri Lankan, very expensive. He knew, because he'd purchased it.

Suddenly, a sharp tone sounded throughout the trauma room. "Full arrest!" cried a nurse.

For a moment, the doctor just stood there, paralyzed by horror and frozen disbelief. Deguello turned toward one of the interns, and now the doctor could see the woman's face: hair matted and askew, eyes open and staring, mouth and nose obscured by the breathing equipment.

His dry mouth worked. "Jennifer," he croaked.

"Losing vitals!" cried the nurse.

"We need lido!" Corbin called. "Lido! **Stat!**"

And then, as quickly as it had come, the paralysis fell away. The doctor wheeled toward a hovering ER nurse. "Defib!" he cried.

She raced to a far corner of the room, wheeled the cart back. "Charging."

An intern approached, injected the lidocaine, stepped back. The doctor grabbed the paddles, barely able to control his trembling hands. This couldn't be happening. It had to be a dream, just a bad dream. He'd wake up and he'd be in the break room, slumped over, Deguello snoring in the next chair.

"Charged!" the nurse called out.

"Clear!" The doctor heard the desperate edge in his own voice. As the workers fell back he placed the paddles on her bare, bloody chest, applied the current. Jennifer's body stiffened, then fell back onto the table.

"Flatline!" cried the nurse monitoring the vitals.

"Charge it again!" he called. A fresh beeping, low and insistent, added its voice to the cacophony.

"Hypovolemic shock," Deguello muttered. "We never had a chance."

They don't know, the doctor thought, as if from a million miles away. **They don't understand.** He felt a single tear gather in his eye and begin to trickle down his cheek.

"Recharged!" the defib nurse said.

He reapplied the paddles. Jennifer's body jumped once again.

"No response," said the intern at his side.

"That's it," Corbin said with a sigh. "Guess you need to call it, Ethan."

Instead, the doctor threw the paddles aside and began heart massage. He felt her body, unresponsive and cool, moving sluggishly under the sharp motions of his hands.

"Pupils fixed and dilated," the monitoring nurse said.

But the doctor paid no attention, his heart massage growing increasingly violent and desperate.

The sound in the trauma room, which had been growing increasingly frantic, now began to die away. "Zero cardiac activity," said the nurse.

"You'd better pronounce her," said Corbin.

"No!" the doctor snapped.

The entire room turned at the anguish in his voice.

"Ethan?" Corbin asked wonderingly.

But instead of responding, the doctor began to cry. Everyone around him went still, some staring in incomprehension, others looking away in embarrassment. Everyone except one of the interns, who opened the door and walked silently down the corridor. The doctor, still crying, knew where the man was going. He was going to get a shroud.

1

THREE YEARS LATER

Growing up in Westport, currently teaching at Yale, Jeremy Logan thought himself familiar with his home state of Connecticut. But the stretch through which he now drove was a revelation. Heading east from Groton—following the e-mailed directions—he'd turned onto US 1 and then, just past Stonington, onto US 1 Alternate. Hugging the gray Atlantic coastline, he'd passed Wequetequock, rolled over a bridge that looked as old as New England itself, then turned sharply right onto a well-paved but unmarked road. Quite abruptly, the minimalls and tourist motels fell away behind. He passed a sleepy cove in which lobster boats bobbed at anchor, and then entered an equally sleepy hamlet. And yet it was a real village, a working village, with a general store and a tackle shop and an Episcopal church with a steeple three sizes too large, and gray-shingled houses with trim picket fences painted white. There were no hulking SUVs, no out-of-state plates; and the scattering of people sitting on benches or leaning out of front windows waved to him as he passed. The April sunlight was strong, and the sea air had a clean, fresh bite to it. A signboard hanging from the doorframe of the post office informed him he was in Pevensey Point, population 182. Something about the place reminded him irresistibly of Herman Melville.

"Karen," he said, "if you'd seen this place, you'd never have made us buy that summer cottage in Hyannis."

Although his wife had died of cancer years ago, Logan still allowed himself to converse with her now and then. Of course it was usually—though not always—more monologue than conversation. At first, he'd been sure to do it only when he was certain not to be overheard. But then—as what had started as a kind of intellectual hobby for him turned increasingly into a profession—he no longer bothered to be so discreet. These days, judging by what he did for a living, people expected him to be a little strange.

Two miles beyond the town, precisely as the directions indicated, a narrow lane led off to the right. Taking it, Logan found himself in a sandy forest of thin scrub pine that soon gave way to tawny dunes. The dunes ended at a metal bridge leading to a low, broad island jutting out into Fishers Island Sound. Even from this distance, Logan could see there were at least a dozen structures on the island, all built of the same reddish-brown stone. At the center were three large five-story buildings that resembled dormitories, arranged in parallel, like dominos. At the far end of the island, partly concealed by the various structures, was an empty airstrip. And beyond everything lay the ocean and the dark green line of Rhode Island.

Logan drove the final mile, stopping at a gatehouse before the bridge. He showed the printed e-mail to the guard inside, who smiled and waved him through. A single sign beside the gatehouse, expensive looking but unobtrusive, read simply CTS.

He crossed the bridge, passed an outlying structure, and pulled into a parking lot. It was surprisingly large: there were at least a hundred cars and space for as many more. Nosing into one of the spots, he killed the engine. But instead of exiting, he paused to read the e-mail once again.

Jeremy,

I'm pleased—and relieved—to hear of your acceptance. I also appreciate your being flexible, since as I mentioned earlier there's no way yet to know how long your investigation will take. In any case, you'll receive a minimum of two weeks' compensation, at the rate you specified. I'm sorry I can't give you more details at this point, but you're probably used to that. And I have to tell you I can't wait to see you again after all this time.

Directions to the Center are below. I'll be waiting for you on the morning of the 18th. Any time between ten and noon will be fine. One other thing: once you're on board with the project, you might find it hard to get calls out with any degree of certainty, so please be sure you've cleared your decks before you arrive. Looking forward to the 18th!

Best,
E. R.

Logan glanced at his watch: eleven thirty. He turned the note over once in his hands. **You might find it hard to get calls out with any degree of certainty.** Why was that? Perhaps cell phone towers had never made it beyond picturesque Pevensey Point? Nevertheless, what the e-mail said was true: he was "used to that." He pulled a duffel bag from the passenger seat, slipped the note into it, and got out of the car.

Located in one of the central dormitory-like buildings, Reception was an understated space that reminded Logan of a hospital or clinic: a half-dozen empty chairs, tables with magazines and journals, a sprinkling of anonymous-looking oil paintings on beige walls, and a single desk occupied by a woman in her mid-thirties. The letters CTS were set into the wall behind her, once again with no indication of what they might stand for.

Logan gave his name to the woman, who in response looked at him with a mixture of curiosity and uneasiness. He took a seat in one of the vacant chairs, expecting a protracted wait. But no sooner had he picked up a recent issue of **Harvard Medical Review** than a door across from the receptionist opened and Ethan Rush emerged.

"Jeremy," Rush said, smiling broadly and extending his hand. "Thank you so much for coming."

"Ethan," Logan replied, shaking the proffered hand. "Nice to see you again."

He hadn't seen Rush since their days at Johns Hopkins twenty years before, when he'd been doing graduate studies and Rush had been attending the medical school. But the man who stood before him retained a remarkable youthfulness. Only a fine tracery of lines at the corners of his eyes bore testament to the passage of years. And yet in the simple act of shaking the man's hand, Logan had received two very clear impressions from Rush: a shattering, life-changing event and an unswerving, almost obsessive, devotion to a cause.

Dr. Rush glanced around the reception area. "You brought your luggage?"

"It's in my trunk."

"Give me the keys, I'll see that somebody retrieves it for you."

"It's a Lotus Elan S four."

Rush whistled. "The roadster? What year?"

"Nineteen sixty-eight."

"Very nice. I'll make sure they treat it with kid gloves."

Logan dug into his pocket and handed the keys to Rush, who in turn gave them to the receptionist with some whispered instructions. Then he turned and motioned Logan to follow him through the open doorway.

Taking an elevator to the top floor, Rush led the way down a long hallway that smelled faintly of cleaning fluid and chemicals. The resemblance to a hospital grew stronger—and yet it seemed to be a hospital without patients; the few people they passed were dressed in street clothes, ambulatory, and obviously healthy. Logan peered curiously into the open doorways as they walked by. He saw conference rooms, a large, empty lecture hall with seats for at least a hundred, laboratories bristling with equipment, what appeared to be a reference library full of paperbound journals and dedicated terminals. More strangely, he noticed several apparently identical rooms, each containing a single narrow bed with literally dozens—if not hundreds—of wires leading to nearby monitoring instruments. Other doors were closed, their small windows covered by privacy curtains. A group of men and women in white lab coats passed them in the hallway. They glanced at Logan, nodded to Rush.

Stopping before a door marked DIRECTOR, Rush opened it and beckoned Logan through an anteroom housing two secretaries and a profusion of bookcases into a private office beyond. It was tastefully decorated, as minimalist as the outer office was crowded. Three of the walls held spare postmodernist paintings in cool blues and grays; the fourth wall appeared to be entirely of glass, covered at the moment by blinds.

In the center of the room was a teakwood table, polished to a brilliant gleam and flanked by two leather chairs. Rush took one and ushered Logan toward the other.

"Can I offer you anything?" the director asked. "Coffee, tea, soda?"

Logan shook his head.

Rush crossed one leg over the other. "Jeremy, I have to be frank. I wasn't sure you'd be willing to take on this assignment, given how busy you are . . . and how closemouthed I was concerning the particulars."

"You weren't sure—even given the fee I charged?"

Rush smiled. "It's true—your fee is certainly healthy. But then your, ah, work has become somewhat high profile recently." He hesitated. "What is it you call your profession again?"

"I'm an enigmalogist."

"Right. An enigmalogist." Rush glanced curiously at Logan. "And it's true you were able to document the existence of the Loch Ness monster?"

"You'd have to take that up with my client for that particular assignment, the University of Edinburgh."

"Serves me right for asking." Rush paused. "Speaking of universities, you **are** a professor, aren't you?"

"Medieval history. At Yale."

"And what do they think of your other profession at Yale?"

"High visibility is never a problem. It helps guarantee a large admissions pool." Logan glanced around the office. He'd often found that new clients preferred to talk about his past accomplishments. It postponed discussion of their own problems.

"I remember those . . . **investigations** you did at the Peabody Institute and the Applied Physics Lab back in school," Rush said. "Who would have thought they'd lead you to this?"

"Not me, certainly." Logan shifted in his seat. "So. Care to tell me just what CTS stands for? Nothing around here seems to give any clue."

"We do keep our cards pretty close to our vest. Center for Transmortality Studies."

"Transmortality Studies," Logan repeated.

Rush nodded. "I founded CTS two years ago."

Logan glanced at him in surprise. "You founded the Center?"

Rush took a deep breath. A grim look came over his face. "You see, Jeremy, it's like this. Just over three years ago, I was working an ER shift when my wife, Jennifer, was brought in by paramedics. She'd been in a terrible accident and was completely unresponsive. We tried everything—heart massage, paddles—but it was hopeless. It was the worst moment of my life. There I was, not only unable to save my own wife . . . but I was expected to pronounce her dead, as well."

Logan shook his head in sympathy.

"Except that I didn't. I couldn't bring myself to do it. Against the advice of the assisting doctors I continued heroic measures." He leaned forward. "And, Jeremy—she **pulled through**. I finally revived her, fourteen minutes after all brain function had ceased."

"How?"

Rush spread his hands. "It was a miracle. Or so it seemed at the time. It was the most amazing experience you can imagine. It was revelatory, life altering. To have pulled her back from the brink . . ." He fell briefly silent. "At that moment, the scales fell from my eyes. My life's work was suddenly revealed. I left Rhode Island Hospital and my practice as an anesthesiologist, and I've been studying near-death experiences ever since."

The life-changing event, Logan thought. Aloud, he said, "Transmortality studies."

"Exactly. Documenting the various manifestations, trying to analyze and codify the phenomenon. You'd be surprised, Jeremy, how many people have undergone near-death experiences and—in particular—how many similarities they share. Once you've come back from the brink, you're never quite the same. As you might guess, it's something that stays with you—and with your loved ones." He swept his hand around the office. "It was almost no effort to raise the money for the Center, all this. Plenty of people who have had near-death experiences are passionately interested in sharing those experiences and learning more about what they might mean."

"So what goes on at the Center, exactly?" Logan asked.

"At heart, we're a small community of doctors and researchers—most with relatives or friends who have 'gone over.' Survivors of NDEs are invited here to stay for a few weeks or months, to document precisely what happened to them and undergo various batteries of tests."

"Tests?" Logan asked.

Rush nodded. "Although we've been operational only eighteen months now, a great deal of research has been conducted already—and a number of findings made."

"But, as you say, you've kept it all pretty hush-hush."

Rush smiled. "You can imagine what the good residents of Pevensey Point would say if they knew exactly who had taken over the old Coast Guard training base down the road, or why."

"Yes, I can." **They'd say you were tampering with fate,** he thought. **Messing with people brought back from the dead.** Now he began to have some idea why his own expertise had been called for. "So exactly what's been going on here that I can help you with?"

A look of surprise briefly crossed Rush's face. "Oh, you misunderstand. Nothing's happening **here**."

Logan hesitated. "You're right—I do misunderstand. If the problem you're experiencing isn't here, then why was I summoned?"

"Sorry to be evasive, Jeremy. I can tell you more once you're on board."

"But I **am** on board. That's why I'm here."

In reply, Rush stood and walked to the far wall. "No." And with a single tug, he opened the blinds, exposing a wall of windows. Beyond lay the airstrip Logan had noticed on his arrival. But from this vantage, he could see the runway wasn't empty after all: it was occupied by a Learjet 85, sleek and gleaming in the noonday sun. Rush extended a finger toward it.

"Once you're on board **that**," he said.

2

There were five people on the plane: a crew of two, Logan, Rush, and a CTS staffer bearing two laptops and several folders stuffed with what appeared to be lab results. Once the jet was airborne, Ethan Rush excused himself and walked to the rear to meet with the staffer. Logan fished the latest issue of **Nature** out of his duffel bag and browsed through it, looking for any new discoveries—or anomalies—that might interest him professionally. Then, feeling drowsy, he set the magazine aside and closed his eyes, intending to doze for five or ten minutes. But when he awoke it was dark outside and Logan felt the disoriented haze of a long, deep sleep. Rush looked over at him from the seat across the aisle.

"Where are we?" Logan asked.

"Coming into Heathrow." He nodded at the staffer, still sitting in the rear. "Sorry about that—like you, I don't know exactly how long I'm going to be away, and there was some CTS business that couldn't wait for my return."

"Not a problem." Logan peered out at the lights of London, spread out like a vast yellow blanket beneath them. "Is this our destination?"

Rush shook his head. Then he smiled. "You know, I found it kind of funny, the way you boarded the plane without question. I thought you'd at least do a double take."

"In my profession you tend to travel a lot. I always carry a passport."

"Yes, I read that in an article about you. That's why I didn't ask you to bring one."

"In the last six months I've been to at least as many foreign countries: Sri Lanka, Ireland, Monaco, Peru, Atlantic City."

"Atlantic City isn't a foreign country," Rush said with a laugh.

"Felt like one to me."

They landed and taxied to a private hangar, where the CTS staffer deplaned with the laptops and the folders to catch a commercial flight back to New York. Rush and Logan ate a light dinner while the jet refueled. When they were once again in the air, Rush took a seat beside Logan, a black leather briefcase in one hand.

"I'm going to show you a picture," he said. "I think it will explain the need for secrecy." Unsnapping the case, he opened it slightly. Rummaging inside, he pulled out a copy of **Fortune** and briefly showed it to Logan.

On the cover was a headshot of a man in his mid-fifties. His thick, prematurely snow-white hair was parted down the middle: a strangely anachronistic look that reminded Logan of a schoolboy from a Victorian-era English public school, Eton or Harrow or Rugby. He was thin, a look accentuated by the heavy backlighting of the photograph. The soft, almost feminine contours of his face were sharply offset by unusually weathered skin, as if by exposure to sun or wind; and though the man was not smiling, there was a faint amused glint in his blue eyes as he stared at the camera, as if at some private joke he was disinclined to share with the world.

Logan recognized the face—and, as Rush had promised, much of the mystery suddenly became understandable. The face belonged to H. Porter Stone, without doubt the most famous—and by far the richest—treasure hunter in the world. Though "treasure hunter" was probably unfair, Logan decided: Stone had been trained as an archaeologist and had taught the subject at UCLA before his discovery of two ships from the Spanish Plate Fleet, sunk in 1648 in international waters. Those vessels—stuffed with silver, gold, and gemstones, on their way back to Spain from the colonies—instantly made Stone not only extremely wealthy but notorious. That notoriety only increased with his subsequent discoveries: an Incan mausoleum and treasure trove hidden in a mountain col twenty miles from Machu Picchu; after that, an immense cache of carved soapstone birds, animals, and human figures beneath a hill complex in the primeval ruins of Great Zimbabwe. Others had followed in remarkably rapid succession. **What ancient civilization,** a banner on the magazine cover asked, **will he pillage next?**

"That's where we're going?" Logan asked incredulously. "A treasure hunt? An archaeological dig?"

Rush nodded. "A little of both, actually. Stone's latest project."

"What is it?"

"You won't be in the dark for long." And Rush opened the case again. As Logan glanced over, he saw the doctor slip the magazine beneath a thin stack of papers. It was only the briefest of glimpses, but Logan noticed the papers were covered with what he thought were hieroglyphs.

Rush closed the case. "I **can** tell you this is his biggest expedition yet. And the most secret. In addition to the usual need to operate below the radar, there are certain . . . unusual logistical issues, as well."

Logan nodded. He wasn't surprised: Stone's expeditions had become increasingly high profile. They tended to attract a lot of attention, both from a curious press and would-be interlopers. Now, instead of supervising the work himself, Stone had become famously reclusive, directing his expeditions **à la distance,** frequently from halfway around the world. "I have to ask. What exactly is your interest in this? It can't have anything to do with your Center: any bodies that interest Stone will definitely be dead. **Long** dead."

"I'm medical officer for the expedition. But I also have another, more indirect interest." Rush hesitated. "Look, I really don't mean to be coy. There are some things you can't learn until you're actually at the site. But I can say there are certain, um, **peculiar** aspects to this dig that have arisen in the last week or so. That's where you come in."

"Okay. Then here's a question that maybe you can answer. Back in your office, you mentioned you were an anesthesiologist before founding the Center. If so, what were you doing working a shift in the emergency room the day your wife was brought in? That should have been years behind you."

The smile on Rush's face faded. "That's a question I used to hear all the time. Before Jennifer's NDE, that is. I always gave a flippant answer. The fact is, Jeremy, I trained as an ER specialist. But somehow, I could never get used to the death." He shook his head. "Ironic, isn't it? Oh, I could handle natural causes all right: the cancer and pneumonia and nephritis. But sudden, violent death . . ."

"For an ER doctor, that's quite a millstone," Logan replied.

"You said it. That fear of death—of dealing with it, I mean—is why I changed fields, became an anesthesiologist instead of an ER doc. But it still haunted me. Running away did no good: I **had** to be able to stare death in the eye. So to keep my hand in, so to speak, I did ER duty every other week. Sort of like wearing a hair shirt."

"Or like Mithradates," Logan said.

"Who?"

"Mithradates the Sixth, king of Pontus. He was in constant fear of being poisoned. So he tried to inure himself by taking sublethal doses every day, until his system was hardened against it."

"Taking poison to develop an immunity to it," Rush said. "Sounds like what I was doing, all right. Anyway, after the experience with my wife, I left medical practice entirely and founded the clinic. I stopped trying to fight my aversion to death. Instead I've put it to positive use: studying those who have escaped its embrace."

"I have to ask. Why found your own clinic? I mean, it's my understanding there are already several organizations devoted to near-death experiences. Graduate students are majoring in NDEs and 'consciousness studies.'"

"That's true. But none of them are as large, as centralized, or as focused as CTS. And besides, we've branched out into some unique avenues of study."

He excused himself and Logan turned to the window, looking out into blackness. It was a clear night, and a brief study of the constellations confirmed they were traveling east. But where, exactly? It seemed Porter Stone had sent expeditions to just about every corner of the globe: Peru, Tibet, Cambodia, Morocco. The man had what the news accounts liked to call the Midas touch: it seemed every project he undertook turned to gold.

Logan thought of the briefcase, and the sheets of paper covered with hieroglyphs. Then he closed his eyes.

When he awoke again, it was morning. He stretched, shifted in his seat, peered once again out the window. Below him now, he could make out a broad brown river, with narrow strips of green fringing its banks. Beyond lay an arid landscape. Then he froze. There, on the horizon, was an unmistakable, monolithic shape: a pyramid.

"I knew it," he breathed.

Rush was seated across the aisle. Hearing this, he glanced over.

"We're in Egypt," Logan said.

Rush nodded.

Despite a carefully cultivated stoicism, Logan felt a shiver of excitement. "I've always wanted to work in Egypt."

Rush sighed—half in amusement and half, perhaps, in regret. "I hate to disappoint you, Dr. Logan," he said. "But actually, it's nothing quite as straightforward as Egypt."

3

Logan had been in Cairo only once before, as a graduate student documenting the movements of Frisian soldiers during the Fifth Crusade. And it seemed to him—as they drove along the highway from Cairo International—as if all the cars he'd noticed twenty years before were still on the road. Ancient Fiats and Mercedes Benzes, sporting dents and broken headlights, jockeyed frantically for position, making their own impromptu lanes at sixty miles per hour. They passed buses, decrepit and rusting, people hanging precariously from empty frames where the passenger entrances ought to have been. Now and then Logan caught sight of late-model European sedans, brilliantly polished and almost invariably black. But aside from these exceptions, the freeway traffic seemed one feverish anachronism, a time capsule from an earlier age.

Logan and Rush sat in the rear of the car, silently taking in the sights. Logan's luggage had been left on the plane, and their driver—a local driving a Renault only slightly less aged than those around them—had expertly navigated the maze of airport access roads and was now headed into Cairo proper. Logan saw block after block of almost identical cement buildings, painted mustard, a half-dozen stories high. Clothes were drying on balconies; windows were covered with canvas awnings displaying a confusing welter of advertisements. The flat roofs were festooned with satellite dishes, and innumerable cables hung between buildings. A faint orange pall hung over everything. The heat, the unblinking sun, were merciless. Logan leaned out the wide-open window, gasping in the diesel-heavy air.

"Fourteen million people," Dr. Rush said, glancing his way. "Crammed into two hundred square miles of city."

"If Egypt isn't our destination, why are we here?"

"It's just a brief stop. We'll be back in the air before noon."

As they approached the city center and left the highway for local roads, traffic grew even denser. To Logan, every intersection seemed like the approach to the Lincoln Tunnel: a dozen cars all struggling to squeeze into one or two lanes. Pedestrians flooded the streets, taking advantage of the gridlock to cross willy-nilly, missing cars by scant inches. Somehow, grievous injury was avoided. Downtown, the buildings were no taller, but the architecture was more interesting, oddly reminiscent of the Rive Gauche. Security became increasingly evident: black-uniformed police were posted in booths at intersections; hotels and department stores had their frontages blocked by concrete fortifications to prevent car bombings. They passed the US Embassy, a fortress bristling with .50-caliber machine-gun posts.

A few minutes later, the car abruptly pulled to the curb and stopped. "We're here," Rush said, opening his door.

"Where's 'here'?"

"The Museum of Egyptian Antiquities." And Rush stepped out of the car.

Logan followed, careful to avoid the press of bodies, the cars that passed close enough to ruffle the fabric of his shirt. He glanced up at the grand facade of rose-colored stone across the entrance plaza. He had been here, too, during his graduate research. The tingle of excitement that he'd first felt on the plane grew stronger.

They crossed the plaza, fending off trinket sellers hawking glow-in-the-dark pyramids and battery-powered toy camels. Bursts of high-speed Arabic peppered Logan from all sides. They passed a brace of guards flanking the main entrance. Just before stepping inside, Logan heard a voice, crackling with amplification, suddenly rise above the din of traffic and the chatter of package-deal tourists: the chant of the muezzin in the local mosque across Tahrir Square, calling the faithful to prayer. As he paused, listening, Logan heard the call taken up by another mosque, then another, the chant moving Doppler-like into greater and greater distances, until it seemed to echo across the entire city.

He felt a tug at his elbow. It was Rush. Logan turned and stepped inside.

The ancient structure was crowded even at this early hour, but the sweaty throngs had not yet warmed the stone galleries. After the fierce sunlight, the interior of the museum seemed exceedingly dark. They made their way through the ground floor, past innumerable statuary and stone tablets. Despite signs bearing warnings against camera usage and forbidding the touching of artifacts, Logan noticed that—even now—many of the exhibits were still open to the air rather than hermetically sealed, and showed signs of extensive handling. Passing the last of the galleries, they mounted a broad flight of stairs to the first floor. Here were row upon row of sarcophagi, laid out on stone plinths like sentinels of the shadow world. Along the walls were glass-fronted cabinets containing funerary objects of gold and faience, the cases locked with simple seals of lead and wire.

"Mind if I take a moment to inspect the grave goods of Ramses III?" Logan asked, pointing toward a doorway. "I believe it's down that passage. I recently read in the **Journal of Antiquarian Studies** of a certain alabaster canopic vase one could use to summon—"

But Rush smiled apologetically, pointed at his watch, and merely urged Logan on.

They made their way to another staircase—this one narrower, missing its banister—and climbed to the next floor. It was much quieter here, the galleries devoted to more scholarly collections: inscribed stelae; fragments of papyri, faded and decaying. The lighting was dim, the stone walls grimy. Once Rush stopped to consult a tiny floor plan he pulled from his pocket, hand-sketched on a scrap of paper.

Logan peered curiously around half-open doors. He saw stacks of papyrus scrolls, shelved floor to ceiling in niches like so many wine bottles in a sommelier's vault. Another room held a collection of masks of ancient Egyptian gods: Set, Osiris, Thoth. The sheer volume of artifacts and priceless treasures, the weight of so much antiquity on all sides, was almost oppressive.

They turned a corner and Rush stopped before a closed wooden door. Inscribed in gold letters so faded as to be almost indecipherable were the words **Archives III: Tanis–Sehel–Fayum**. Rush glanced back briefly at Logan, then over his shoulder and down the empty hall. And then he opened the door and ushered Logan inside.

The room beyond was even darker than the hall-way. A series of windows arrayed just below the high ceiling grudgingly admitted shafts of sunlight, heavily filtered through countless years of grime. There was no other illumination. Bookcases covered all four walls, stuffed to bursting with ancient journals, bound manuscripts, moldy leather-covered notebooks, and thick bundles of papyri, fastened together with desic-cated leather stitching and in apparent disarray.

As Rush closed the door behind them, Logan took a step into the room. It smelled strongly of wax and decaying paper. This was precisely the kind of place he could find himself very much at home in: a clearinghouse for the distant past, a repository of secrets and riddles and strange chronicles, all wait-ing patiently to be rediscovered and brought into the light. He had spent more than his fair share of time in such rooms. And yet his experience was primar-ily in medieval abbeys and cathedral crypts and the restricted collections of university libraries. The arti-facts here—the histories and the narratives, and the dead language most of them were written in—were very, very much older.

In the center of the room was a single research table, long and narrow, surrounded by a half-dozen chairs. The room had been so dark and still that Logan had believed them to be alone. But now, as his eyes adjusted, he noticed a man in Arab garb seated at the table, his back to them, hunched over an ancient scroll. He had not moved at their entrance, and did not move now. He appeared completely engrossed in his reading.

Rush took a step forward to stand beside Logan. Then he quietly cleared his throat.

For a long moment, the figure did not move. Then he turned slightly in their direction. The old man—for it was clear to Logan he was an elderly scholar—did not bother to make eye contact; rather, he simply acknowledged the new presences. He was dressed in a formal but rather threadbare gray thawb, with faded cotton pants and a hooded linen robe that partially concealed a plain black-and-white patterned ghutra fringing his forehead. Beside him, a tiny cup of Turkish coffee sat on a worn earthenware coaster.

Logan felt an inexplicable stab of annoyance at this presence. Rush had clearly brought him here to consult some private document: How were they going to keep their business confidential from an elderly scholar, even one who was so insolent as to barely acknowledge them?

Then—to Logan's surprise—the old man pushed his chair away from the desk and, very deliberately, stood up to face them. He was wearing a pair of old reading glasses, cracked and dusty, and his seamed face was hidden behind the folds of the hood. He stood, regarding them, eyes indistinguishable behind the ancient spectacles.

"I'm sorry we're late," Rush said.

The man nodded. "That's all right. This scroll was just getting interesting."

Logan looked from one to the other in confusion. The stranger standing before them had replied in perfect English—American English, in fact, with the faintest whiff of a Boston accent.

Now, slowly and carefully, the old man pulled back his hood, revealing a shock of brilliant white hair combed carefully beneath the ghutra. He took off the glasses, folded them, and slipped them into a pocket of his robe. A pair of eyes stared back at Logan. Even in the faint light of the archives, they were as pale blue as a swimming pool on the first fresh day of summer vacation.

Suddenly, Logan understood. The man he was looking at was Porter Stone.

4

Logan took a step backward. He saw Rush's hand approach his elbow and instinctively brushed it aside. Already the shock was passing, replaced by curiosity.

"Dr. Logan," Stone said, "I'm sorry to surprise you like this. But, as you can no doubt appreciate, I am forced to keep the very lowest of profiles."

He smiled, but the smile did not extend as far as his eyes. Those eyes were far more piercing, more brilliant, than the pointillist photo on the cover of **For-**

tune had conveyed. Behind them clearly burned not only a fierce intelligence but an unslakable hunger—for antiquities or wealth or merely knowledge, Logan could not surmise. The man was taller than he'd expected. But the frame beneath the Arab garb was just as thin as the photos in the press had led him to believe.

Stone nodded to Rush. As the doctor turned to lock the door, Stone shook Logan's hand, then gestured for him to have a seat. Logan drew no particular impression from the handshake—just a fierce energy out of keeping with such a gaunt frame and almost effeminate features.

"I didn't expect to find you here, Dr. Stone," he said as he sat down. "I thought you kept yourself far removed from your projects these days."

"That is what I would like people to believe," Stone replied. "And for the most part, it's true. But old habits die hard. There are times even now when I can't resist doing a little digging, getting my hands dirty."

Logan nodded. He understood perfectly.

"Besides, whenever possible I prefer to talk personally to key members of a new team—especially on a project as important as this one. And of course, I was very curious to meet you face-to-face."

Logan was aware the blue eyes were still scrutinizing him. There was something almost pitiless in their intensity: here was someone who had taken the measure of many, many men.

"So I'm a key part of the team?" Logan asked.

Stone nodded. "Naturally. Although, to be honest, I hadn't expected you to be. You're something of a late addition."

Rush took a seat across the table from them. Stone put aside the scroll he'd been reading, revealing a narrow folder beneath it. "I knew of your work, of course. I'd read your monograph on the Walking **Draugen** of Trondheim."

"That was an interesting case. And it was nice to be able to publish—I'm so rarely allowed to."

Stone smiled his understanding. "And it seems we already have something in common, Dr. Logan."

"Call me Jeremy, please. What might that be?"

"Pembridge Barrow."

Logan sat up in surprise. "You don't mean to say you read—"

"I did indeed," Stone replied.

Logan looked at the treasure hunter with fresh respect. Pembridge Barrow had been one of Stone's smaller, but historically more spectacular, discoveries: a burial pit in Wales that contained the remains of what most scholars agreed was the first-century English queen Boadicea. She had been found buried in an ancient war chariot, surrounded by weapons, golden armbands, and other trinkets. In making the find, Stone had solved a mystery that had plagued English historians for centuries.

"As you know," Stone continued, "the scholarly elite always maintained Boadicea met her end at the hands of the Roman legions in Exeter, or perhaps Warwickshire. But it was your own graduate dissertation—in which you argued she survived those battles to be buried with full warrior's honors—that led me to Pembridge."

"Based on projected movements of Roman search parties far removed from the Watling Road," Logan replied. "I guess I should feel honored." He was impressed with Stone's thoroughness.

"But I didn't summon you here to speak of that. I wanted you to understand just what you're getting yourself involved in." Stone leaned forward. "I'm not going to ask you to sign a blood oath or anything so melodramatic."

"I'm relieved to hear it."

"Besides, somebody in your unique line of work can be trusted to keep a confidence." Stone leaned back again. "Have you heard of Flinders Petrie?"

"The Egyptologist? He discovered the New Kingdom at Tell el-Amarna, right? And the Merneptah stele, among other things."

"That's right. Very good." Stone and Rush exchanged a significant glance. "Then you probably know that he was that rarest of Egyptologists: a true scholar, endowed with a limitless appetite for learning. In the late 1800s, when everybody else was frantically digging up treasure, he was searching for something else: **knowledge**. He loved to stray from the obvious dig sites—the pyramids and the temples—searching far up the Nile for potsherds or bits of clay pictographs. In many ways, he made

Egyptology a respectable science, discouraging looting and haphazard documentation."

Logan nodded. So far, this was all relatively common knowledge.

"By 1933, Petrie was the grand old man of British
archaeology. He'd been knighted by the king. He'd
offered to donate his head to the Royal College of
Surgeons so that his unique brilliance could be studied in perpetuity. He and his wife retired permanently
to Jerusalem, where he could spend his twilight years
among the ancient ruins he loved so much. And so
the story ends."

A brief silence fell over the archives. Stone pulled
out the grimy spectacles, fiddled with them a moment,
placed them on the table.

"Except that it **doesn't** end. Because in 1941—
after years of sedentary retirement—Petrie abruptly
left Jerusalem, bound for Cairo. He told none of his
old colleagues at the British School of Archaeology
about this new expedition of his—and there can be
no doubt that it **was** an expedition. He took a bare
minimum of staff: two or three at most, and those
I suspect only because of his age and growing infir-
mity. He made no request for grants; it would appear
he sold several of his most prized artifacts to finance
the trip. None of these things were in character for
Petrie—but strangest of all was his **haste**. He had
always been known for careful, deliberate scholarship. But this trip to Egypt, with North Africa already
deep in the throes of war, was the polar opposite of

deliberation. It seems to have been frantic—almost desperate."

Stone paused to take a sip from the tiny cup of coffee. The air was briefly perfumed with the scent of **qahwa sada**.

"Where exactly Petrie went—why he went—was not known. What **was** known is that he returned to Jerusalem five months later, alone, funds depleted. He would not speak of where he'd been. His air of desperation remained, yet the journey had sorely weakened an already enfeebled body. He died not long afterward in Jerusalem, in 1942, apparently while raising funds for yet another return to Egypt."

Stone replaced the cup on its earthenware coaster, then glanced at Logan.

"None of that is in the historical record," Logan said. "How did you find this out?"

"How do I find anything out, Dr. Logan?" Stone spread his hands. "I peer into the dark corners others don't bother to examine. I search public and private records, hunting for that one lost document accidentally shoved behind the others and forgotten. I read anything and everything I can get my hands on—including, I might add, obscure graduate dissertations."

Logan put one hand to his heart, made a mock bow.

"People talk about the secret of my Midas touch." Stone uttered these last words contemptuously. "What tripe. There's no secret beyond plain hard work. The fortune I made from the Spanish Plate Fleet gave me the resources to do things my way: send scholars and investigators to all corners of the world, searching quietly for that tantalizing gap in the historical record, that scrap of ancient rumor, that might prove to be of interest—and, perhaps, more than **just of interest**."

As quickly as it came, the bitterness left Stone's voice. "In the case of Flinders Petrie, I obtained a battered diary, purchased as part of a lot in an Alexandrian bazaar. The diary had been kept by a research assistant of Petrie's during his last years in Jerusalem: a young man who wasn't asked to go along on that final expedition and afterward, in vexation, joined the army. He died in the Battle of the Kasserine Pass. Of course the story described in his diary piqued my interest. What could have possessed Petrie—who cared little for treasure, who had earned a large measure of scholarly fame, not to mention every right to enjoy an old age of ease—to leave the comfort of his home and enter a war zone at almost ninety years of age? It was a mystery." Stone paused. "But you must understand, Dr. Logan: I have a hundred, **two** hundred, such mysteries in the vault of my research lab in Kent. Some I discovered myself; others I have paid well to have unearthed. They are all interesting. But my time is finite. I will not commit to a project until I feel confident I have sufficient knowledge to guarantee success."

The Midas touch, Logan thought. Aloud, he said, "I take it, then, this research assistant of Petrie's wasn't the last word on the subject?"

Stone smiled again faintly, and, as he returned Logan's gaze, the stark, appraising look returned to his eyes. "Petrie's housekeeper. One of my associates learned of her existence, traced her whereabouts, and interviewed her shortly before her death, in a hospice for the aged in Haifa. This was six years ago. She was rambling, semilucid. But under gentle questioning, she clearly recalled one particular afternoon in 1941, when Petrie was displaying a portion of his vast collection of antiquities to a guest. It was a guest of no importance, and Petrie entertained in this fashion frequently. In any case, on this particular occasion the housekeeper clearly recalled Petrie and the nameless guest exploring the contents of a wooden crate from one of the Egyptologist's earliest excursions up the Nile. All of a sudden Petrie sat bolt upright, as if galvanized by an electric shock. He stammered for a minute. Then he quickly got rid of his visitor with some excuse. And then he closed and locked the door to his study—something he had never done before. That's what made the housekeeper remember the incident. Within days, he departed on his final trip to Egypt."

"He found something," Logan said, "in his storehouse of artifacts."

Stone nodded. "Something that had been lying there, in plain sight, all along. Or more likely, never

carefully examined before the day that guest arrived—
Petrie had amassed such a large collection that he
barely knew its extent."

"And I'm assuming—since we're here—that you
found that artifact."

"I found it," Stone said slowly.

"May I ask how?"

"You may not." If this was meant as a joke, it
didn't show. "My methods are, shall we say, pro-
prietary? Suffice to say it was a long, arduous, vex-
ing, boring—and expensive—task. If you assumed
I spent a lot of money to discover the journal and
the housekeeper—and I did—I spent twenty times
as much to learn what it was Petrie uncovered on that
day in 1941. But I **am** willing to share the artifact
with you—briefly." And Stone reached for the cup of
coffee, raised it to his lips.

Logan waited, expecting Stone to produce some
carefully sealed relic case, or perhaps instruct Dr.
Rush to retrieve an artifact from some secret corner
of the dusty room. But instead, Stone simply took a
sip from the tiny cup. Then he nodded at the worn
coaster on the table, now stained with a faint damp
ring of coffee.

"Pick it up," he said.

5

For a moment, Logan hesitated. He wasn't sure he understood. Stone merely returned his gaze, cup in hand, his expression unreadable.

Logan began to reach for the worn coaster, paused, then extended his hand—gingerly—and picked it up. As he did so he realized it was not earthenware, after all, but a thin piece of limestone, badly chipped at the edges. Turning it over, he saw faint pictographs drawn in pale brown ink.

"Not the original, of course," Stone said. "But an exact copy." He paused. "Do you know what it is?"

Logan turned it over in his hands. "It looks like an ostracon."

"Bravo!" Stone turned toward Rush. "Ethan, this man impresses me more by the minute." He looked back at Logan. "If you know it's an ostracon, then you'll also know its purpose."

"Ostraca were discarded bits of leftover stone, pottery, almost anything, used for unimportant writings. Antiquity's version of the notepad."

"Precisely. With emphasis on 'unimportant.' They might have been used for bills of sale or for grocery lists. Which is precisely why I was using that as a coaster. A melodramatic touch, but it makes a point. To someone like Flinders Petrie, ostraca were a dime a dozen: occasionally interesting in the light they could throw on humdrum, everyday life in the ancient world, but otherwise of little significance."

"Which is why Petrie would never have noticed it before." Logan looked down at the faded limestone inscription. There were a total of four pictographs, badly scratched and faded. "I know very little about hieroglyphs. What makes this so special?"

"I'll give you the short version. Have you heard of King Narmer?"

Logan thought a moment. "Wasn't he the pharaoh who many believe unified Egypt?"

"That's right. Before Narmer came along there were two kingdoms: upper and lower Egypt. 'Upper' meant farther up the Nile and actually lay to the south. Each had its own ruler, with his own crown. The kings of upper Egypt wore a white, conical crown, shaped almost like a bowling pin, while the kings of lower Egypt sported a red crown with a peak at the back. Around 3200 BC, Narmer—the ruler of upper Egypt—came north, killed the king of lower Egypt, and in so doing unified the country, with himself as pharaoh. It's my belief that he was the first god-king of a long line that followed; and—who knows?—perhaps only a god could have united the two Egypts. He was certainly believed to have power over both life and death." Stone paused. "Anyway, he unified something else, too. He unified the **crowns** of the two kingdoms. You see, Dr. Logan, the crown of the Egyptian pharaoh was a uniquely important symbol of power. Narmer of course was aware of this. So once Egypt had become a single kingdom, he wore a double crown—a combination of the white and red crowns, symbolic of his dominion over both lower and upper Egypt. And for the next three thousand years, every pharaoh that followed in his wake did the same."

He drained the tiny cup, put it to one side. "But back to Narmer. The unification of Egypt was memorialized on a large siltstone tablet, depicting his defeat of the rival king. Scholars have referred to this Narmer Palette as 'the first historical document in the world.' It depicts the earliest representation of Egyptian kings ever found. It also contains primitive—and **very** distinctive—hieroglyphs."

Stone held out his hand and Logan gave him the limestone fragment.

"What Petrie saw on this ostracon were hieroglyphs dating from that very early period. As you can see, there are a total of four." Extending a slender finger, Stone pointed to them in turn.

"What do they say?" Logan asked.

"You'll understand if I'm a little reticent about the details. Let's just say that this is no insignificant laundry list. Quite the opposite. This ostracon is the key to the biggest—and I mean **the** biggest—archaeological secret in history. It tells us what King Narmer took with him when he journeyed to the underworld."

"You mean, what's actually buried in his tomb?"

Stone nodded. "But you see, here's the rub. Narmer's tomb—we know where it is, a rather sad little two-chamber affair in Abydos, Umm el-Qa'ab to be precise—held none of the things described on this ostracon."

"Then what . . ." Logan paused. "You're telling me the known tomb isn't a tomb at all."

"Oh, it's a tomb, all right. But it's not **the** tomb. It might be an early example of a cenotaph—a symbolic, rather than actual, tomb. But I prefer to think of it as a decoy. And when Flinders Petrie saw this ostracon—and understood that . . . well, that's the reason he dropped everything at a moment's notice;

abandoned the comforts of retirement; and risked his health, his safety, and his fortune—in an attempt to find Narmer's **real** tomb."

Logan thought about this. "But what could possibly be so valuable—"

Stone raised a hand by way of interruption. "I won't tell you that. But once you know the location of the tomb—I'll leave that to Dr. Rush to explain—you'll understand why, hypothetically, even if we didn't know what the tomb contained, we would be **utterly** convinced of its incredible importance."

Stone leaned forward, tented his fingers. "Dr. Logan, my methods are unusual. I've implied as much to you already. When I undertake a new project, I spend most of the total time and at least half the total expense merely in preparation. I research every possible avenue of success, bring overwhelming scholarly and investigative pressure to bear, before a spade first breaks ground. So it probably would not surprise you to learn that—once this ostracon and its message were in my possession—I gave the project a green light. In fact, it became my highest priority."

He leaned back again, glanced at Rush.

The doctor spoke for the first time. "Where Petrie failed, we succeeded. We're triangulating the location of the tomb. Everything is in place; all assets are on the ground. Work is proceeding."

"Proceeding very quickly," Stone added. "We are under some significant time pressure."

Logan shifted in his chair. He was still trying to

fully grasp the enormity of the find. "You've learned of the real tomb's existence. You know where it is. You've started excavation. So why do you need me?"

"I'd rather you find that out for yourself, on site. It would serve no purpose for me to prejudice you or color your judgment. Let's just say there are complications that fall under your area of expertise."

"In other words, something strange, perhaps inexplicable, and probably frightening is taking place at the dig site. Such as a curse."

"Isn't there always a curse?" Stone asked quietly.

This was greeted by a silence.

After a moment, Stone continued. "These **complications** need to be analyzed, understood, and dealt with. Ethan here can give you some more background on your way to the site."

"And where, exactly, is this site?"

"That, my dear doctor, just may be the strangest element in a very strange story. But enough background." Stone stood up and again shook Logan's hand. His grasp was cool and slight. "It's been a pleasure to meet you. Ethan will take over from here. He has every confidence in your unique talents—and, having met you, I do as well."

This was an unmistakable sign that the meeting was over. Logan nodded, turned to go.

"And Dr. Logan?"

Logan turned back.

"Work quickly. **Quickly.**"

6

The plane climbed steeply out from Cairo Airport, banking immediately toward the Nile. They flew south, following the lazy turnings of the river. Logan stared out the window, down toward the lazy, chocolate-colored surface. They were flying at only a few thousand feet, and he could make out dhows and riverboats cutting through the water, leaving wakes through red patches of lotus petals. Along the shore, and stretching inward beside a tracery of canals, were thin green ranks of banana and pomegranate plantations.

Rush excused himself and went forward to talk with the crew. This was fine with Logan: he wanted a little time to digest what he had just heard.

He found himself deeply impressed with the thin, almost frail-looking Porter Stone. First impressions were rarely so misleading. The passion and determination it must have taken to follow this fragile trail of evidence to its conclusion were awe-inspiring.

Just as impressive was the discovery itself: the true tomb of Egypt's first pharaoh, the god-king Narmer, and its mysterious contents—this was perhaps the holy grail of Egyptology.

Gradually, the greenery along the riverbanks drew thinner, the lush palms and grasses giving way to papyrus sedge. Rush wandered back from the cabin. "Okay," he said with a smile. "I promised myself I wouldn't ask. But I just can't resist. Just how the hell do you do it?"

"Do what?" Logan replied coyly.

"You know. What it is you do. Just how, for example, did you exorcise the legendary 'ghost' that haunted Exeter University for six hundred years? And how—"

Logan raised a hand to forestall further questions. He had known this would come up eventually—it always did. "Well," he considered, "I'd have to swear you to secrecy, of course."

"Of course."

"You understand you can't tell a soul."

Rush nodded eagerly.

"Very well." Logan glanced around conspiratorially, then leaned forward as if to impart a secret. "Two words," he whispered. **"Clean living."**

For a moment, Rush looked at him blankly. Then he chuckled and shook his head. "Serves me right for asking."

"In all seriousness, it's not usually about garlic clusters or vials of pixie dust. It just requires a rather extensive knowledge of certain subjects—some of them obvious, like history and comparative theology, some not so obvious, like astrology and the, ah, secret arts. Also, a willingness to keep an open mind. You've heard of Occam's razor?"

Rush nodded.

" **'Entia non sunt multiplicanda praeter necessitatem.'** The simplest explanation is most often the correct one. Well, in my line of work, I take the opposite approach. The correct explanation is often the **least** expected, the most unusual one—at least for people like us: modern, Western educated, out of sync with nature, and impatient with past practices and beliefs." He paused. "Take the Exeter ghost you mentioned. With sufficient research into ancient town records, and by asking the locals about old legends, I learned enough about a certain community-sanctioned murder of a supposed witch, circa 1400, to give me what I required. After that, and after securing the location

of the witch's grave site, it was just a matter of bringing certain rituals—and certain chemicals—to bear."

"You mean . . ." Rush looked nonplussed. "You
mean there actually **was** a ghost?"

"Naturally. What did you expect?"

This was greeted by silence. After a minute or
two, Logan shifted. "But let's get back to the topic
at hand. Stone's story is remarkable, but it raises as
many questions as it answers—and not just about
what's in the tomb. For example, how did he discover
its actual location? I mean, that ostracon is a fascinating artifact—but it's not exactly a road map."

For a moment, Rush's thoughts seemed to go far
away. Then he shook himself back to the present. "I
don't know all the details myself. Tremendous finan-
cial and organizational resources were brought to
bear—discreetly, of course. I do know that he started
by studying Petrie's movements. Once he'd deci-
phered the ostracon, how would the old Egyptologist
have known where to look? He wouldn't have rushed
off to Egypt in such a hurry without having a pretty
good idea. So Stone began putting the known facts
together. And he began his search around the Temple
of Horus at Hierakonpolis."

"Where?"

"The capital of upper Egypt. King Narmer's home
before he invaded the lush lands to the north and
unified the country. That's where the Narmer Palette
was discovered around the turn of the twentieth cen-

tury. And Petrie had been known to journey as far south as Hierakonpolis in his early expeditions."

"Narmer's capital city," Logan said. "Home of the Narmer Palette—and, I assume, that ostracon as well. And a focus of Petrie's explorations, to boot. So that's the location of Narmer's tomb—Hierakonpolis?"

Rush shook his head. "But it **was** the location of the document that led to the true site."

Logan thought for a minute. "That's right," he said. "It couldn't be Hierakonpolis. Because you said the site was nothing as straightforward as Egypt." He glanced sidelong at the doctor. "What exactly did you mean by that?"

Rush chuckled. "I was wondering when you'd ask. We'll talk all about it on the boat."

"The boat?"

As Rush nodded, Logan felt the aircraft begin a gentle descent. Looking out the window again, he noticed the Nile had widened into Lake Nasser. In another fifteen minutes they had landed at an unnamed airstrip just past the lake: a single pitted runway, surrounded by featureless desert. They deplaned and climbed into a waiting jeep. The driver put Logan's bags and a large, unlabeled metal case from the plane's belly into the back, then got in and drove them west, toward the river. The sun was a pitiless white ball, baking the parched ground with midafternoon light. Within minutes they reached the river itself. Scattered ibis flew low over the water. Somewhere in the distance a hippopotamus bellowed. The jeep pulled up to a long wooden pier that seemed as deserted as the airstrip. Rush got out and led the way down to the strangest vessel Logan had ever seen.

It was at least eighty feet long but with a beam remarkably narrow given its length. For its size it rode extremely shallow: Logan estimated a draft of two feet at most. The superstructure consisted of a single, two-story construction that took up most of the deck. At either side of the bow were two small platforms, open to the air and suspended out over the water, that reminded Logan of crow's nests. But the boat's single most remarkable feature was at its stern: a massive, conical cage of steel, narrow end forward, as big as a Gemini space capsule and roughly the same shape. It enclosed a large, cruel-looking five-bladed propeller. The entire assembly was fixed permanently atop the stern section of the main deck.

"Good lord," Logan said from the dock. "An airboat on steroids."

"A description apt enough," came a gruff voice. Logan glanced up to see a man appear in a doorway at the front of the superstructure. He was fiftyish, of medium build, with deep-set eyes and a closely cropped white beard. He stepped up to the waiting gangplank and ushered them aboard.

"This is James Plowright," Rush said. "The expedition's senior pilot."

"Quite a vessel," Logan said.

"Aye." The man nodded.

"How does she handle?" Logan asked.

"Well enough." Plowright had a rough Scottish burr and the Scotsman's economy of words to go with it.

Logan looked back at the propeller assembly. "What's the powerplant?"

"Lycoming P-fifty-three gas turbine. Retrofitted from a Huey jetcopter."

Logan whistled.

"This way," Rush said. He turned to Plowright. "You can cast off when ready, Jimmy."

Plowright nodded.

Rush led the way back along the deck. Given the size of the superstructure and the craft's slim beam, the decking was very narrow, and Logan was glad of the railing alongside. They passed several doors, then Rush ducked through an open doorway and ushered Logan into a dimly lit space. As his eyes adjusted, Logan found himself in a pleasantly appointed saloon, furnished with couches and banquettes. A variety of framed nautical scenes and sporting prints hung on the walls. The space smelled strongly of polished leather and insect repellent.

The driver of the jeep deposited Logan's bags and the metal case in one corner, bowed, then returned to the deck.

Logan pointed at the case. "What's in there?" he asked.

Rush smiled. "Hard disks containing the case

files from the Center. I can't completely ignore my full-time job while I'm out here."

Within a minute, Logan heard faint sounds from the direction of the stern: the jet engine started up with a howl and the vessel drew away from the dock, its frame throbbing slightly, heading upriver toward the Sudan.

"We have two of these craft, specially built for the expedition," Rush said as they settled onto one of the banquettes. "We use them for ferrying things to the site. Things too bulky or fragile for airdrop: high-tech equipment, for example. Or specialists."

"I can't imagine any site that would require a craft like this."

"When you see it, you'll understand all too well—I promise."

Logan sat back on the rich leather seat. "Okay, Ethan. I've met Stone. I know what you're looking for. Now I think it's time you told me where we're going."

Rush smiled faintly. "You know the term 'hell on earth'?"

"Of course."

"Well, prepare yourself. Because that's exactly where we're headed."

7

Rush leaned forward in the banquette. "Have you heard of the Sudd?"

Logan thought a moment. "It rings a distant bell."

"People assume that the Nile is just a wide river, snaking its way unimpeded out from the heart of Africa. Nothing could be further from the truth. The early British explorers—Burton and Livingstone and the others—found that out the hard way when they encountered the Sudd. But take a look at that—it'll describe the place far more eloquently than I can." And Rush gestured to a book on a nearby table.

Logan hadn't noticed it before and now he picked it up. It was a battered copy of Alan Moorehead's **The White Nile**. It was a history of the exploration of the river; he vaguely remembered leafing through a copy as a child.

"Page ninety-five," Rush said.

Logan flipped through the book, found the page, and—as the saloon throbbed around him—began to read.

> **The Nile . . . is a complicated stream. [It] proceeds through the desert on a broad and fairly regular course. . . . [But ultimately] the river turns west, the air grows more humid, the banks more green, and this is the first warning of the great obstacle of the Sudd that lies ahead. There is no more formidable swamp in the world than the Sudd. The Nile loses itself in a vast sea of papyrus ferns and rotting vegetation, and in that foetid heat there is a spawning tropical life that can hardly have altered very much since the beginning of the world; it is as primitive and hostile to man as the Sargasso Sea. . . . [The] region is neither land nor water. Year by year the current keeps bringing down more floating vegetation, and packs it into solid chunks**

**perhaps twenty feet thick and strong
enough for an elephant to walk on. But
then this debris breaks away in islands and
forms again in another place, and this is
repeated in a thousand indistinguishable
patterns and goes on forever. . . . Here
there was not even a present, let alone a
past; except on occasional islands of hard
ground no men ever had lived or ever could
live in this desolation of drifting reeds
and ooze, even the most savage of men.
The lower forms of life flourished here
in mad abundance, but for . . . men the
Sudd contained nothing but the threat of
starvation, disease and death.**

Logan put the book down. "My God. Such a place
really exists?"

"It exists all right. You'll see it before dark." Rush
shifted on the banquette. "Imagine: a region thousands of square miles across, not so much swamp as
a labyrinth of papyrus reeds and waterlogged trunks.
And mud. Mud everywhere, mud more treacherous than quicksand. The Sudd isn't deep, often just
thirty or forty feet in places, but in addition to being
horribly honeycombed with braided undergrowth, its
water is so full of silt, divers can't see an inch beyond
their faces. The water's full of crocodiles by day, the
air full of mosquitoes by night. All the early explorers
gave up trying to cross it and eventually went around.

The Sudd may not be quite as remote or impassable today as it was in the times Moorehead wrote of, but it's no picnic. It's in a wide, shallow valley. And every year it spreads. Just a little, but it spreads. It's like a living thing—that's why we need such a narrow craft. Trying to traverse the Sudd is like threading a needle through the bark of a tree. Every day we have a recon helicopter that charts the shifting eddies, maps new paths through it. And every day, those routes change."

"So the vessel acts sort of like an icebreaker," Logan said. He was thinking of the strange equipment he'd seen at the bow.

Rush nodded. "The shallow draft helps clear underwater obstructions, and the propeller at the stern provides the raw power necessary to push through tight spots."

"You're right," Logan said. "It **does** sound like hell on earth. But why are we . . ." He stopped. "Oh, no."

Rush nodded. "Oh, yes."

"Good lord." Logan fell silent a moment. "So Narmer's tomb is there. But why?"

"Remember what Stone said? Think about it. Narmer went to unprecedented lengths to conceal the location of his tomb. He actually went out of Egypt proper, past the six cataracts of the Nile, into Nubia—a dangerous journey into hostile lands. Given how early in Egyptian history this was—remember, this is the Archaic Period, the First Dynasty—it's an accomplishment on the order of the Great Pyramid.

Not only that, but Narmer is the only pharaoh **not** buried in Egypt—as you probably know, all pharaohs had to be entombed on Egyptian soil."

Logan nodded. "That's why Egypt never colonized."

"Given all this, Jeremy—all this incredible effort and expense and risk—do you really think it likely that Narmer's tomb contains little of value?"

"But an impenetrable swamp . . ." Logan shook his head. "Think of the logistics involved in tomb building—especially for a primitive culture, operating in a hostile region."

"That's the fiendish beauty of the thing. Remember how I said the Sudd spreads a little every year? Narmer knew that. He could build his tomb on what was then the **edge** of the Sudd, keeping its location secret. There's a vast system of volcanic caves just below the surface of the Sudd valley. After his death, the swamp, expanding ever outward, would hide all traces of his tomb. Nature would do the job for him." Rush's face took on a troubled look. "Almost too well."

"What do you mean?"

"You heard Stone. The site is up and running, smooth as clockwork. All the experts are in place, the technicians and archaeologists and mechanics and the rest. Only . . ." He hesitated. "Only the precise location proved a little more difficult to find than Stone's experts assumed." Rush sighed. "Of course there is the usual need for a low profile—not as much as on a typical site, of course, but it's there nonetheless. And it's the worst time of the year to work, too: the rainy season. It makes the Sudd that much more difficult and unpleasant and unhealthy a place to work."

Logan remembered Stone's words: **We are under some significant time pressures**. "So why the frantic pace? Why not just wait for the dry season? The tomb has sat there for five thousand years—why not another six months?"

As if in answer, Rush stood and beckoned Logan to follow him out of the saloon. They regained the deck and walked carefully forward to the bow. The sun was sinking toward the horizon, the pitiless white ball now an angry orange. The Nile spread out from the prow in thick undulating lines. The cry of waterbirds was giving way to strange trumpetings from either bank.

Rush spread his hands. Glancing ahead, Logan saw a range of hills rising on both sides of the river, widening to form a vast amphitheater ahead of them, marching on into the distance where sight failed. "You see that?" Rush asked. "Beyond those is the Af'ayalah Dam. Already it's nearing completion on this, the Sudanese side of the frontier. In five months, all this—everything, the whole useless godforsaken place—will be underwater."

Logan peered into the gathering gloom. Now he understood the hurry.

As he peered thoughtfully into the water ahead, he began to notice bracken floating in the lazy current.

First, just bundles of papyrus reeds. But then the reeds began forming small islands, attaching themselves to promontories of mud that rose out of the river like miniature volcanoes.

"The dam provides us with a great cover story," Rush went on. "We're posing as a team researching the ecosystem, documenting it before it's gone forever. But that layer of phoniness costs extra money, and, again, the longer it continues, the more difficult the deception becomes."

The boat began to slow as the debris grew thicker. Now Logan could see huge logs, twisted together as if in titanic struggle, moss and rotting weeds hanging from their flanks like so much webbing. A stench of decay and overripe verdure began rising around them. A door in the superstructure opened and two mates appeared, each carrying a strange, harpoonlike weapon attached to pneumatic hoses. They took up positions in the platforms on each side of the bow, leaning out over the water, devices at the ready.

Suddenly, a floodlight snapped on in the forecastle, sending a shaft of surreal blue light ahead of the bow. The turbine throttled back still further. A light rain had begun to fall. The vegetation was growing ever thicker, a nearly impenetrable carpet of weeds and papyrus and branches and vile muck that now surrounded them. The men in the bow began using their pneumatic devices to violently push the heavier logs and clots of fibrous matting out of the way. Their machines made deep, ugly **snuck, snuck** noises. Ahead, in the narrow lane of open water the boat was following, Logan caught sight of a small light, bobbing in the swamp, flashing quickly in the reflected glow of the vessel's searchlight. One of the mates fished it out as they passed.

"The daily search chopper drops beacons as it charts a fresh path through this hell," Rush explained. "It's the only way for the boats to get through."

They crawled forward into an ever-thicker tangle of logs and bracken. The noises from the riverbanks—if indeed there were still any banks to be found in this morass—had all but ceased. It was as if they were now surrounded by an infinite riot of flora, dead and dying, all wedged into one colossal tangle. They waited in the bow, barely speaking, as the boat followed the line of flashing beacons. Now and then the path seemed to Logan to lead to a dead end; but each time, after making a blind turn, the fetid tangle of vegetation widened once again. Frequently, the boat had to use its own superstructure to push aside the oozing warp and weft.

At one point they reached a spot through which there was no clear passage. Up in the pilothouse, Plowright, the captain, goosed the turbine; the vessel lifted bodily into the air and forced its way over the matted surface—twenty-five, fifty feet forward—with a horrible clanging and scraping along the underside. It became clearer than ever to Logan why the boat's motive power, the huge fan, had been mounted **atop** the deck: any normal propeller would have been snagged in a minute. The two mates leaned forward over the bow, plying their pneumatic prods. The cloying heat, the stench of rotting vegetation, grew overpowering.

"It's been a long day," Rush said suddenly, out of the fading light. "Tomorrow, you'll meet some of the key members. And you'll get what I think you've been waiting for the most."

"What's that?"

"The last piece of the puzzle. The one that answers your other question: why you, of all people, are here."

Here? Logan glanced ahead. And then, quite suddenly, he understood.

The boat had made a sharp turn through a vast screen of knotted limbs and papyrus, and now a most unusual sight greeted Logan's eyes. Ahead, floating on at least a half-dozen vast pontoon platforms, lay what appeared to be a small city. Lights twinkled from beneath countless mosquito nets. Canvas tarps the size of football fields were erected over the structures, shielding them from the sky. There was a faint hum of generators, barely louder than the whine of insects that hovered and dove in clouds around their boat. It was an outrageous sight, here in this most remote and dreadful of spots: an oasis of civilization that might just as well have been set down on one of Jupiter's moons.

They had arrived.

8

The airboat slowed to a crawl, gave a blast of its horn. Almost at once, a rectangle of lights came on beneath one of the huge tarps. Logan watched, fascinated despite his weariness, as a bank of mosquito netting was drawn back from beneath the tarp like a curtain from a theater stage. Slowly, they glided beneath the tarp and into a covered marina. To their left was another huge airboat identical to the one they were on; to their right, moored to short, floating piers, were numerous smaller craft and Jet Skis.

Plowright maneuvered the vessel into its slip, and somebody in shorts and a flowered shirt trotted down the pier to tie them up. With a whisper, the external netting was drawn back into place. Logan glanced at it: beyond the glow and sparkle of the marina lights, the Sudd was a wall of blackness.

Dr. Rush led the way down the gangplank and onto the pier. "This way," he said, ushering Logan onto a walkway made of stamped metal, then through a doorway and down a long, tunnel-like floating pier and onto what seemed to be an immense, barge-like structure covered by another vast sheet of what appeared to be opaque Mylar, almost in the fashion of a circus tent.

"Seven p.m., local time," Rush added. Even at this hour the air was sticky and oppressive. From the darkness beyond the netting, Logan could hear, amid the patter of raindrops, a strange fugal drone of insects, frogs, and other less-identifiable creatures.

He looked around. "Does this thing have a name?"

Rush laughed. "Nothing official. Most people just call it the Station—after **Heart of Darkness,** I suppose. The six primary floating structures, the 'wings,' that make up the base are color coded, and they're referred to by their colors. The one we're entering now is Green. It's where the back-office work of the expedition is done: interfacing with suppliers, transportation coordination, vessel and equipment maintenance, that sort of thing. It's also the, ah, public face of the expedition—such as it is."

They were now walking down a narrow passage-way, rather grimy and scuffed, studded with open doors. It was cooler inside this enclosed structure, and Logan noticed that the walls were, in fact, painted green. He peered curiously into the rooms on either side. They were full of computers, video cameras on tripods, whiteboards covered with diagrams and legends. Messy-looking laboratories—apparently, eco-logical and biological setups—had complete suites of scientific equipment and paraphernalia for collecting samples. The rooms all had one thing in common: they were dark, devoid of any activity.

"What's all this?" Logan said, nodding toward one of the open doors.

"The public face I mentioned."

Logan shook his head. "Unique or not, why study something as godforsaken as this place?"

Rush chuckled. "That's exactly what the local government thinks—and what we want them to think. Why document a swamp that's been univer-sally reviled ever since it was first discovered? But of course they were happy to take some money in exchange for the necessary permits. That's probably the only benefit of being situated here—nobody's likely to drop in for a surprise visit. We had an offi-cial flown in when the site first went active. We didn't make it easy to get here, and we were sure to turn off the air-conditioning while he was on location. We don't expect any future interruptions—but of course, if necessary, these decoy labs and offices could be up and running within five minutes."

They made their way along Green's central passageway, now passing offices that were, it appeared, real: Logan made out someone typing at a terminal, another speaking into a field radio. They turned down another passage, which led to a dark, circular opening covered by wide, ceiling-to-floor strips of semiopaque plastic. Logan was reminded of the mouth of a baggage carousel. Rush pushed his way past the plastic strips, and Logan followed. Suddenly, he was outdoors again, in a narrow tube of mosquito netting, supported by pontoons. It was pitch-black, and—if anything—the insect noise had increased, completely overwhelming the drone of the generators. Listening, Logan didn't think he could bear to spend a night outdoors with such an infernal racket.

As they traversed the long walkway, it rocked back and forth, and Logan could hear sucking, sopping noises emanating from beneath their feet. Clearly, they were moving from one of the primary floating barges to another.

"All these structures are anchored to the bed of the Sudd," Rush said. "Very precisely anchored, too—there can be no shifting, not even by so much as half a meter. Our work is dependent on GPS positioning. But you'll see that for yourself soon enough."

"Remarkable."

"The most remarkable part isn't even visible. As

you might imagine, a swamp like the Sudd throws off a lot of methane. There are collection devices underneath each of the wings. The methane is concentrated and processed into clean-burning fuel in special chambers. Then it's piped out to the two external generators. It's also used as fuel for everything from the boats to the Bunsen burners. We're almost completely energy independent."

"That's amazing. Why doesn't everyone do it?"

"Well, rotting vegetation doesn't cover the rest of the earth—thank God."

"Of course." Logan laughed. "Isn't it a little dangerous?"

"Having natural gas pipes running through your house is probably dangerous, too. It's a closed system, monitored twenty-four seven, the whole thing set up with a safety mechanism that's fully automatic. And flying in thousands of gallons of oil and gas on a regular basis might raise eyebrows. Besides, Stone not only likes to fly below the radar but prefers to leave no trace behind, do as little damage to the environment as possible. This helps accomplish that."

They passed through another barrier into a second vast enclosure, this one painted a pale azure, the dome high overhead arching over cubicles with seven-foot walls. "This is Blue," Rush said. "Crew quarters."

Activity here was more pronounced. They passed a recreation room with pinball machines and shuffleboard layouts; then a minilibrary with comfortable chairs, magazines, and racks of paperbacks; next, a lounge where several groups of four were sitting around card tables, immersed in games. Logan could hear laugher, snippets of conversation in French, German, and English.

"Believe it or not, bridge has become a tradition on Porter Stone's digs," Rush said. "It's encouraged during off-hours. Stone believes that it gets people's minds off the day's stress, helps prevent brooding over the isolation and the separation from loved ones, while at the same time keeping the mind sharp."

"How many people are on the site?"

"I don't recall the exact number. Somewhere around a hundred and fifty."

They paused outside what appeared to be half commissary, half mess. "Want a bite to eat before I show you to your quarters?" Rush asked.

Logan shook his head. "I'm fine."

"Let me get you something anyway, just in case." Rush disappeared inside. Logan waited in the corridor, observing the activity within. There were at least a dozen people in the mess, eating dinner. The atmosphere was remarkably heterogeneous: scientists in lab coats were practically bumping elbows with rough-looking roustabouts begrimed by mud or motor oil.

Rush reappeared in the doorway with a paper bag. "Here's a BLT, an apple, and a can of iced tea," he said. "Just in case you get peckish."

He led the way around a bend and into a dormitory area. The chatter was louder here: conversations, laughter, the blare of music from digital players, movies playing on laptops or flat-screen monitors.

Rush stopped before a closed door marked 032. "This is yours," he said, opening the door and ushering Logan inside. Beyond lay a room, spartan but neat, furnished with a desk, bed, two chairs, a closet, and a set of drawers flush with the wall.

"They'll bring your luggage 'round in a few minutes," Rush said. "And tomorrow we'll get you officially processed and start the orientation. But now you must be tired."

"Make that overwhelmed."

Rush smiled. "I have to check in with Medical. Want to meet for breakfast? Say, eight o'clock?"

"Sure."

"I'll see you then." Rush grasped his shoulder, then turned and left, closing the door behind him.

The soundproofing was better than expected: the noises in the hallway immediately sank to a murmur. Logan was setting his watch to local time when there came a knock on the door and his luggage was brought in by a young man with a thatch of carrot-colored hair. Logan thanked him, closed the door, then lay down on the bed. He wasn't fatigued, exactly, but he needed a while to sort out in his head all the surprises and revelations of the last thirty-six hours. It seemed almost unbelievable: here he was, in a vast complex of platforms, connected by walkways, shrouded by

canvas and mosquito netting, and everything floating atop a dismal swamp, hundreds of miles from
anywhere. . . .

Five minutes later he was fast asleep, dream-
ing that he was standing atop a pyramid, alone and
marooned, surrounded by an endless sea of heaving,
steaming quicksand.

9

The following morning passed in a blur of activity. Logan met Rush for breakfast, as agreed. Afterward, Rush led him back to Green, where he was officially processed, issued an ID card, and given a twenty-minute orientation by a no-nonsense woman with a Home Counties accent. The entire process was efficient and clinical, with an almost military precision: clearly, this was a machine oiled and streamlined over many previous missions. At the end of the orientation, he was asked to hand over his cell phone, being informed he'd get it back at the conclusion of his stay. **Once you're on board with the project, you might find it hard to get calls out with any degree of certainty,** Rush had written in his introductory e-mail. Now Logan understood why: Stone and his fanatical obsession with secrecy. Although it seemed unlikely that anybody's cell phone would get a signal in such a remote wasteland.

"You'll be meeting with Tina after lunch," Rush told him as they stepped back out into the narrow corridor.

"Tina?"

"Dr. Christina Romero. She's the head Egyptologist. She'll fill in the rest of the blanks, get you up to speed. She can be a bit prickly at times, and she has very strong opinions about looting grave goods, but she's the best at what she does." He hesitated a moment, as if about to say something. "Meanwhile, I thought you might like to see the work in process."

"Sure," Logan replied. "Especially if it'll give me some idea what I'm doing out here."

The two made their way past more offices, labs, and equipment sheds. Logan quickly became disoriented in the mazelike interiors. They passed lab-coated scientists, a machinist in coveralls, and—surprisingly— a burly, bearded man sporting boots and a cowboy hat.

"Roustabout," Rush said, as if that explained everything.

They crossed through another pontoon-supported walkway, encased in Mylar and mosquito netting, floating just inches above the surface of the swamp, and the doctor pushed past another makeshift wall of vertical plastic panels. Logan followed suit—then stopped abruptly. Beyond lay a vast room. Along one yellow wall was a rank of lockers, perhaps two dozen, painted battleship gray. Along the opposite wall was a bank of instrumentation: rack-mounted servers, oscilloscopes, what appeared to be highly sophisticated depth finders and sonar devices, and a dozen still-more-exotic pieces of equipment. Leads, power cables, and data conduits snaked underfoot, all converging at the center of the huge space, where a large circular hole had been cut in the floor. This well-like hole was surrounded by a railing and more instrumentation.

"This is Yellow," Rush said, waving a hand, a note of pride in his voice. "The face of the dig."

He led the way toward the center of the room. Logan followed, picking his way carefully over the sea of cabling. Several people were arrayed around the central hole: some monitoring instruments, others in dive suits sitting on benches and conversing in low tones. A woman in a nurse's uniform sat at a small medical station, typing on a laptop.

Logan approached the hole and peered in gingerly. It was at least eight feet in diameter. He could see the brownish-green surface of the Sudd not eighteen inches beneath his feet. Its miasmic vapor rose like a fetid breath to his nostrils. Two ladders descended into its murky depths, along with several thick cables.

Rush nodded toward the hole. "Our interface with the swamp. We call it the Maw."

"The Maw?"

Rush smiled grimly. "Rather appropriate, don't you think?"

Logan had to agree that it was.

On the far side of the Maw was a huge flat-panel monitor, connected to a bank of CPUs. On it was displayed something that looked to Logan like a cross between a chessboard and some kind of alien lottery ticket: a grid of squares, ten by ten, in a variety of colors. Some of the squares contained odd symbols; others, small logos and lines of text. Others were empty.

Beside this monitor was an industrial rolling ladder, the kind used for stocking warehouse shelves. Standing atop it, hands folded over a barrel-like chest, stood a man, cigar in mouth despite the NO SMOKING signs posted everywhere. He was bald, his dome shining brilliantly under the large surgical-bay lights, and he'd clearly spent so many years in the sun that his skin was the color of chewing tobacco. Although he was no more than five feet tall, he radiated confidence and authority.

Dr. Rush made his way around the Maw and stopped at the base of the ladder. "Frank?" he said to the man atop it. "There's someone I'd like you to meet."

The man on the safety ladder looked down at

them. Then he peered carefully around the room, scrutinizing everything, as if to assure himself everything was under control. Then at last he descended the ladder, puffing on the cigar.

"Jeremy, this is Frank Valentino," Rush said. "Dive and dig site honcho."

Valentino took out the cigar, looked meditatively at the soggy end, then put it back in his mouth and held out a meaty paw.

"Frank, this is Jeremy Logan," Rush continued. "He arrived with me last night."

Valentino's look grew slightly more interested. "Yeah, I heard of you," he said. His voice was remarkably deep and free of accent. "The spook doctor."

For a moment, Logan stood utterly still. Then, quite abruptly, he spread his palms outward and leaned toward Valentino. "Boo!" he said.

Valentino shrank back. **"Madonna,"** he murmured, crossing himself. Out of the corner of his eye, Logan saw Rush suppress a smile.

In the background, behind the low chatter of the engineers and divers, Logan could hear the squawk of an occasional electrified voice coming over a radio on the far side of the large monitor. It sounded again: "Romeo Foxtrot Two, on descent."

"Romeo Foxtrot, roger," said a man seated at the radio console. "Your signal is five by five."

Rush gestured at the Maw. "Until the actual tomb is located, this is where all the exploratory and cartographical work is based."

"But the Sudd is so vast," Logan said. "How did you know where to establish the site?"

"Tina Romero can explain. Suffice it to say that the location was initially established as a square, several miles to a side. Scholarship and, ah—other considerations—narrowed that down to one mile."

"One square mile," Logan repeated, shaking his head in admiration.

Rush directed Logan's attention to the huge flat panel. "What you see there is a reproduction of the ground along the bottom of the Sudd: the square mile beneath us, broken into a ten-by-ten grid. Using a GPS satellite to ensure pinpoint accuracy, we're exploring each square in turn. Divers go down to scour the site, explore any hits."

"Romeo Foxtrot, Echo Bravo," said the radioman. "Give me an update."

After a moment, the radio squawked again. "Romeo Foxtrot. At minus thirty feet and descending."

"Bubble status?"

"Eighty-two percent."

"Watch that bubble, Romeo Foxtrot."

"Roger."

"What you're hearing are communications from the current dive team," Rush explained. "They dive in pairs for safety's sake. And they use special equipment to maintain their orientation. You can't imagine what it's like to descend into the Sudd—completely black, the mud and quicksand around you like a suffocating blanket, no way of telling up from down . . ." He paused.

"You talked about scouring the site," Logan said. "About exploring hits."

"Yes," Rush said, glancing back at him. "You see, this was once the site of a prehistoric volcano. Even in Narmer's day, the volcano was long gone. But traces of it remained behind in the form of subterranean lava pipes. Our belief is that the pharaoh selected a suitable lava tube for his tomb and had his workers expand and fortify it as necessary. Once it was sealed, the encroaching muck and water of the Sudd would do the rest. Anyway, when we first move to a new section of the Grid, the thing that must be done initially is to blast away the accretion of silty deposits from the swamp bed."

"That's Big Bertha's job," Valentino said with a smile. He jerked one thumb over his shoulder, where—in the shadowy depths of the hangarlike space—Logan could make out a hulking machine that looked half Zamboni, half snowmobile.

"Narmer thought his tomb would remain hidden away for all time," Rush said. "But he could never have imagined the technology we're bringing to bear—remote-sensing radar, scuba gear, global positioning devices."

"This is Romeo Foxtrot," the harsh metallic voice intruded. "The bubble mechanism's acting a bit flaky. Status stands at forty-three percent."

The radioman looked over at Valentino, who nodded. "Depth?" he said into the radio.

"Thirty-five feet."

"Keep a close watch," said the radioman. "Abort if it drops below twenty-five percent."

"Roger that."

"Big Bertha does the scouring," Rush resumed. "Then, the grid square is examined for hits—holes or tunnels in the swamp bed. If there aren't any, the square is marked as explored and we move to the next square on the Grid. If tunnels are found, they're flagged as Search for the next team of divers."

"Might find a sinkhole," said Valentino. "Might find nothing. But we got to check each one. Sometimes the tunnels, they branch out. Then we have to map it—map it all."

Rush nodded at the monitor again. "And the results are recorded on that—and on the main cartographic display in the Operations Center—with archaeological precision."

"Found anything yet?"

Rush shook his head.

"And how much of the Grid have you explored so far?"

"Forty-five percent," Valentino replied. "By tonight, Madonna willing, fifty percent."

"That's fast work," Logan said. "I had assumed—"

He was interrupted by a loud voice over the radio. "This is Echo Bravo. There's a problem with my regulator."

"Check the purge valve," the man at the radio said.

"I did. Nothing."

Logan glanced quickly at Rush.

"It's probably nothing," the doctor said. "As you can imagine, diving in these conditions is tough on equipment. In any case, the respirators are designed to fail open—even if one malfunctions it will keep delivering air."

"Echo Bravo to base," came the voice. "I'm not getting air!"

Immediately, Valentino walked over to the radio and took the handset himself. "This is Valentino. Use your backup second stage."

"I am! I am! I'm getting nothing. I think the dust cap is blocked!" Even over the radio, the panic in the man's voice was evident.

"Romeo Foxtrot," Valentino said into the radio, "do you see Echo Bravo? His regulator's malfunctioning and his octopus is apparently detached. You need to share air. Do you see him? Over!"

"Romeo Foxtrot here," came the other amplified voice. "No sign of him. I think he's purging, heading topside—"

"Oh, Christ," said Rush. "Forsythe is panicking. Forgetting the rules." He turned to the nurse. "Get a crash cart and an emergency team here—right now. And bring the water seal."

"What's the problem?" Logan asked.

"If he remembers his basic training, nothing. But if he panics, holds his breath as he surfaces . . ." Rush fell silent a moment. "For every thirty-three feet you descend, the air in your lungs loses half its volume to pressure. They were at thirty-five feet at last report. If he surfaces with all that air in him—"

"It will expand to twice its size," Logan said.

"And rupture his lungs." Grim faced, Rush hurried to the medical station, where the nurse was talking rapidly into a phone.

10

They gathered around the dark, yawning circle of the Maw: tense, tight-lipped. At Valentino's clipped order, additional lights were snapped on overhead, throwing the shivering, quaking surface below into sharp relief. As Logan stared down at it, it seemed to him that the Sudd was a living thing, its brownish surface the skin of some vast beast, and that their perching on it like this was an act of monumental folly. . . .

And then one of the cables leading down into the mire jerked spasmodically, and a strange gargling noise sounded over the radio.

Valentino ran back to the transmitting station. "Echo Bravo? **Echo Bravo!**"

"Romeo Foxtrot here," came the disembodied voice. "Still no sign of him. It's black as hell down here, can't see a thing—"

With a clatter, two white-clad medics appeared at the entrance to Yellow, each pushing large carts full of medical equipment.

There was another jerk on the cable as the radio sounded again. "Romeo Foxtrot to base, I see him. I've got hold of him. Surfacing now."

Suddenly, the mottled surface of water and decayed vegetation began to churn and heave. A moment later, a black-gloved hand abruptly broke the surface, grasping a rung of one of the ladders. This was followed by a neoprene hood and mask. Despite the air of crisis, Logan was momentarily arrested by the strangeness of the image: the emerging diver seemed like an insect, struggling to break free from some primordial ooze.

Beside him, Dr. Rush had been waiting, tense and silent, like a coiled spring. Now he dashed forward and—with the help of one of the medical technicians—began to free the man from the Sudd's grip. The diver had his arm around a second neoprene-clad man, who was struggling weakly. The two were pulled up out of the Maw and onto the floor of the Staging Area. Both were covered head to foot with matter the consistency of oatmeal. The room suddenly reeked of decay and dead fish.

"Hose them down," Valentino ordered.

But even as a team rushed to blast the muck from the divers, Dr. Rush was shifting the injured man to a waiting stretcher. He plucked the mask and hood from his face, then—with a scalpel—slashed the neoprene suit open from neck to navel. The man moaned and thrashed on the stretcher, bloody foam flecking his lips.

Quickly, Rush placed a stethoscope on the man's bare chest.

"He panicked," the other diver said as he came over, wiping his face and hair with a towel. "A rookie mistake. But diving in that shit, you forget—"

Rush raised a hand for silence. He moved the stethoscope around the chest, listening. His movements were jerky, almost violent. Then he straightened. "Extravasation of air," he said. "Resulting in pneumothorax."

"Doctor," said the nurse, "we can take him to Medical, where the—"

"There's no time!" Rush snapped as he pulled on a pair of latex gloves. The man on the stretcher twitched, clawing at his throat, gargling inarticulately.

Rush turned toward the medics. "A needle aspiration would be insufficient. Our only option is a thoracoscopy. Give me the chest tube, stat!"

Logan looked on with mingled surprise and

apprehension. Up to this point, Ethan Rush had been the epitome of calm assurance. But this—the sudden, almost frantic movements, the impatience and barked orders—was a Rush he had not seen before.

While one of the medics turned to his crash cart, Rush swabbed an area beneath the diver's left arm with iodine and a topical anesthetic, and then—with another swipe of the scalpel—made a two-inch incision between the ribs. "Hurry up with that chest tube!" he said over his shoulder.

The medic brought it over, unwrapping it from the sterile covering. Rush knelt before the struggling man and carefully threaded it into the incision he had made. He checked the placement, grunted, then rose.

"Chest drain," he rapped.

Another medic trotted over, pushing a floor stand that held a white-and-blue plastic device that, to Logan, looked like a blood-pressure monitor on steroids. It had several vertical gauges, and two clear plastic tubes led away from its upper housing.

"Suction-control stopcock?" Rush barked.

"On."

"Fill water seal to two millimeters."

"Yes, Doctor."

As the medic added water to the device, Logan saw the reservoir chamber turn blue. Meanwhile, Rush attached one of the plastic tubes to the line inserted into the injured diver's chest. Logan glanced over at the diver: his struggles were weaker now, his movements erratic.

"Catheter in place," Rush said. "Initiating suction. Setting pressure at minus twenty cm H_2O." He snapped a switch on the device, then began turning a stopcock on the unit's housing. Instantly, the liquid in the suction control chamber began to bubble. Rush turned the stopcock farther; the bubbling increased. The tube leading from the incision in the diver's side began to fill with mingled water and blood.

"If we can get the fluid out of the thoracic cavity quickly enough, the lungs might reinflate," Rush told the medical tech. "There's no time to operate."

The large room fell silent except for the hum of the machine and the bubbling of water draining from the tube.

Rush looked from the man on the stretcher to the water seal and back again in growing agitation. "He's becoming cyanotic," he said. "Increase vacuum pressure to negative fifty mmHg."

"But such a high level—"

Rush rounded on the tech. "Damn it, just **do** it." Then, walking briskly around the stretcher, Rush opened the now-motionless diver's mouth and began administering artificial respiration. Fifteen seconds passed, then thirty. And then, quite suddenly, the diver's limbs jerked; he coughed up blood and water and then took a deep, ragged breath.

Slowly, Rush straightened. He looked at the diver,

then at the water seal. "Dial it back to negative twenty," he murmured.

He glanced around at the assembled faces, then pulled off the gloves. "Keep an eye on the collection chamber," he told the nurse. "I'll go prep medical for a thorough evaluation." And without another word, he turned on his heel and strode out of the Staging Area.

As lunchtime approached, Logan found that his feet—he'd been wandering around the facility, trying to get his bearings—had brought him unbidden to what appeared to be the medical center. If there were really only a hundred and fifty people on the project, Medical seemed to him larger than necessary—until he recalled how far they were from any kind of help.

The center seemed quiet, almost somnolent. Logan walked down the central corridor, looking through the open doorways, at the empty beds and unused equipment. A woman at the nurse's station was making notations on a clipboard. He passed a large open area labeled OBSERVATION. The injured diver was here, surrounded by various diagnostic machines.

Logan continued, stopping at the next room. This was apparently Rush's office; the doctor was inside, his back to the door, speaking into a digital voice recorder.

"A catheter was inserted into the thoracic cavity and tension pneumothorax alleviated before the condition could degrade to a mediastinal shift or air embolism," he recited, "either of which might have caused the case to terminate fatally, due to the fact that under the circumstances it would have been unfeasible to . . ."

Realizing someone else was in the office, Rush snapped off the recorder and turned around. Logan was shocked by what he saw: the man's face was gray, his eyes puffy and red. It looked almost as if he had been crying.

The doctor gave a small smile. "Jeremy. Have a seat."

"That was good work," Logan said.

The smile faded. "An interesting way to usher in your stay."

Logan nodded. "Yes. Witnessing an accident like that."

"Accident," Rush repeated. "**Another** accident." For a moment, he appeared lost in thought. Then he brightened slightly. "I'm sorry you had to—well, to see me like that."

"You saved a life."

Rush waved a hand as if to deflect this. "Ever since that experience with my wife, I've been dealing solely with people who have cheated death. This is the first time I've had to deal with a life-or-death emergency since . . . I guess since she was brought into the Providence ER. I didn't know it would affect me like that." He paused, then looked at Logan. "I wouldn't say this to anybody else, Jeremy, but I hope Porter Stone didn't make a mistake signing me up as chief medical officer."

"No mistake. Stone chose a fine doctor. And you wait and see: this will be the only medical crisis you'll face. From now on it'll be clear sailing. Now, how about a bite of lunch before I have to face this Tina Romero?"

Another, more genuine, smile crossed Rush's face. "Give me five minutes to finish up this report. Then I'm your man."

11

Christina Romero's office was situated in Red, the container facility devoted to the med center and the various science labs. It reminded Logan more than a little of his own office back at Yale: orderly and clean, with row after row of books sorted by author and subject matter on long metal shelves. A large desk in the middle of the room was littered with artifacts and notebooks, yet somehow managed to look tidy; more artifacts were stored against the rear wall in a stack of carefully labeled plastic containers. Several diplomas and framed prints hung on the other three: a photo of an Egyptian wall painting; a print of Turner's **Regulus**, and—bizarrely—a very childlike depiction of the Sphinx.

If the office seemed vaguely familiar, however, Dr. Romero herself was a surprise. She was thin and very young—no more than thirty. Logan realized he'd been expecting a frowsy old woman in tweeds, a female Flinders Petrie. Romero could not have been more different. She was dressed in blue jeans and a black mock turtleneck with its sleeves pushed up to her elbows. She had kinky, shoulder-length black hair, parted in the middle, and it flared away from her face, looking not unlike the headdress of an Egyptian king. As Logan entered, she was seated behind the desk, absorbed in filling a fountain pen from a bottle of blue-black ink.

He knocked politely on the doorframe. Romero jerked in surprise, almost dropping the pen.

"Shit!" she said, grabbing for a tissue to wipe up the spilled ink.

"Sorry," Logan said, remaining in the doorway. "Get ink on yourself?"

"That's nothing," she said. "I might have ruined **this**." She held the pen up for him to see. "You know what this is? A Parker Senior Duofold in mandarin yellow, vintage 1927, the first year of production. **Very** scarce. Look—it even has the yellow threads on the barrel, before they switched to black." She waved it at him like a baton.

"Very impressive. Although I always preferred Watermans, myself."

She put the pen down and looked at him. "The silver overlays?"

"No. The Patricians."

"Oh." She screwed the cap onto the pen and slipped it into the pocket of her jeans, then stood up to shake his hand.

The handshake told Logan even more about Romero than the office decor did. He held her grasp just a shade longer than was typical.

"What do you want?" she asked. "I haven't seen you around before."

"That's because I just got here last night. The name's Jeremy Logan."

"Logan." She frowned.

"We have an appointment."

She brightened. "Oh, of course. You're the ghost—" She fell silent, but her green eyes twinkled with private amusement.

The same old silliness. Logan was used to it. "I prefer the term 'enigmalogist,' myself."

"Enigmalogist. Yes, that does lend an air of legitimacy." She looked him up and down, an expression on her face somewhere between skepticism and veiled hostility. "So—where is it? In that duffel bag you're carrying?"

"Where is what?"

"Your stuff. You know: the ectoplasm detector, crystal ball . . . and a dowsing rod. Surely you've got a dowsing rod around somewhere."

"Never carry one. And by the way, crystal balls can be very useful—not for clairvoyance necessarily but for emptying the mind of needless thoughts and distractions, say prior to meditation, depending, of course, on the impurities in the stone and its refractive index."

She seemed to consider this a minute. "Won't you come in and have a seat?"

"Thanks." Logan stepped inside, chose a seat before the desk, and placed his bag on the floor.

"I'm sorry, I don't mean to be flippant. It's just that I've never met an . . . **enigmalogist** before."

"Most people haven't. I'm never at a loss for conversation at cocktail parties."

She shook out her black hair and leaned back. "What is it you do, exactly?"

"More or less what it sounds like. I investigate phenomena that lie outside the normal bounds of human experience."

"You mean, like poltergeists?"

"On occasion. But more commonly, scientific or psychical activity that can't be easily explained through traditional disciplines."

Her eyes narrowed. "And you do this full-time?"

"I also teach history at Yale."

This seemed to interest her. "Egyptian history?"

"No. Medieval history mostly."

The interest died as quickly as it had come. "Okay."

"As long as we're playing twenty questions, why don't you fill me in on your background?"

"Sure. Got my PhD in Egyptology at the University of Cairo." She waved a hand at the diplomas. "Studied under Nadrim and Chartere. I assisted them in the Khefren the Sixth excavation."

Logan nodded. These were very impressive credentials. "Is this your first project with Porter Stone?"

"Second."

Logan shifted in his seat. "Dr. Rush said you'd fill me in on the background. What you found at Hierakonpolis when you searched the Temple of Horus. How you managed to locate this particular spot for the tomb."

Romero slid her hands into her pockets. "Why do you want to know?"

To Logan, this translated to **Why should I waste my time telling you?** Aloud, he said, "It might help me with my investigation."

She paused. Then, slowly, she sat forward. "I'll make this brief. Porter Stone managed to locate something called an ostracon—"

"He showed the replica to me."

"Good, that'll save time in explanations. Stone learned, from the ostracon and from several other scholarly investigations, that Narmer used Hierakonpolis as his staging point for building his tomb." She looked at him. "You do know who Narmer was, right?"

Logan nodded.

"The first king of a unified Egypt."

"I believe there's been some debate about that. In the past, scholars believed King Menes should be credited with the unification."

"Many scholars—myself included—believe that Narmer and Menes are one and the same." She peered at him again. "So you **do** know ancient Egypt."

Logan shrugged. "In my business, it's helpful to know a little bit about everything."

"And how far does this erudition extend exactly?"

Logan nodded toward the framed Egyptian wall painting. "Enough to guess that dates to the Amarna Period."

"Really? What gives you that idea?"

"The busyness of the scene, the overlapping of bodies. The emphasis on the feminine form: hips, breasts. You don't see that in earlier Egyptian art."

For a moment, she looked at him. Then a smile slowly broke across her face. "Okay, Mr. Ghostly Detective. You're clearly more than just a face from a magazine. Touché."

Logan grinned in return.

She sat up again. "All right. Using geophysical analysis and remote aerial sensing techniques, we were able to identify what appeared to be the site of a funerary quarry. This was unusual, because the very early Egyptians usually buried their dead—even nobility and royalty—in sand pits. So as a result, March began a targeted excavation."

"March?"

"Fenwick March. The head archaeologist for the project. He runs the show when Porter Stone isn't around."

"What did you find?"

"At first, what you'd expect. Early black-top pots with carbonized rims, pollen, paleozoological remains. But as work continued we realized just how large the site was."

"Big enough to be the city where tomb builders and engineers were based?"

"Bingo. And then, we found **this**." She stood up, walked over to a filing cabinet, and opened a drawer. Pulling out two rolled-up sheets, she walked back to the desk and handed one to him.

Logan unrolled it. He saw a color photograph of an ancient Egyptian inscription, incised and painted. It showed a seated ruler, along with lines and arrows and a variety of early pictographs.

"Recognize it?" Romero asked.

He glanced up. "It looks like some kind of stela."

"Very good. A slab stela, to be precise. Know what's written on it?"

Logan smiled. "My erudition only goes so far."

"It's a road map."

"A road map? To where?"

Romero raised one hand, index finger extended. Then, very slowly, she pointed straight down, between her feet.

"My God," Logan said.

"You must know how advanced the ancient Egyptians were in astronomy, in terms of mapping the sky. This stela was a map to show the engineers and builders how to get to the site of Narmer's tomb during its construction. No doubt it was supposed to be destroyed, smashed to dust, once the tomb was complete. Lucky for us it wasn't, because it allowed us to triangulate the tomb's location to within a few miles. Once on the site, geological and scholarly analysis allowed us to narrow it down even farther."

Logan thought of the Grid he'd seen on the flat-screen monitor in the dive Staging Area. "Incredible. Vintage Porter Stone."

"Indeed. But Stone found something else. On the far side of that site."

"What's that?"

"A giant, square piece of black basalt. Apparently, the plinth for some kind of statuary—perhaps of Narmer himself. It had been polished to an agate gleam, even after all the intervening centuries. It contained something, too." And she handed him the other sheet.

Logan took it. It was a photograph of another inscription, somewhat shorter.

"What is it?" Logan asked.

"It's the reason you're here."

Logan looked at her. "I don't understand."

She returned the look with a smile, but this time the smile didn't extend as far as her eyes. "It's a curse."

12

"A curse," Logan repeated.

Christina Romero nodded.

Porter Stone had alluded to a curse. Logan had been wondering when the other shoe would drop.

"You mean, like the one supposedly on King Tut's tomb? 'Death shall come on swift wings' and all that? That's just a lot of rumormongering."

"In the case of King Tut, you may be right. But curses were quite common in the Old Kingdom—and not only for private tombs. As the first king of a unified Egypt, Narmer wasn't going to take any chances. His tomb could not be allowed to be desecrated—it could mean the dissolution of his kingdom. And so he left behind this curse as a warning." She paused. "And what a warning."

"What does it say exactly?"

Romero took back the photo of the inscription, glanced at it. "'Any man who dares enter my tomb,'" she translated, "'or do any wickedness to the resting place of my earthly form will meet an end certain and swift. Should he pass the first gate, the foundation of his house will be broken, and his seed will fall upon dry land. His blood and his limbs will turn to ash and his tongue cleave to his throat. Should he pass the second gate, darkness will follow him, and he will be chased by the serpent and the jackal. The hand that touches my immortal form will burn with unquenchable fire. But should any in their temerity pass the third gate, then the black god of the deepest pit will seize him, and his limbs will be scattered to the uttermost corners of the earth. And I, Narmer the Everliving, will torment him and his, by day and by night, waking and sleeping, until madness and death become his eternal temple.'"

She replaced the sheet on the desk. For a moment, the office was silent.

"Quite a bedtime story," Logan said.

"Isn't it a beaut? Only a first-class bloodthirsty tyrant like Narmer could have invented it. Although come to think of it, his wife could have done the job, too. Niethotep. Talk about a match made in heaven." Romero shook her head.

"Niethotep?"

"Now **she** was something. One of those bathe-in-the-blood-of-a-hundred-virgins psychos, supposedly. Narmer imported her from Scythia, royalty in her own right." Romero turned back to the photograph. "Anyway, about the curse. It's the longest example I've come across. It's also by far the most specific. You heard the reference to the god of the deepest pit?"

Logan nodded.

"Notice he's not identified by name. Not even Narmer, a god in his own right, dared do that. He's referring to An'kavasht—He Whose Face Is Turned Backwards. A god of nightmare and evil that the earliest Egyptians were scared to death of. An'kavasht dwelled Outside, 'in the endless night.' Do you know what 'Outside' meant?"

"No, I don't."

"It meant the Sudd." She paused to let this sink in. Then she took the two sheets, rolled them up again, and returned them to the filing cabinet. "Within fifty years or so, the advancing waters of the Sudd would have made any secrecy unnecessary. The swamp took care of the hiding for him." She looked over at him. "But you know what? I don't think Narmer was particularly worried about concealment. Remember, he was considered a god, and not just in a ceremonial way. Anybody messing with the tomb of a god is asking for trouble. He had an army of the dead—and this curse—to guard him. Nobody, not even the most brazen tomb robber, would dare defy such a curse."

"What is that business about the three gates?"

"The gates are the sealed doors of a royal tomb. So it would appear that Narmer's tomb had three chambers—three important chambers, at least."

Logan shifted in his chair. "And this curse is the reason I'm here."

"There have been several—how would March put it?—**anomalous** events since work started. Equipment malfunctioning. Items disappearing or turning up in the wrong place. An unusually high number of odd accidents."

"And people are starting to get spooked," Logan said.

"I wouldn't say spooked. Restless, yes. Demoralized, maybe. See, it's bad enough being out here in the middle of nowhere, floating in the world's nastiest swamp. But with these strange happenings . . . well, you know how talk gets started. Anyway, maybe with you poking around, people will calm down."

Poking around. As she was speaking, Romero's initial skepticism, if not outright hostility, had slowly returned.

"So I'm to be a rainmaker," he said. "I may not do any good, but it's comforting to see me on the job." He glanced at her. "Now I know where I stand. Thanks for your candor."

She smiled, but it wasn't a particularly friendly smile. "You got a problem with candor?"

"Not at all. It clears the air. And it can be very bracing—even enlightening."

"For example?"

"For example, you."

"What about me?" she asked sharply. "You don't know the first thing about me."

"I know quite a bit, actually. Although some of it is, admittedly, conjecture." He held her gaze steadily. "You were the youngest child in your family. I'd imagine your older siblings were boys. I'd further imagine that your father devoted most of his attention to them: Boy Scouts, Little League. He wouldn't have had much time for you—and if your brothers noticed you at all, it would be to belittle you. That would account for your instinctive hostility, your academic overcompensation."

Romero opened her mouth to speak, then shut it again.

"There was a famous, or at least distinguished, woman a few generations back in your family: an archaeologist, perhaps, or maybe a mountain climber. The way you hang your diplomas carelessly on the wall, slightly askew, suggests an informal approach to academics—we're all one big happy family, whether we have impressive doctorates or not. And yet the very fact you brought your diplomas at all suggests a deep insecurity about your standing on this expedition. A young woman, one of few among men, on a physically demanding mission in a harsh and unforgiving environment—you worry about being taken seriously. Oh, and your middle name starts with **A**."

She looked at him, eyes blazing. "And just how the hell do you know **that**?"

He gestured over his shoulder with one thumb. "It's on your nameplate on the door."

She stood up. "Get out."

"Thanks for the chat, Dr. Romero." And Logan turned and left the office.

13

Logan's schedule was free until the following morning, so he spent the rest of the afternoon wandering around the Station getting his sea legs: trying to get a feel for the place and its occupants. Since he'd already seen the offices, residency, and dive staging areas, he decided to visit the science labs in the Red wing. Though the labs themselves were small, he was astonished by their diversity: not only archaeology but geology, organic chemistry, paleobotany, paleozoology, and several others. The laboratories were modular: each was a stainless-steel box approximately eighteen feet square. While some were occupied, others were mothballed: apparently, Porter Stone cherry-picked the labs he thought might be useful for a particular expedition and then activated them on an as-needed basis.

Next he visited White, which he learned was command and control. Although there were the obligatory secure areas and locked doors, the site seemed refreshingly informal: there were very few guards, and the ones he met were friendly and candid. He did not speak of the curse or his reason for being on the project; judging from the curious looks he occasionally received, however, it was clear that at least a few had been briefed.

The nerve center of White was a large space, staffed by a lone technician sitting at a terminal in a far corner. His back was to Logan, and he was so surrounded by monitors that he was reminiscent of a pilot in a cramped cockpit.

"Catch any shoplifters?" Logan said, stepping into the room.

The tech whirled around, neighing in surprise. A book that had been sitting on his lap flew to the floor, spinning around and coming to rest in a corner.

"Judas H. Priest!" the man said, one hand plucking at the collar of his lab coat. "You trying to give a guy a heart attack or something?"

"No. I imagine that would ruin Dr. Rush's day."

He stepped forward and extended his hand with a smile. "Jeremy Logan."

"Cory Landau." From the mangy thatch of black hair, and the way he'd lounged in his chair, Logan had guessed even from the doorway that the tech was young. But seeing him face-to-face was a surprise. Landau couldn't have been more than twenty-two or twenty-three. He had brilliant blue eyes, the fresh, peach-colored complexion of a cherub, and—a bizarrely incongruous addition—a narrow Zapata-style mustache. A can of grape-flavor Jolt and a thick pack of chewing gum sat on the desktop before him.

"So," Logan said. "What do you do around here?"

"What do you think?" the youth replied, leaning back in his chair, surprise giving way to an affected breeziness. "I run the joint." He took a sip of Jolt. "What did you mean by that crack about catching shoplifters?"

Logan nodded at the array of screens that surrounded Landau. "You've got enough LCDs here for the security pit at the Bellagio."

"Security pit, my aunt Fanny. It all begins and ends right here." Suddenly Landau's brow creased with suspicion. "Who are you, anyhow?"

"Don't worry. I'm one of the good guys." And Logan flashed his ID.

"In that case, check this out." Landau waved at the forest of glass panels and the half-dozen keyboards arrayed beneath them. "Here's where all the data gets entered, all the numbers get crunched by autonomous programs."

"I thought that was taken care of at the Maw."

Landau waved a dismissive hand. "You kidding? They're just the piano builders. I'm the artist who **plays** the instrument. Watch."

With a quick flurry of keystrokes, Landau brought up an image on one of the monitors. "See, we receive sensor, sonar, and visual information from the ongoing diving missions. It all comes into a program, here, that maps out the underwater terrain. It's a beast of a program, too. And this is the result."

Logan followed the outstretched hand toward the image on the screen. It was indeed remarkable: a fantastically complex wireframe CAD image of an undulating, almost lunar, landscape, thickly honeycombed with tunnels and boreholes.

"That's what it looks like, forty feet below us," Landau explained. "With each new dive, our representation of the swamp bed—and the caverns below it—expands." He demonstrated how the image could be manipulated, zoomed and panned, rotated on the X, Y, and Z axes. "You mentioned the Maw. You seen it yet?"

Logan nodded.

"While you were there, did you get a chance to check out the Grid?"

"You mean, that thing that looks like a bingo card on steroids?"

"That's it. Well, what I've got here is the other

half of the equation. The Grid is a two-D representation of what's been explored so far. And this shows its exact topology." Landau patted the display with almost fatherly pride. "When we find the—the target, we'll use this to ensure it is fully mapped and explored."

Logan murmured his appreciation. "Is this your first assignment for Porter Stone?"

The youth shook his head. "Second."

Logan waved a hand around. "Is this unusual? All this equipment, tools, expensive setups—just for a single expedition?"

"It's not for a single expedition. Stone's got a warehouse somewhere in the south of England. Maybe more than one. That's where he stores all the stuff."

"You mean, the vehicles and electronics? Portable labs?"

"So they say. Everything he might possibly need for a particular site."

Logan nodded. It made sense: like the inactive labs, such an arrangement would allow Stone to get up and running quickly, with as little time wastage as possible, in almost any conceivable climate or terrain.

It was refreshing to chat with someone who hadn't heard of him before, who didn't pester him with a hundred questions. Logan gave a smile of thanks. "Nice talking to you."

"Sure. Mind tossing me that book on your way out?"

Logan walked over to the book that had fallen

from the tech's lap. Picking it up, he saw it was William Hope Hodgson's exceptionally weird novel **The House on the Borderland**.

He handed it to Landau. "Sure this is the kind of book you want to be reading out here?"

"What do you mean?" Laudau took the book and cradled it protectively.

"The Sudd's bizarre enough. Reading stuff like that besides may rot your mind."

"Huh. Maybe that explains it." And Landau turned around and resumed his typing.

From White, Logan crossed another floating tube into Maroon, which housed—according to a small sign at the far end of the access vent—the historical archives and exotic sciences. Although Logan had no idea what "exotic sciences" were, he began to get an idea as soon as he peeked into some of the additional modular labs that had been installed in this wing. One darkened lab was stocked with ancient books and manuscripts about alchemy and transmutation; the walls of another were plastered with maps of Egypt and Sudan, as well as photographs of pyramids and other structures, each image overspread with a tangle of lines and circles, intersecting at odd geometric angles. Clearly, Stone would explore any avenue of knowledge, no matter how abstruse, to help make his finds. Logan wondered if he should feel insulted that his own office was located here.

As he made his way down the corridor, he stopped before a room whose door was ajar. Although Maroon seemed to hold very few people at present, this particular room was occupied. It was dimly lit. Logan could make out a hospital bed, from which dozens of leads snaked down to various monitoring devices at its foot. It reminded him of the setups in the vacant rooms he'd seen back at the Center for Transmortality Studies.

The bed in this room, however, was not empty. Logan could see that a woman was lying on it: perhaps the most beautiful woman he had ever seen. Something about her—some quality he could not quite analyze—made him stop, rooted in his tracks. Her hair was a very unusual color, a rich, dark cinnamon. Her eyes were closed. Probes were set at her temples, and others were fixed to her wrists and ankles. On the wall beside her was a very large mirror, brilliantly polished. The faint lights of the medical devices were reflected in it in myriad points of tiny color.

Logan stood there, mesmerized by this unusual sight: the woman, almost ethereal looking in the faint light of the vast arsenal of instrumentation. She lay absolutely motionless; there was not even any indication of breathing. She almost seemed to have passed from life into death. He had the distinct feeling he'd met her sometime in the past. This feeling was not in itself unusual; with his unusually sharp perception, Logan found déjà vu to be a frequent companion. This time, however, the sensation was unusually strong.

There was motion by the monitors at the foot of the bed. Logan glanced toward it and was surprised to see Dr. Rush. He adjusted a dial, peered at a gauge. And then—as if with some sixth sense—he turned toward the doorway and saw Logan.

Logan began to raise his arm in greeting. But he could tell from the look on Rush's face, from the man's body language, that this was not the time to linger and that his presence was not welcome. So instead Logan turned away and continued down the hallway, in search of his own office.

14

Logan found his office in a far corner of the Exotic Sciences wing. It was modular, like the others, and contained a desk, two chairs, a laptop computer, and a single empty bookcase. He noted—with faint amusement—that there was no other equipment.

Placing his large duffel bag on the guest chair and opening it, he put a dozen or so books in the bookcase. Then he removed several pieces of equipment and placed them on the desk. Next, he removed two quotations in small frames and hung them on the wall with pushpins. Then he closed the duffel and turned to the laptop.

He logged in with the password and ID he'd been given during that morning's processing. The site's network was relatively easy to navigate, and he immediately saw there were three e-mails awaiting him. The first was a generic welcome, explaining the layout of the Station and the whereabouts of important locations (Medical, cafeteria). The second e-mail was from the HR woman who had processed him, laying out a few ground rules (no straying from the site, no unauthorized sat-phone communications). And the third e-mail was from a person who identified himself as Stephen Weir, assistant to Porter Stone. It was essentially an aggregation of all the strange, unanticipated, or unfortunate events that had occurred since the site went live two weeks before—in other words, the reason he was here.

Logan read over the list twice. Many of the items could be immediately discounted—lights flickering, systemic effects like nausea or dizziness—but several others remained. Firing up the laptop's word processor, he began to make a list.

Day 2: On a routine reconnaissance, the engine of one of the Jet Skis abruptly went wild and refused to cut off. The occupant was forced to leap off to save himself, breaking a leg in the process. When the boat was finally recovered, the engine would not work at all. The following day, however, it operated normally.

Day 4: Three people, using the library late in the evening, reported hearing a strange, dry voice whispering to them in an unknown language.

Day 6: A cook reported two sides of beef missing from the meat locker—almost two hundred pounds. A careful search yielded nothing.

Day 9: Cory Landau was found wandering the marsh outside the perimeter after nightfall. When questioned, he said he'd seen a strange form in the distance, beckoning to him.

"Huh," Cory had said to him not half an hour before. "Maybe that explains it."

Day 10: Every electrical object, computer, and other equipment in Green shut down spontaneously at 3:15 p.m. Attempts to restart them were unsuccessful. At 3:34 p.m., they resumed functioning normally. No explanation was found.

Day 11: Tina Romero reported that the outfit of an Egyptian high priestess was missing from a closet in her office.

Day 12: Several eyewitnesses in Oasis, the drinks lounge, reported seeing strangely colored lights flickering near the horizon, accompanied by an ominous chanting, barely audible.

Day 13: A worker in the communications room reported strange noises and a machine that suddenly sprang to life when it should have been dormant.

Day 14: A machinist reported seeing a strange woman in Egyptian garb at a distance, walking across the Sudd at nightfall.

Day 15: An as-yet-undiagnosed equipment problem forced a diver to panic and surface, causing him severe injury.

Logan looked up from the screen. He already knew about the last one, of course. He'd witnessed it himself.

His thoughts drifted to King Narmer's curse. **Any man who dares enter my tomb will meet an end certain and swift. . . . His blood and his limbs will turn to ash and his tongue cleave to his throat. . . . I, Narmer the Everliving, will torment him and his, by day and by night, waking and sleeping, until madness and death become his eternal temple.** There was something the recitation of incidents had in common. Except for the diver and the Jet Ski rider, nobody had been hurt. That did not jibe with the details of the curse.

Of course, Logan thought to himself, nobody had yet found—or entered—Narmer's tomb. . . .

For perhaps the dozenth time, he wondered what Narmer's tomb might contain. Why had the pharaoh expended such effort, made such lavish sacrifices of gold and men's lives, bestowed such a curse, to make sure his remains were never violated, his most important possessions undisturbed? What was Porter Stone keeping from him? What would a god take with him to the next world?

There was a quiet sound behind him. Logan turned from the laptop screen to see Ethan Rush standing in the doorway.

"Mind if I come in?" the doctor asked with a smile.

Logan took his duffel bag from the guest chair and placed it on the floor. "Help yourself."

Rush stepped in, glanced around. "Rather spartan accommodations."

"I guess the interior decorators were uncertain just how to stock the lair of an enigmalogist."

"Funny thing about that." Rush took the empty seat, glanced toward the bookshelf. "Interesting selection of books: Aleister Crowley, Jessie Weston, Stowcroft's **Organic Chemistry, The Book of Shadows**."

"I have eclectic interests."

Rush peered at a particularly old and moth-eaten book, bound in leather. "What's this?" He reached out, glanced at the title. "**The Necro—**"

"Don't touch that one," Logan said in a quiet voice.

Rush pulled back his hand. "Sorry." He turned his attention to the two framed quotations. " 'The most beautiful thing we can experience is the mysterious,' " he read from one of them. " 'It is the source of all true art and science. Whoever does not know it and can no longer wonder, no longer marvel, is as good as dead. Einstein.' " He glanced at Logan. "Message?"

"Only that it sums up my vocation rather well. You could say I've got one foot in the world of science—Einstein's world—and the other in the world of the spirit."

Rush nodded. Then he turned to the other frame. " '**Forsan et haec olim meminisse iuvabit.**' "

"It's Virgil. From the **Aeneid**."

"I don't read Latin."

When Logan didn't offer to translate, Rush turned to the objects on the desk. "What exactly are those?"

"You use scalpels, forceps, and blood-oxygen meters, Ethan: I use tri-field EM detectors, camcorders, infrared thermometers, and—yes—holy water. Which reminds me: Do you think you can scare up a key for this desk drawer?"

"I'll talk to Supplies." Rush shook his head. "Funny. I guess I never thought of you as using instruments at all."

"That's not all I use. But then, we all have our professional secrets."

This was met with a brief pause.

"I suppose," Rush said, "you're referring to what you saw in my examination room a few minutes ago."

"Not necessarily. Although I am curious."

"I wish I could tell you. But I'm afraid that research is of a rather, ah, sensitive nature."

"So is mine." He thought of what Romero had said: **Maybe with you poking around, people will calm down.** "I'm on-site now. If I'm to be of any use at all here, you can't be keeping things from me."

This was followed by another, longer silence.

"Oh, **hell**!" Rush suddenly burst out. "You're right, of course. It's just that Stone is so into compartmentalization, he lives and breathes secrecy . . ." He paused. "Listen. I've told you of our work at the Center."

"In general terms. You're doing research on people who have undergone near-death experiences. And you implied you'd made some very interesting findings."

Rush nodded. "And our primary interest lies in one of those findings: that the experience of 'going over' has, in many cases, a direct effect on a person's . . . well . . . psychic abilities."

"Indeed? Manifested how?"

Rush broke into a broad smile. "Thank you, Jeremy. Nine times out of ten, the moment I mention the word 'psychic' I get the hairy eyeball."

Logan nodded. "Go on."

"The manifestations are quite broad. The bulk of our research at CTS is devoted to codifying it. That's what separates us from other organizations or universities studying NDEs. There's no pseudoscience or new age mumbo jumbo about this, Jeremy—we're using extremely sophisticated statistical algorithms to quantify it. In fact, we have developed a way to very precisely rank a person's psychic ability. We call it the Kleiner-Wechsmann scale, after the two researchers at the Center who developed it. In some ways it's not unlike an intelligence test, but extremely subtle and complex. The scale takes into account an entire battery of tests for psychic sensitivity—divination, telekinesis, cold reading, ESP, astrological prediction, telepathy—half a dozen others. Naturally, the scale compensates for such things as standard deviation, probability, and simple luck."

Rush stood up and began pacing the small room. "Here's an example of how it works. Let's say I've got five bills in my pocket—a one, a five, a ten, a twenty, and a fifty. I pull one out at random and ask you to guess what it is. Assuming a null hypothesis—that is, no psychic ability at all—the base success ratio would be one in five, or twenty percent. On the Kleiner-Wechsmann scale, that equates to twenty. This would be the ranking of your man on the street. On the same scale, a person with some psychic ability ranks, oh, around forty. A person with pronounced psychic power ranks sixty. A person with psychic power developed to a remarkable degree might rank eighty—he or she would guess correctly four times out of five."

He stopped pacing and turned to Logan. "But here's what we've discovered. Of the people we've tested who've 'gone over' and returned successfully, the **average** ranking is close to sixty-five."

"That's impossible—" Logan began, then stopped himself.

Rush shook his head. "I know. It's hard to believe, even for you. Why would having an NDE affect one's psychic ability? But it's fact, Jeremy—we've got hard data, and the data doesn't lie. Oh, of course, it doesn't always happen. And the particular psychic gifts vary from person to person. Not everyone's going to be able to guess, for example, what kind of bill I'm going to pull from my pocket. Some are better at extra-sensory perception. Others at clairvoyance. But that doesn't change the fact that the numbers we've accumulated, based on the testing of over two hundred subjects to date, show the **average** K-W score of a person having undergone a near-death experience is unusually high."

He sat down again. "And there's something else we've discovered. By and large, the longer the period of time the person 'went over,' the **higher** their ranking on the scale." He paused. "My wife Jennifer's heart stopped, her brain activities ceased, for fourteen minutes before I revived her. That's the longest period of time of anyone we've tested at the Center. And her ranking on the Kleiner-Wechsmann scale is also the highest of anyone we've tested: one hundred and thirty-five."

"One hundred and thirty-five?" Logan said. "But that can't be possible. According to the criteria you mentioned, a score of one hundred would mean a correct guess one hundred percent of the time. How can anyone beat a perfect score?"

"I can't explain that, Jeremy," Rush said. "Because we're not exactly sure ourselves. This is a new science. I can only tell you that we've checked and rechecked our findings. Basically, it goes beyond naming the bill you pull from your pocket—it means naming the bill **even before you put your hand in your pocket**." He shook his head, as if despite everything he still found it a little hard to believe himself. "And she's demonstrated it time and time again. Her particular gift is retrocognition."

"Retrocognition," Logan repeated. He thought a moment. Then he glanced at Rush. "And that was your wife? In the testing chamber?"

Rush nodded.

"But then what is she doing here? What use could Porter Stone have for heightened psychic abilities— even remarkably advanced psychic abilities?"

Rush coughed delicately into his hand. "Sorry. There are some things I really don't think I should tell you—at least, for now."

"I understand. This has been very interesting, thanks." **More than interesting,** he thought. **Perhaps I'll look into this on my own.**

All of a sudden, the ground beneath them trembled, as if a giant hand had seized the entire facility and given it a violent shake. In the distance came the boom of an explosion. For a moment, the two men looked at each other in surprise. Then a shrill claxon began to sound in the hallway outside the office.

"What's that?" Logan cried, jumping to his feet.

"Emergency alarm." Rush was also on his feet, reaching for the portable two-way radio clipped to his belt. Even as he did so, it began beeping shrilly.

"Dr. Rush," he said, bringing it to his lips. He listened for a moment. "My God," he said into it. "I'll be right there."

"Let's go," he said to Logan, clipping the radio back to his belt.

"What's happened?"

"Generator two is on fire." And Rush ran out of the office, Logan at his heels.

15

They ran at top speed out of Maroon, through the welter of corridors that made up Green, and then out into the large, echoing marina. The piers, which had seemed so sleepy and deserted the day before, were now crowded with people. There was a confused overlap of conversation, shouted orders. Logan could smell acrid smoke in the loam-heavy air.

He followed Rush as he raced down a gangway leading along the far wall and out through the wall of camouflaged netting. Suddenly they were outside, on a narrow walkway that angled into the swamp and disappeared around the corner of the vast pontoon structure supporting the marina. It was three o'clock, and the sun felt like a burning blanket across Logan's neck and shoulders. Above the netted roofline of the marina, he could see clouds of thick black smoke rising into the blue of the sky.

They rounded the corner of the pontoon and there—some thirty yards ahead—Logan could see the generator. It was a large, hulking structure, suspended above the swamp on floating pilings. Angry flames shot from a grille on its near side and licked upward, coating the metal housing in heavy soot. Men on Jet Skis surrounded the platform, directing streams of water toward it from portable tanks on their backs. Even at this distance, Logan could feel the heat of the inferno come over him in waves.

There was a commotion behind them, and Logan turned to see Frank Valentino and two men in coveralls coming up fast. One of the men held a heavy-duty drainage pump; the other had coils of industrial hose draped over one shoulder.

The three ran past, toward the small knot of workers bunched together at the end of the walkway. "Hurry up with that pump!" Valentino ordered.

Kneeling, the first engineer placed the pump on the metal of the walkway and flung the intake hose down into the Sudd, while the second engineer affixed the other end to the pump's spigot. Gingerly inching closer to the generator, the man aimed the hose at the flames, while the other pulled the pump's starter. Its engine coughed into life and a thin stream of brown, viscous water looped toward the flames.

"**Affanculo!**" Valentino shouted. "What's the matter?"

"It's this swamp," one of the engineers said. "It's too damn thick!"

"Shit," Valentino muttered. "Go get a number three filter—**hurry!**"

The man dropped the hose and ran back down the walkway.

Now Valentino turned to a tall man of about sixty with thinning blond hair who seemed to be in charge. "What about the methane in-link?" Logan heard Valentino ask.

"I've checked with Methane Processing. The relief valves in each wing are closed, the safety protocols fully engaged."

"Thank God for that," Valentino said.

Rush had begun walking closer to the knot of people at the end of the walkway, and Logan instinctively followed. Suddenly, he stopped dead in his tracks, as abruptly as if he'd encountered an invisible wall. Without warning, he'd become aware of a presence, hanging over the generator and its immediate surroundings: a foul, malignant, evil thing, ancient and implacable. In the heat of the swamp and flames from the generator, Logan shivered with a sudden chill. The foul stench of a charnel seemed to fill his nostrils. He sensed somehow that the thing—entity, spirit, force of nature, whatever it might be—knew of his presence, of all their presences, and felt a deep and abiding hate for all: a hate almost lustful in its strength and depth. He took an instinctive step backward, then another, before mastering himself.

Logan took a deep breath and stifled this sudden reaction; he had long ago learned that his sensitive gift had the capacity to produce either scorn or fear in others. He concentrated on listening to the conversations around him.

"Christ!" Valentino was saying. "The auxiliary tank!" The chief turned and shouted at one of the men on Jet Skis. "Rogers, quick—go uncouple and float that aux tank free before the heat ignites it!"

The man nodded, put down his hose, and moved his Jet Ski into position on the far side of the generator. But just as he was reaching toward the tank with a boat hook, a massive explosion sent a cloud of thick smoke roiling toward them. The walkway trembled violently, and Logan was knocked to his knees. As he rose to his feet again, he could hear a desperate, ragged screaming. The smoke began to clear and he made out the figure of Rogers. The man was coated in burning diesel, his clothes and hair afire. As a half-dozen workers jumped into the swamp and began swimming toward him, he writhed—screaming—off his Jet Ski and began to sink, still afire, beneath the brown and murky surface of the Sudd.

16

Oasis was the name of the Station's lone watering hole. Half canteen, half cocktail lounge, it was located in a far corner of Blue, overlooking the vast, bleak expanse of the Sudd. And yet, Logan noticed as he entered the bar, the windows facing the swamp were covered with bamboo blinds, as if to obscure, rather than emphasize, the fact they were smack in the middle of nowhere.

The lounge was dark, lit indirectly in blue-and-violet neon, and almost empty. Logan wasn't surprised. In the wake of the generator fire, the mood of the Station had grown subdued. There were no bridge games that evening, no merry chatter in the mess. Most people had retreated to their quarters, as if to deal with what had happened in solitude.

Logan felt just the opposite. The overwhelming sense of pervasive evil he had felt as the generator collapsed in flames had alarmed and unnerved him. His empty lab, his quiet room—these were the last places he wanted to be at the moment.

He walked up to the bar and took a seat. Charlie Parker was playing from invisible speakers. The bartender—a young man with short dark hair and a **Sgt. Pepper** mustache—came over.

"What can I get you?" he asked, placing a crisp cocktail napkin on the bar.

"Got any Lagavulin?"

With a smile, the man gestured toward an impressive array of single-malt scotches on the mirrored wall behind him.

"Great, thanks. I'll take it neat."

The bartender poured a generous dram into a glass and placed it on the napkin. Logan took a sip, admiring the heft of the heavy-bottomed glass, enjoying the peaty taste of the scotch. He took a second sip, waiting for the sharp memory of the fire, the smell of burnt flesh, to ease just a little. Rogers had suffered third-degree burns over 25 percent of his body: he'd been evacuated, of course, but the nearest burn center was hundreds of miles away and his prognosis was guarded.

"Buy a girl a drink?"

He looked over and saw that Christina Romero had entered the bar and taken a seat beside him.

"That's a good question. Can I?"

"This isn't the woman who reamed you out earlier. This is an upgrade. Christina Romero, release two point zero."

Logan chuckled. "All right. In that case, I'd be happy to. What'll you have?"

She turned to the bartender. "Daiquiri, please."

"Frozen?" the bartender asked.

Romero shuddered. "No. Shaken, straight up."

"You got it."

"Shall we move to a table?" Logan asked. When Romero nodded, he led the way to a table near the wall of windows.

"There's something I want to say up front," she told him as they sat down. "I'm sorry about being such a bitch, back in my office. People always tell me I'm arrogant, but I usually don't parade it around like that. I guess, your being pretty famous and all, I wanted to appear like I wasn't in awe. I overdid it. Big-time."

Logan waved a hand. "Let's forget it."

"I'm not trying to make excuses. It's just—you know—the stress. I mean, nobody talks about it, but we haven't found a damn thing yet in two weeks of digging. I've got a couple of major league a-holes to deal with here. And then, these—these strange goings-on. People seeing things, equipment malfunctioning. And now this fire, what happened to Rogers." She shook her head. "It gets on your nerves after a while. I shouldn't have taken it out on you."

"That's okay. You can pay the bar tab."

"It's free," she said with a laugh.

They sipped their drinks.

"Did you always want to be an Egyptologist?" Logan asked. "I wanted to be one myself, as a kid, after seeing **The Mummy**. But then—when I learned how hard it was to read hieroglyphics—I lost interest."

"My grandmother was an archaeologist—but then, you already knew that somehow. She worked on all sorts of digs, everywhere from New Hampshire to Nineveh. I always idolized her. I guess that's part of it. But what really gave me the bug was King Tut."

Logan looked at her. "King Tut?"

"Yup. I grew up in South Bend. When the King Tut expedition came to the Field Museum, my whole family drove to Chicago to see it. Oh, my God. My parents had to tear me away. I mean, the death mask, the golden scarabs, the treasure hall. I was only in fourth grade, and it haunted me for, like, months. Afterward I read every book about Egypt and archaeology I could get my hands on. **Gods, Graves, and Scholars**; Carter and Carnarvon's **Five Years' Explorations at Thebes**—you name it. I never looked back."

She grew more animated as she spoke, until her

green eyes practically flashed with excitement. She wasn't pretty, exactly, but she had a kind of inner electricity, and a refreshing candor, that Logan found intriguing.

She finished her cocktail with a mighty slug. "Your turn."

"Me? Oh, I became interested in history my freshman year at Dartmouth."

"Don't be evasive. You know what I'm talking about."

Logan laughed. It wasn't something he usually talked about. But, after all, she had sought him out, apologized. "I guess it started when I spent the night in a haunted house."

Romero signaled the bartender for another drink. "This isn't going to be bullshit, is it?"

"Nope. I was twelve. My parents were away for the weekend, and my older brother was supposed to look after me." Logan shook his head. "He looked after me, all right. He dared me to spend the night in the old Hackety place."

"The old, haunted Hackety place."

"Right. It had been empty for years, but all the local kids said a witch lived there. People talked about strange lights at midnight, about how dogs avoided the place like the plague. My brother knew how stubborn I was, how I could never resist a dare. So I took a sleeping bag and a flashlight, and some paperbacks my brother gave me, and I went down the street to the deserted house and sneaked in a first-floor window."

He paused, remembering. "At first it seemed like a breeze. I laid out the sleeping bag in what had been the living room. But then it got dark. And I started to hear things: creaks, groans. I tried to distract myself by looking into the books my brother gave me, but they were all ghost stories—it figures—and I put them aside. That was when I heard it."

"What?"

"Steps. Coming up from the basement."

The cocktail arrived, and Romero cradled it in her hands. "Go on."

"I tried to run, but I was petrified. I couldn't even stand up. It was all I could do to switch on the flashlight. I heard the footsteps move slowly through the kitchen. Then a figure appeared in the doorway."

He took a sip of scotch. "I'll never forget what I saw in the gleam of that flashlight. A crone, white hair wild and flying in all directions, her eyes just hollows in the glare. My heart felt like it was going to explode. She started walking toward me. And then I started to cry. It was all I could do not to wet my pants. She stretched out a withered hand. That's when I knew I was going to die. She'd hex me, and I'd just shrivel up and die."

He paused.

"Well?" Romero urged.

"I didn't die. She took my hand, held it in hers. And suddenly I—I **understood**. It's . . . it's hard to explain. But I realized she wasn't a witch. She was just an old woman, lonely and scared, hiding in the basement, living on tap water and canned food. It was as if I could . . . I could **feel** her fear of the outside world, feel her miserable existence in the cold and dark, feel her pain at having lost everyone she cared about."

He finished his drink. "That was it. She retreated into the dark. I rolled up my sleeping bag and went home. When my parents got back, I told them what happened. My brother got grounded for a month, and the cops checked out the Hackety place. She turned out to be Vera Hackety, a mentally handicapped woman whose family had been taking care of her. Her last surviving relative had died eighteen months before. She'd been living in the basement ever since."

He looked at Romero. "But a funny thing happened. Something about that encounter changed me. I became fascinated by tales of real-life ghosts, of haunted mansions and treasures with curses, and Bigfoot, and everything else you can imagine. And one of those books—the ghost stories my brother had so thoughtfully given me to scare me even worse—turned out to be a book by E. and H. Heron called **Flaxman Low, Occult Psychologist**. It was a book of stories about a supernatural sleuth."

"A supernatural sleuth," Romero repeated.

"That's right. A kind of Sherlock Holmes of the spirit realm. As soon as I finished that book, I knew what I wanted to do with my life. Of course, it usually isn't a full-time job—hence the professorship."

"But how did you develop your—your skills?"

Romero asked. "I mean, there aren't exactly any grad-uate courses in enigmalogy."

"No. But there are lots of treatises on the subject. That's where being a medieval historian comes in handy."

"You mean, like the **Malleus Maleficarum**?"

"Exactly. And many others, even older and more authoritative." He shrugged. "As with anything else, you learn by doing."

The skeptical look began to creep back into Rome-ro's face. "Treatises. Don't tell me you believe all that stuff about familiars and astrology and the philoso-pher's stone."

"Those are just Western European examples you mention. Every culture has its own supernatural apparatus. I've studied just about all that have been documented—and some that haven't. And I've ana-lyzed the elements they have in common." He paused. "What I believe is that beyond the natural, visible world there are elemental forces—some good, others evil—that always have and always will exist in coun-terpart to ourselves."

"Like a curse on a mummy's tomb," Romero said. She pointed at Logan's glass. "How many of those did you have before I got here?"

"Think of atoms or dark matter: we can't see them, but we know they exist. Why not elemental beings—or creatures we simply haven't yet encoun-tered? Or, for that matter, forces we simply haven't learned how to harness?"

Romero's skeptical look deepened.

Logan hesitated for a second. Then he reached over, plucked the plastic straw from Romero's drink, and placed it on the white linen tablecloth between them. He placed his hands on both sides of it, palms downward, fingers spread slightly. He breathed in, slowly exhaled.

At first, nothing happened. Then the straw shuddered slightly. And then—after another, more violent shudder—it rose slowly off the table; hovered—trembling—half an inch above it for a few seconds; then dropped back onto the cloth, rolling once before falling still again.

"Jesus!" Romero said. She peered at the straw, then gingerly picked it up, as if it might burn her fingers. "How did you do that? That's one hell of a magic trick."

"With the proper training, you could probably do it, too," Logan replied. "But not as long as you think of it as a trick."

She looked dubiously at the straw, then put it back down on the table, took a thoughtful sip of her drink. "Just one other question," she said. "Back at my office—everything you said about me was true. Down to the fact that I was the youngest child. How did you know so much about me?"

"I'm an empath," Logan replied.

"An empath? What's that?"

"Somebody with the ability to absorb the feelings and emotions of others. When I shook your hand, I received a series—a flood, really—of very strong memories, notions, thoughts, concerns, desires. They're nonselective—I have no control over what impressions I receive. I only know that, when I come into physical contact with another person, I will receive impressions, in greater or lesser measure."

"Empathy," Romero said. "Sounds like something right up there with aromatherapy and crystals."

Logan shrugged. "Then you tell me: How **did** I know all that?"

"I can't explain it." She looked at him. "How do you become an empath?"

"It's inherited. It has a biological aspect and a spiritual one, as well. Sometimes it remains dormant in people their entire lives; frequently it is awakened by a traumatic experience. In my case, I believe it was the touch of Vera Hackety." He fiddled with his empty glass. "All I can tell you for sure is that it's proven critical to my work."

She smiled. "Levitation, reading thoughts . . . can you predict the future, too?"

Logan nodded. "How's this: I predict that, if we don't get to the mess in ten minutes, they're going to stop serving dinner."

Romero glanced at her watch. Then she laughed. "That's the kind of prediction I can understand. Let's go, Svengali."

And as they stood up from the table, she picked up the cocktail straw and slipped it into the pocket of her jeans.

17

The following morning at nine o'clock, a conference was called to perform a postmortem on the prior day's accident. Logan wasn't invited, but—learning about it from Rush at breakfast—he managed to slip into Conference Room A in White on the doctor's coattails.

The room was large and windowless, with two semicircles of chairs. One wall was covered by several whiteboards; another sported dual digital projector screens. A huge satellite map of the Sudd hung from an overhead support, decorated with pushpins and handwritten legends scribbled on Post-it notes. Logan recognized a few of the assembled faces: Christina Romero was there, and so was Valentino; the chief of the digging operation was surrounded by a small knot of his techs and roustabouts.

Logan helped himself to a cup of coffee, then took a seat in the second tier of chairs, behind Rush. No sooner had he done so than the older man with thinning blond hair—the one he'd seen at the generator the previous day—cleared his throat and spoke.

"All right," he said. "Let's talk about what we know." He turned to a man wearing a white coverall. "Campbell, what's the status of our power grid?"

The man named Campbell sniffed. "We've ramped up generator one to ninety-eight percent of rated load. Our core nominal output is down to sixty-five percent."

"Status of the methane gathering and conversion system?"

"Unaffected. The scrubbers and interface baffles are at peak efficiency. In fact, with generator two out, we've had to dial back fuel production."

"Thank God they're still functional." The older man turned to someone else—a short woman with a tablet computer on her lap. "So output's down by thirty-five percent. How does that affect Station functionality?"

"We've scaled back on nonessential services, Dr. March," she replied.

Logan looked at the man with fresh interest. **So that's Fenwick March,** he thought. He'd heard of March: he was the head archaeologist for the dig. He was, according to Romero, second in command in Stone's absence—and he seemed to enjoy hearing the sound of his own voice.

"What about the primary search operation?" March asked the woman.

"Unaffected. We've diverted power and personnel, as necessary."

Now March turned to a third person. "Montoya? What about a replacement?"

The man named Montoya shifted in his chair. "We're putting out inquiries."

March's expression changed abruptly, almost as if he'd caught a whiff of something foul. "Inquiries?"

"We have to be tactful. A six-thousand-kilowatt generator isn't a common item around here, and we can't afford to increase our visibility in Khartoum or—"

"Damn it," March interrupted, "don't give me excuses! We need that replacement generator—and we need it now!"

"Yes, Dr. March," the man replied, ducking his head.

"We're on a tight schedule—we can't afford any snags, let alone the loss of half our power output."

"Yes, Dr. March," the man repeated, ducking his head farther, as if he wanted it to vanish between his shoulders.

March looked around, his gaze landing next on Valentino. "You've examined what's left of generator two?"

Valentino nodded his burly head.

"And?"

Valentino shrugged. He clearly was not intimidated by the head archaeologist—and March seemed to sense it.

"Well?" March pressed. "Can you tell me what caused the explosion?"

"It's hard to say. The unit was torn apart, the mechanism half melted. Maybe a stator fault, maybe a turn-to-turn failure in one of the coils. Either way, overheating spread to the couplers and collector rings, and from there to the aux tank."

"The auxiliary tank." March turned to Rush, almost as an afterthought. "Have you heard any more about Rogers's condition?"

Rush shook his head. "Last I heard he was in critical condition in Coptic Hospital. I'm waiting for the nurse's report now."

March grunted. Then he turned back to Valentino. "Can you at least tell me whether this was caused by mechanical failure or structural weakness or if some . . . external element was involved?"

At this, Christina Romero looked up and caught Logan's eye. She gave him an expression that was half smile, half smirk.

"External element," Valentino said. "You mean, like sabotage?"

"That's one possibility," March said carefully.

Valentino thought about this for a moment. "If it was sabotage—and, yes, it's possible some **figlio di puttana** monkeyed with the works—the fire would have destroyed any evidence."

"What makes you think of sabotage, Fenwick?" Rush said in a quiet voice. "You of all people know how carefully the entire crew was vetted."

"I know," March replied, lowering his eyes. "But I've never been on an expedition where so much has gone wrong. It's as if—" He paused. "It's as if someone **wants** our mission to fail."

"If that were the case," Rush went on, "there are much easier ways to accomplish that than compromising a generator."

Slowly, March raised his eyes and looked meaningfully at Rush. "That's true," he said. "That's very true."

18

Jack Wildman hung suspended, thirty-five feet below the surface, as he watched his dive partner, Mandelbaum, prepare to fire up Big Bertha. "Watched" wasn't exactly the right term, he decided: Mandelbaum was little more than the vaguest blur in the muddy horror that surrounded them on all sides, a smudge, black against black, detectable only because it was in motion.

"Able Charlie to base," Mandelbaum spoke into his radio. "We're ready to start scouring grid G three."

"Able Charlie, roger," came the squawked reply from up top. "Bubble status?"

"Eighty-nine percent."

Wildman glanced at the digital readout on the device strapped to his forearm. "Whiskey Bravo here," he said into his own radio. "Bubble at ninety-one."

"Roger that," came the response from base. "Proceed."

There was a low drone as Mandelbaum started up Big Bertha. Immediately, Wildman felt the resulting pressure as thick muck was eddied past him by the machine's jets of compressed air. It was like standing in a vat of molasses.

Actually, it was worse than that. Because the muck and mire that surrounded them were treacherous. He had to constantly watch his step: sticks and bracken were hidden everywhere, often sharp, ready to pierce his suit. And the Sudd was so damned thick, every move was an effort, like trying to work in an atmosphere of 10 g's. . . .

"Able Charlie to base," Mandelbaum radioed. "Scouring under way."

Now Wildman turned on the heavy spotlight fixed to his right shoulder and approached the stone face: the freshly bared bed of the Sudd, scoured temporarily clean by Big Bertha. It was Mandelbaum's job to operate Big Bertha; his own job to examine the scoured areas it left behind for any evidence of caverns, lava pipes, or ancient construction. He felt like an astronaut on some nightmare gas planet, with his heavy wet suit and its powerful light and the helmet video camera and the bubble apparatus all conspiring to weigh him down.

Actually, he was glad about the bubble. Very glad. It kept him oriented in this soup. If not for the bubble, you could easily lose your bearings, forget which way was up. He couldn't stop thinking about what happened to Forsythe: panicking over a blocked regulator, trying desperately to surface. . . . The thought chilled him. If you got disoriented in this black ooze, lost your guide cable—forget it. Your only hope was that your dive buddy would find you. Otherwise, you were dead meat. . . .

His foot slipped in the greasy muck of the bottom and he slid backward, only to feel something hard strike him in the calf. He reached down, felt it. A stick. Since he was unable to make out anything unless it was inches before his mask, he brought it up into visual range. Sure enough. Goddamn Sudd. Good thing the stick hadn't penetrated his suit—the one time that had happened, the smell had been so awful it had taken him three showers to get rid of it.

He went back to examining the scoured area.

"Able Charlie," Mandelbaum said into the radio. "I think Big Bertha needs another cleaning. I'm having trouble keeping the throttle steady."

"Roger that," repeated the voice from the surface.

Pushing mud and ooze away from his face, Wildman moved to his right, preparing to examine a fresh area. The feeling of muck streaming past his limbs in the wake of the machine's air jets was horrible. A few days before, one of the divers on another crew had had his mouthpiece jarred loose by his partner's elbow. The poor sap got a mouthful of the shit, started puking his guts out, and had to do an emergency surface before he aspirated. . . .

"Able Charlie," Mandelbaum said again, "I'm afraid we need to terminate the dive. I'm having more trouble with Big Bertha—"

As he spoke, Wildman heard Bertha's engine suddenly roar, the throttle going wide open. Mandelbaum quickly killed the throttle, but not before an irresistible wave of black muck, thrown up by the jets, knocked Wildman back a foot into the dense soup. Again, he felt something hard prod him, this time in the lower back. **Shit.** Reaching around, he grabbed for it, felt his hands close over the slippery stick. He brought it around toward his mask. He ought to beat Mandelbaum over the head with it. The thought brought a smile to his face until he got a look at the thing and found it wasn't a stick, after all.

It was a bone.

19

Late that afternoon, a small group gathered in the forensic bay of Rush's tidy medical suite. In addition to Rush himself, there was an assisting nurse, Tina Romero, and Jeremy Logan. When Logan had entered, Rush opened his mouth—apparently to protest, given Porter Stone's standing order for compartmentalization—but then he simply shrugged, smiled faintly, and gestured him forward.

The archaeological team had finished their initial

examination of the skeleton discovered by the dive team—now it was up to Rush to perform what would be, in essence, a postmortem.

The collection of bones themselves sat in a blue plastic evidence locker, set upon a wheeled cart of stainless steel. As the others watched, Rush snapped on a pair of latex gloves, then pulled the ceiling-mounted microphone toward him, pressed the Record button, and began to speak.

"Examination of remains found on day sixteen of project, in a shallow cave within grid square G three. Ethan Rush performing the analysis, with Gail Trapsin assisting." A pause. "The matrix of silt and mud surrounding the remains has apparently acted as a preservative, and the skeleton is in very good condition, considering. Nevertheless, there is considerable decay."

He took the cover from the evidence locker, then began carefully removing the bones and placing them on the nearby autopsy table. "The cranial and facial bones are intact, as are those of the rib cage, arms, and vertebral column. Dive teams have searched for the remainder of the skeleton, without success, finding only a few leathery fragments of what might once have been sandals. The archaeological team has speculated that only the upper portion of the body was preserved in the silty matrix, and that the lower section has completely decayed and is no longer extant."

He placed the bones on the table, roughly in anatomical order. Logan looked at them curiously. They were a dark brown, almost mahogany, as if varnished by their five-millennium-long mud bath. As Rush worked, bringing out more bones, the room began to smell of the Sudd: peat, vegetal decay, and an odd, sweetish smell that made Logan feel faintly nauseous.

Rush spoke into the microphone again. "Radio-carbon dating by mass spectrometer indicates that the bones are approximately fifty-two hundred years old, with a two percent margin of error due to the natural contaminants in the surrounding matrix."

"Contemporaneous with Narmer," Romero said quietly as she toyed with her ever-present fountain pen.

"Found with the body was a round shield, badly deteriorated, and the remains of what appears to be a mace."

"Equipment of the pharaoh's personal bodyguard," Romero added.

"While, as I mention, the shield is in poor condition," Rush continued, "the archaeology team has used reverse-investment casting, in concert with digital enhancement, to sharpen the remains of what seems to be ornamentation on the shield's face. Archaeology believes the ornament to be a serekh, enclosing two symbols: a fish, and what appears to be a tool of some kind."

"A catfish and a chisel," Romero said. "The phonetic representation of Narmer's name. At least, that's what I assume—if March would ever let me take a look at the damn thing."

Rush pressed the button on the microphone. "Christina, would you mind reserving your comments until after I've finished my report?"

Romero inclined her head and pressed her fingers lightly to her forehead in mock genuflection. "Sorry."

Rush addressed the microphone again. "As for the bones themselves, the skull is relatively intact, the neurocranium and the splanchnocranium suffering the least amount of damage. The temporal bones are missing. The mandible, hyoid bone, and clavicle show somewhat more deterioration. Most of the teeth are missing, and those that remain show the advanced caries common to the period." He paused to examine the rest of the bones. "The articulated vertebra grow increasingly damaged and decayed as we move from the cervical to the thoracic to the lumbar. The last extant vertebra is L two—the sacral and coccygeal vertebrae are entirely missing. Ribs one through eight are extant. While the lower of the existing ribs become increasingly damaged, there are distinct marks on the anterior of rib six"—here he paused again for a closer look—"that suggest the scraping of a knife or sword. This would lead one to assume the manner of death to be homicide."

"I **knew** it!" Romero shouted in a triumphant voice.

This sudden outburst, in marked contrast to Rush's even, reasoned tone, caused Logan to jump. Once again, Rush turned off the microphone, an irritated look crossing his face. "Christina, I have to insist that you—"

"But you're wrong about the manner of death," Romero interrupted again. The note of triumph had not left her voice. "It wasn't murder. It was suicide."

Rush's look of irritation turned to something closer to disbelief. "How can you possibly know—"

"And that isn't all. Not far away—maybe fifty, maybe a hundred yards north of where this was discovered—we're going to find more skeletons. A whole hell of a lot more skeletons. I'm off to tell Valentino where to concentrate his divers." And without another word she turned and walked briskly out of the medical bay, leaving Logan and Rush to look at each other in bafflement.

20

The discovery of the skeleton had another effect beyond boosting the spirits of the searchers and raising the level of excitement across the Station—it also heralded the approach of Porter Stone himself. Arriving sometime late that evening under cover of darkness, he called for a Station-wide meeting the following morning. All work—even the diving itself—would take a thirty-minute recess while Stone addressed the expeditionary team.

The meeting was to be held in the largest space on the Station: the machine shop in Green. As Logan stepped into the shop at precisely ten o'clock, he looked around curiously. Metal racks stretched from floor to ceiling on three of the walls, containing every imaginable part, tool, and piece of equipment. Several Jet Skis sat on lifts in various stages of disassembly. A half-dozen other large sections of engines and diving equipment were arrayed on metal tables. In one corner sat what looked like part of the ruined generator, its flanks blackened and ugly under the bright work lights.

Logan's glance shifted from the room itself to those standing within it, waiting for Stone. It was an incredibly diverse crowd: scientists in lab coats, technicians, divers, roustabouts, cooks, electricians, mechanics, engineers, historians, archaeologists, pilots—a throng of some one hundred and fifty people, all gathered here at the whim of a single man: a man with a crystal clear vision of what he wanted to accomplish and with the iron will to see that vision through.

As if on cue, Stone stepped into the machine shop. The crowd broke into spontaneous applause. Stone moved through the multitude, shaking hands, murmuring fragments of sentences to people who stopped him. He had abandoned the Arab garb for a linen suit, but if he had been wearing a leather bomber jacket and a pith helmet he would have looked no more the adventurer: something about his tanned, heavily weathered skin and the way his tall, lean body moved with an almost animal grace seemed to exude exploration and discovery.

Reaching the back of the room, he turned to face the group, smiling broadly, and raised his hands. Gradually, the crowd fell into a restive silence. Stone glanced around, still smiling, allowing the drama to build. And then at last he cleared his throat and began to speak.

"My first experience as a treasure seeker," he said, "took place when I was eleven. In the Colorado town where I grew up, there was a local legend about a band of Indians that had once lived in the fields just outside town. Boys like myself, college students, even professional archaeologists had visited those fields again and again, dug holes and test trenches, swept the area with metal detectors—all without finding so much as a single bead. I was among them. I must have wandered over those fields a dozen times, eyes on the ground, searching.

"And then one day I raised my eyes from the ground. I looked—really **looked**—at the place for the first time. Beyond the fields, the land fell gently down to the Rio Grande, about a mile away. There were stands of cottonwoods along the river, and the grass was lush and thick.

"In my youthful mind's eye I traveled back two hundred years. I saw a band of Indians, camped on the river's edge. There was water for drinking and cooking, abundant fish, sweet grass for the horses, shade and shelter beneath the trees. Then I looked at the dry, barren field in which I stood. Why, I wondered, would Native Americans make their camp here—when another, more favorable spot was so close by?

"So I hiked the mile down to the river and began poking around in the dirt and grass by the riverbank. And within ten minutes I discovered **this**." Reaching into his pocket, he drew something out and held it up for the crowd to see. Logan saw it was an obsidian arrowhead, perfectly flaked: a real beauty.

"I went back to that site many more times," Stone continued. "I found more points, along with clay pipes, stone pestles, and a host of other things. But nothing, before or since, has ever filled me with such excitement as the discovery of that very first arrowhead. These days, I never go anywhere without it." He replaced it in his pocket, then glanced at the throng, his eyes roving from person to person, before speaking again.

"It wasn't just the thrill of discovery. It wasn't just uncovering something of beauty, something of value. It was using my **intellect,** my ability to think outside the scholarly box, to unravel the riddles of the past. All the many others before me had accepted as gospel the stories of where those Native Americans had camped. I, too, started out that way—but then I learned an important lesson. A lesson I've never forgotten."

Putting his hands in his pockets, he began to stride back and forth as he spoke. "Archaeological excavation, my friends, is like a mystery story. The past likes to keep its secrets. It doesn't want to yield them up. So it's my job to play detective. And any good detective knows that the best way to solve a mystery is to bring as many tools, as much evidence, as much investigation, to bear as possible."

He stopped abruptly, ran a hand through his white hair. "As you know, I've done this many times before—with results that speak for themselves. I'm doing it again here and now. I have spared no expense on research or equipment—or talent. All of you standing before me are the best at what you do. I have done my part—and, with the discovery of this skeleton, almost without doubt the personal bodyguard of the pharaoh Narmer—we find ourselves once again on the very cusp of success. I am convinced we are days, mere days, from finding the tomb—and in so doing, learning more of those secrets that the past tries so hard to conceal."

He glanced again over the silent group. "As I said, I have done my part. Now—now that we are so close—it is time to do yours. Our window of opportunity is short. I am relying on you all to give me one hundred and ten percent effort. Whatever your position here—whether you lead a dive team or you wash dishes in the mess—you are an integral, a **critical** part of a machine. Every last one of you is vital to our success. I want you to remember that in the coming days."

Stone cleared his throat once again. "Somewhere beneath our feet are the unguessable treasures that

Narmer gathered around himself, that he placed in his tomb to accompany him into the afterlife. Our discovery, and our study, of these treasures will not only make you all famous—they will make you rich. Not necessarily in monetary terms, though of course that is part of it. But most important, they will expand our knowledge of the earliest Egyptian kings a thousandfold—and **that** is the kind of richness that we, as the detectives of history, can never get enough of."

There was another burst of applause. Stone let it continue for fifteen seconds, then thirty, before finally raising his hands again.

"I won't keep you any longer," he said. "You all have jobs to do. As I've said, over the next several days I'll be wanting, and expecting, your very best. Are there any questions?"

"I've got one," Logan heard himself say into the silence.

As a hundred and fifty heads turned to look at him, Logan wondered what on earth had made him speak up. It was something he'd been mulling over privately—but he hadn't intended to voice his speculations aloud.

Porter Stone didn't appear to have expected any questions, because he had already turned away to speak with March. At the sound of Logan's voice, however, he turned back, searching the crowd.

"Dr. Logan?" Stone said, spotting him.

Logan nodded.

"What's on your mind?"

"It's something you said just now. You said that Narmer gathered his treasures around himself, placed them in his tomb, so they could accompany him to the next world. But I was wondering—isn't it possible that, in building such a remote and secret tomb, he wasn't simply amassing his valuables but hiding them, **protecting** them, as well?"

Stone frowned. "Of course. All kings tried to protect their earthly goods against vandals and tomb robbers."

"That wasn't the kind of protection I meant."

There was a brief silence. Then Stone spoke again. "An interesting conjecture." He raised his voice, spoke to the assembled group. "Thanks again for your time. You may all return to your stations now."

As the crowd began to break up and move away, heading for the machine shop exit, Stone turned once again to Logan. "Not you," he said. "I think we should talk."

21

Porter Stone's private office, at the end of one of the interior corridors of White, was a small but highly functional space. There was no power desk, no framed magazine covers sporting his image. Instead, there was a single round table surrounded by a half-dozen chairs; a few laptops; a shortwave radio. A single shelf held several books on Egyptology and the history of the dynastic line. There were no artifacts, grave goods, or decorations of any kind. The only thing on the wall was a single page displaying the current month, ripped roughly from a calendar and taped behind the conference table, as if to underscore the time pressure they were under.

Stone waved Logan toward the table. "Have a seat. Would you care for coffee, tea, mineral water?"

"I'm fine, thank you," Logan said as he sat down.

Stone nodded, then took a seat across the table. For a moment he regarded Logan with his pale blue eyes, so prominent in the tanned face. "I wonder if you'd care to clarify what you said, back there in the machine shop."

"I've been studying Narmer's curse—and how it compares to other ancient Egyptian curses. It led me to think about something."

Stone nodded. "Go on."

"Many pharaohs owned priceless treasures—probably much more valuable than those of Narmer, who after all was a very early ruler. And yet none of them took anywhere near the trouble Narmer did to hide himself and his possessions. Certainly, they built pyramids in Giza, they built tombs in the Valley of the Kings—but they didn't have themselves buried beyond their borders, in potentially hostile countries, hundreds of miles from their seats of power. They didn't build false tombs to throw would-be looters off the scent. And Narmer's curse, as dreadful as it is, is unusual: it doesn't mention riches and gold. It all makes me wonder: Did Narmer have some other, overbearing concern, beyond merely keeping his valuables close?"

Stone had listened without moving. "Are you implying that, even more than his descendants, Narmer couldn't risk having his sarcophagus defiled? He'd unified Egypt, but it was still a shaky unification; he couldn't allow his tomb to be ransacked and his dynasty threatened?"

"That's part of it. But not all. The incredible lengths he went to keep his tomb a secret—to me, it seems the work of a man who was protecting something, hiding something—something that was as valuable to him as life, or afterlife, itself. Something whose absence, in fact, might **jeopardize** the afterlife."

For a moment, Stone simply looked at Logan. And then his face broke into a smile, and he laughed. Watching him, Logan had the distinct impression that he had just been tested—and had passed.

"Damn it, Jeremy—may I call you Jeremy?—this is the second time you've surprised me. I like the way your mind works. Sometimes I believe my specialists are so good at what they do, at their own little spheres of knowledge, that they forget there are other ways of looking at things." He leaned forward. "And, as it happens, I believe that you're exactly right."

He stood up, walked to the door, opened it, and leaned out, asking his secretary for coffee. Then he returned to the table and pulled something from the pocket of his suit.

"What—the arrowhead again?" Logan said.

"Hardly." Stone palmed something to Logan. It

was the ostracon he'd seen in the reading room of the Museum of Egyptian Antiquities.

"Do you remember this?" Stone asked. "The ostracon that once belonged to Flinders Petrie?"

"Of course."

Stone placed it on the table. "You remember it contains four hieroglyphs?"

"I remember that you were coy about their meaning."

A soft knock, and the secretary entered with Stone's coffee. He took a sip, then turned back to Logan. "Well, I'm not going to be coy anymore. You've graduated to the inner circle." He regarded his guest, his eyes dancing with the same private amusement Logan had noticed before. "You recall that Narmer was—according to most Egyptologists—the unifier of upper and lower Egypt?"

"Yes," Logan said.

"And you recall that he wore the 'double' crown, representing the red and the white crowns of the two Egypts—the sacred relics of the unification?"

Logan nodded.

Stone let his gaze roam slowly around the office for a moment. "It's a very curious thing, Jeremy. Did you know that no crown of an Egyptian pharaoh has ever been found—not one? Even King Tut's tomb, which was discovered intact and unlooted, containing absolutely everything he needed to take with him on his journey to the next world, contained no crown."

He let this fact settle in a moment before going on. "There are several theories why. One is that the crown had magical properties that somehow prevented it from passing into the next world. Another—more popular among scholars, naturally—is that there was never more than one such crown in existence, passed down from one king to the next: thus it was the one thing that couldn't be taken on the journey to the underworld. But the fact is, **nobody** knows for sure why one has never been found."

Stone picked up the disk again, turned it over in his hand. "What Petrie saw on this ostracon were four hieroglyphs dating from a very early period." Extending a finger, Stone pointed to them in turn. "This first is a representation of the red crown of upper Egypt. The second is the white crown of lower Egypt. The third is a hieroglyph of a vault, or resting place. And the last is a primitive serekh containing Narmer's name."

In the silence that followed, Stone put the ostracon back on the table, inscription side down, and placed his coffee cup atop it.

Logan barely noticed. His mind was working quickly. "Do you mean to tell me . . ."

Stone nodded. "This ostracon is the key to the biggest—and I mean **the** biggest—archaeological secret in history. It's why Petrie dropped everything and left his comfortable retirement to undertake a long, dangerous, and ultimately unsuccessful search. It tells us that King Narmer was buried with the **original** two crowns of Egypt: the white and the red."

22

The senior staff lounge, located down the corridor from Oasis in the Station's Blue wing, was a space in which the movers and shakers of the expedition could gather for relaxation and friendly chat. The fact that lower-level staff were denied admittance meant that even sensitive aspects of the work could be discussed informally without fear of betraying any secrets.

Jeremy Logan entered the lounge with a distinct feeling of curiosity. He'd been unable to visit it before, but his newfound status with Porter Stone meant that all doors—most, anyway—were now open to him. The lounge was better appointed than the other spaces he'd seen, even Stone's own office. The walls were covered in a veneer of dark wood, and chairs and sofas of burgundy leather were arranged over thick Turkish rugs. These appointments, along with the heavy brass lamps, gave the lounge the feeling of an Edwardian men's club.

Logan put down his duffel on an empty chair and glanced around. Urns of coffee and hot water stood on a long table in the back, along with cucumber sandwiches and madeleines. One wall was lined with bookshelves; the others displayed framed landscapes and sporting prints. He wandered over to the wall of books and briefly scanned their titles. There were numerous current thrillers, lots of nineteenth-century English novels, and biographies, histories, and works of philosophy. In fact, there was everything, it seemed, except anything on Egypt or archaeology. It was almost as if this room was meant as a determined escape from the project at hand. He thought back to the bridge games he'd observed, recalled what Rush had told him about Stone's belief in diversion from the business at hand.

Three people were sitting around a table, speaking in low tones. Logan saw Fenwick March, Tina Romero, and a cinnamon-haired woman whose back was to him. Tina smiled at him; March gave a curt nod, as if to imply Logan's presence in the lounge was at the second-in-command's own sufferance.

Logan chose a magazine at random from one of the tables and sat down, loath to intrude on their conversation, but Tina waved him over. "Come on, Jeremy," she said. "Maybe you'll learn something."

Logan retrieved his duffel and joined the group. As he did so, he saw the face of the other woman. It was Jennifer Rush. Seeing her up close made him briefly go weak at the knees. She had her hair in a severe French twist—precisely the style his own wife had always favored. Except that, even to his hardly objective eyes, Jennifer Rush was far more beautiful. She had an oval face, with high cheekbones and a narrow, sculpted chin, and amber eyes. The combination was exotic, and in a way Logan thought she resembled an Egyptian princess herself.

Jennifer Rush smiled briefly at him. "You must be Dr. Logan," she said.

"The enig**ma**logist," March said. "You two should have a lot in common." He turned back to Tina Romero. "In any case, I think you and Stone are wrong. We're not going to find the crown inside the tomb."

"So you say," Tina replied. "And what makes you so sure?"

"Because no such thing has ever been found in any tomb." He leaned forward. "What kinds of things are traditionally discovered in later pharaonic tombs?

Offerings of food and drink. Ushabti. Statuary. Jewelry. Gaming pieces. Canopic jars. Funerary offerings. Inscriptions from **The Book of the Dead**. Even boats, for God's sake. And what do they all have in common? Just one thing: they aid the pharaoh in his journey from our world to the next and they provision him for that next world." He waved a hand dismissively. "Crowns—they are of **this** world."

"Sorry, but I don't buy it," Tina said. "He would be pharaoh in the next world, just as he had been here. He would need his trappings of power."

"If that is true, then why have no crowns ever been discovered—even in unlooted tombs?"

"Be as skeptical as you want," Tina said, her voice a notch higher. "But the fact remains: Narmer went to incredible trouble, unheard-of trouble, to keep his tomb secret. Other First Dynasty pharaohs were content with the mud-brick tombs at Abydos. But not Narmer. His tomb wasn't even a cenotaph, like the royal tombs at Saqqara—a symbolic grave—it was a goddamn **fake**! Think of the lengths he went to, the dangers he took, the lives he sacrificed, to keep the location of his real burial chamber a secret. So tell me, Fenwick, old boy: If it isn't the double crown that's hidden in that tomb—**then what is buried down there beneath the Sudd?**"

And she sat back, a triumphant look on her face.

March looked at her, an arch smile on his lips. "A very good question. What—if anything?"

Tina's triumphant look morphed into a scowl.

March turned to Jennifer Rush. "But maybe we should be asking you that question. What secrets have come to you from beyond, pray tell?"

The faint tinge of sarcasm in the archaeologist's voice was impossible to miss. Nevertheless, Jennifer Rush didn't rise to the bait. "My findings are confidential between my husband, me, and Dr. Stone," she replied. "If you want to know more—ask them."

March waved a hand. "That's all right. I hope you don't mind my skepticism, Mrs. Rush—but as an empirical scientist, who bases his beliefs on reproducible evidence, I have a hard time placing much credence in parapsychology and pseudoscience."

Something in March's haughtily dismissive attitude got Logan's goat. "An empirical scientist," he interjected. "And reproducible evidence might scour that dubious tone from your voice?"

March glanced toward him, as if sizing up a potential opponent. "Naturally."

"What about Zener cards, then?" Logan said.

For a moment, Jennifer Rush's eyes fell upon him, before glancing away again.

March frowned. "Zener cards?"

"Otherwise known as Rhine cards. Used in experiments on extrasensory perception." He pulled his duffel toward him, rummaged in it for a moment, then pulled out a set of oversize cards and showed them to the group. Each held one of five different designs against a white background: a circle, a square, a star, a cross, and three wavy lines.

"Oh. Those." March rolled his eyes.

Tina laughed. "So **that's** what the supernatural sleuth carries in his bag of tricks."

"Among other things." Logan glanced at Jennifer Rush, motioning with the cards, as if to say: **Do you see where I'm going with this? Are you okay with it?**

She shrugged. Taking the cards, Logan moved to a seat between March and Tina so the three of them could see the cards but Jennifer Rush could not.

"I'll hold up a total of ten cards, one at a time," Logan told the group. "Mrs. Rush will try to identify them."

He began by holding up a card with a star on it.

"Circle," Jennifer Rush said instantly, staring at its back.

Logan held up a second: a card with the wavy lines.

"Cross," Jennifer Rush said.

A smirk came over March's face.

Logan took a deep breath. Then he held up a card containing a circle.

"Star."

With increasing embarrassment, Logan went through the cards. Each time, Jennifer Rush got it wrong. Logan thought back to what her husband had told him: about the Kleiner-Wechsmann scale, about her ranking being the highest of anyone ever tested. **Something's very wrong here,** he thought. His professional instincts began to sense charlatanism at work.

He put the ten cards facedown on the table. As he did so, he saw Jennifer Rush's gaze turn to March's smug expression. For a moment, she was silent. Then she spoke. "They were all wrong, weren't they?" she said.

"Yes," Logan replied.

"Once more, please. This time I'll get them all right."

Logan picked up the cards, began raising them again, one at a time, in the same order.

"Star," said Jennifer Rush. "Waves. Circle. Cross. Star. Square."

It was a flawless performance. Not once did she get a card wrong.

"Holy shit," Tina Romero muttered.

Now Logan understood. Jennifer Rush had deliberately gotten the cards wrong on the first try. She had rubbed March's nose in his own skeptical words. It was a bravura performance. Logan looked at the woman with renewed respect.

"Empirical evidence, Dr. March?" he said, turning to the archaeologist. "Care to have the results reproduced?"

"No." March rose. "I'm not a fan of parlor tricks." Then, nodding curtly to each of them in turn, he left the lounge.

"What a piece of work that guy is," Tina said, shaking her head and looking at the door March had just exited through. "And did you hear what he said? 'What's buried beneath the Sudd—**if anything**?'

Trust Stone to bring someone like him along as lead archaeologist."

"You mean March thinks this is all a wild-goose chase?" Logan fell silent. It had never occurred to him that Stone's fabled research might be flawed—that this entire vast undertaking might be built upon a false assumption.

"Why did Stone hire him, then?" he asked after a moment.

"Because March might be a prick, he might be an intellectual snob, but he's the best at what he does. Stone's brilliant that way. Besides, he likes someone who questions his assumptions. Maybe that's why he likes you." Tina stood up. "Well, I have to get back to work. If I'm right, March is going to get some news soon that'll put his nose even more out of joint." She glanced at Jennifer Rush. "Thanks for the show." Then she turned to Logan. "You ought to show her your trick with the straw. The two of you may have more in common than you realize."

Logan watched her leave, then turned back to Jennifer Rush. "I've been looking forward to meeting you, Mrs. Rush," he said.

"Call me Jennifer," she replied. "My husband has told me about you."

"He's told me about you, as well. How you were the inspiration for the Center he founded. And about your remarkable abilities."

The woman nodded.

"I have to say, your performance with the Zener

cards just now—it's unparalleled in my experience. I've overseen the test hundreds of times, but I've never seen greater than a seventy, seventy-five percent success rate."

"I doubt Dr. March has, either," she replied. She had a low, silky voice that was out of keeping with her small, slender frame.

"If Ethan has told you about me, you probably know that my business is with unusual phenomena, things not easily explained," he said. "So naturally I'm fascinated with the phenomenon of the NDE, of 'going over.' I've read the literature, of course, and I know all about the remarkable consistency in what people encounter: the feeling of peace, the dark tunnel, the being of light. You experienced all those, I assume?"

She nodded.

"But for me, of course, reading and actually experiencing are such different things . . ." He paused. "As an investigator, it seems I'm always on the outside, looking in after the fact. That's why I almost envy you—personally undergoing such an extraordinary event, I mean."

"Extraordinary event," Jennifer repeated, her voice barely audible. "Yes—you could call it that."

Logan looked at her closely. In another person, such a reply would have seemed cold, distant. But he sensed something different in her. He sensed unhappiness, a private discomfort. He knew from personal experience that not all gifts were welcome—or even, at times, tolerable. Her amber eyes had a remarkable depth and a curious hard, agate quality. It was as if they had seen things no other human had seen—and, perhaps, that no human being should have.

"I'm sorry," he said. "I don't know you well enough to speak of such things. Let me just say that I understand the skepticism and disbelief you must face from people like March. I've faced it, too. For the record, I believe—and I look forward to working with you."

Jennifer Rush had been watching him. As he spoke, something in the agate eyes softened slightly. "Thank you," she said, with a small, gentle smile.

Then—as if with one thought—they rose from their chairs. They stepped toward the door of the lounge; Logan opened it and Jennifer Rush stepped through.

In the hallway, Logan extended his hand for a farewell handshake. After the briefest of delays, she grasped it lightly. As she did so, Logan felt a sudden, searing flash of emotion, so powerful and overwhelming he was almost physically staggered. He withdrew his hand, struggling to conceal his shock. Jennifer Rush hesitated. He ventured a smile, and then—with a disjointed farewell—he turned and made his way down the corridor.

23

"This was three nights ago," Logan said to the young man operating the airboat.

The man—his name was Hirshveldt—nodded. "It was dusk. I was on the catwalk outside Green, checking the methane-conversion feeder ducts. I dropped a wrench. When I bent down to pick it up, I looked out over the swamp. And I saw . . . **her**."

They were perhaps a quarter mile out from the Station, heading northeast at a painful crawl over the skeletal vegetation of the Sudd. It was a bizarre, arduous trip through several elements—mud, water, bracken, air—as the airboat forced its way through an otherworldly tangle. One minute, they were wallowing in viscous black mud that seemed to suck the vessel downward; the next, they were taking small, jarring leaps over knots of clotted reeds, dead stumps, water hyacinth, and long, whiplike grass. It was dusk, and a smoky sun was setting into the marshland behind them.

Hirshveldt brought the airboat to a shuddering halt. He looked around, glanced back toward the Station. "It was more or less here."

Logan nodded, looking at him. He'd read up on Hirshveldt. Machinist Second, he'd been on three prior expeditions with Porter Stone. His expertise was in fixing and running complex mechanical systems of all kinds, with particular emphasis on diesel engines. His psych profile—Stone ran profiles on all prospective employees—showed a very low coefficient of divergent thinking and disinhibition.

In other words, Hirshveldt was probably the last person one would expect to start seeing things.

Now that they had stopped moving, legions of mosquitoes and other biting insects began hovering around them in increasing numbers. The smell of the Sudd—a raw, earthy, putrescent stench—was inescapable. Opening his duffel, Logan slipped out his digital camera, adjusted the settings manually, and took several shots of the vicinity. This was followed by a slow pan with a video camera. Returning these to his bag, he brought out a half-dozen test tubes, took samples of the mud and vegetation, then stoppered the tubes and put them aside. Finally, he pulled a small handheld device from the duffel. It sported a digital readout, an analogue knob, and two toggle switches. Stepping carefully into the bow of the airboat, Logan switched it on, then adjusted the knob, sweeping the device slowly in an arc ahead of him.

"What's that?" Hirshveldt asked, his professional curiosity aroused.

"Air ion counter." Logan examined the display, adjusted the knob again, did a second sweep. He'd done a basal reading back on the Station before getting into the airboat. The air here was more ionized, but not significantly enough to be alarming—approximately five hundred ions per cubic centimeter. He pulled a notebook from his pocket, made a notation, then replaced the ion counter in his bag.

He turned to Hirshveldt. "Can you describe what you saw, please? I'd appreciate as much detail as possible."

Hirshveldt paused, obviously combing his memory. "She was tall. Thin. Walking slowly, right about here, over the surface of the swamp."

Logan looked out over the labyrinthine tangle of vegetation. "While walking, did she stumble or slip?"

The machinist shook his head. "It wasn't normal walking."

"What do you mean?"

"I mean it was slow, really slow—as if she was in a trance, maybe, or sleepwalking."

Logan wrote in his notebook. "Go on."

"There was this faint blue glow around her."

Glow—the glow of sunset, the glow of imagination, or the glow of an aura? "Describe it, please. Was it steady, like incandescent light, or did it waver like the aurora borealis?"

Hirshveldt slapped away a mosquito. "It wavered. But that was slow, too." A pause. "She was young."

"How do you know?"

"She moved like a young person moves. Not like an old woman."

"Skin color?"

"The glow made it hard to tell. It was pretty dark out, anyway."

Logan made more notations. "Can you describe what she was wearing?"

A pause. "A dress. High-waisted, almost translucent. A long ribbon was tied around her waist and trailed down past her knees. Over it was a—a triangular kind of thing that hung down around her shoulders. Same material, I think."

Egyptian shawl cape, Logan thought as he made notes. The garb of nobility, or perhaps of a priestess. Like the one Tina Romero claimed had gone missing from her office. He'd asked her about it; she told him she planned to wear it to the celebratory closing party Stone always held at the end of a successful expedition. "Would you recognize her if you saw her again?" he asked.

Hirshveldt shook his head. "It was too dark. Anyway, the thing on her head made it hard to see her face. Even when she looked at me."

Logan stopped in midnotation. "She looked at you?"

The machinist nodded.

"**At** you? Or just in the direction of the Station?"

"As I stared, she stopped walking. Then—just as slowly—she turned her head. I could see the glow of her eyes in the dark."

"You said she had a thing on her head. What did it look like?"

"It looked like **. . .** the body of a bird. A feathered bird with a long beak. It covered her head like a hat. The wings came down on both sides, over her ears."

A Horus falcon, mantling. Priestess, without a doubt. Logan made a final note, then slipped the notebook into the duffel bag. "When she looked at you, did you get any kind of feeling or sensation?"

Hirshveldt frowned. "Sensation?"

"You know. Like, a welcome? An acknowledgment?"

"Funny you should mention that. When I first saw her out there in the swamp, she seemed . . . well, sad, almost. But then she turned to look at me and I felt something else."

"Yes?" Logan urged.

"I felt anger. Real anger." Another pause. "I don't

know why I felt that. But a funny feeling came over me then. My mouth went all dry, like I couldn't swallow. I looked away a minute, wiped the sweat from my eyes. When I looked back—she was gone."

Logan thought back to the curse of Narmer. **His tongue will cleave to his throat.** Looking around in the gathering dark, he felt his skin prickle. It was back again: that evil he'd felt so strongly when the generator caught fire. It was almost like a physical presence, whispering to him malevolently over the drone of insects.

He turned back to Hirshveldt. "I think it's time for us to get back to the Station. Thanks for your time."

"You bet." The machinist seemed just as eager to leave the swamp. He fired up the airboat and they made their way painfully back toward the welcoming lights.

24

From the vantage point of Mark Perlmutter—in the "Crow's Nest" atop Red—the two figures in the airboat looked ridiculous, bumping and thumping their way back toward the Station across the godforsaken swamp. What the hell were they doing out there, anyway—testing a malaria vaccine, maybe?

As if in response to this conjecture, a buzzing sounded in his ear and he quickly shooed the insect away. **Better get busy or I'll be one big mosquito**

bite myself. Anyway, it wasn't Perlmutter's business what those two were up to—this was only his second Porter Stone assignment, but already he'd learned that so many crazy things went on, it just didn't make sense to ask questions.

Turning away from the gathering dusk, he focused his attention on the mast—the periscope-like metal structure that enclosed the various microwave antennas and pieces of broadcasting/receiving apparatus the Station depended on for its link to the outside world. The low-frequency radio transmitter had been acting a bit wonky, and—as communications assistant—it was Perlmutter's job to climb up the damn mast, all the way to the Crow's Nest above the canvas that enclosed Red, and see what was what. Who else was going to do it? Not Fontaine, communications chief and his boss—at two hundred and seventy pounds, the guy probably wouldn't make it past five rungs.

It was getting dark fast, and he switched on a flashlight to examine the transmitter. He'd already checked out the wiring, circuit board, and transceiver down below in the communications room, and had found nothing; he was betting the problem lay with the transmitter itself. Sure enough—a two-minute inspection uncovered a frayed wire whose end had come loose from the main assembly.

This would be a snap. Perlmutter paused a moment to apply some more bug dope to his neck and arms, then he reached into his utility satchel for the cordless soldering gun, heat sink, solder, and flux.

Balancing the flashlight on the mast, he cut off the damaged end with wire cutters, then—once the gun was hot—applied the flux and, carefully, the solder.

Putting the soldering gun aside, he scrutinized his work with the flashlight. Perlmutter was proud of his soldering skills—sharpened by years of working with ham radio equipment as a youth—and he nodded to himself as he inspected the clean, shiny joint. He blew on the wire gently to help it set. He'd test things out once he got back to the communications room, of course, but he felt 100 percent sure this was the problem. Of course, over dinner he'd elaborate a bit on the difficulty of the repair for Fontaine's benefit. If the dig succeeded, there would be bonuses, big bonuses—and Fontaine would have a say in the size of Perlmutter's own.

He slipped the housing back over the equipment, then turned away, glancing once again over the landscape as he waited for the gun to cool down. The airboat had vanished, and the Sudd spread away in all directions, black and endless. It looked as if yet another rain shower was going to start any minute. The lights of the Station, scattered below him across the six separate wings, twinkled brightly. From his vantage point, he could see the long strands of light marking the marina curtain; the faint glow from the windows of Oasis; the endless little rows of dancing white that marked the exterior catwalks and the pontoon walkways that joined the wings to each other. It was a cheerful sight—and yet Perlmutter did not feel cheered. The little city of lights merely punctuated the countless miles of dark wilderness that surrounded them, merely helped underscore the fact that they were hundreds of near-impassable miles from help or even a trace of civilization. On the inside—in the dormitory housing, at work in the communications room, or relaxing in the library or lounge—it was almost possible to forget just how alone they were. But up here . . .

Despite the warmth of the night, Perlmutter shivered. **If the dig succeeded . . .** Talk of the curse of Narmer had been growing in recent days. At first—as the project got under way, and word of what they were after slowly filtered out among the crew—the curse had been a joke, something brought up over beers to get a laugh. But as time went on, the talk had grown more serious. Even Perlmutter, who was the most committed atheist you'd ever want to see, had started to get the heebie-jeebies—especially after what had happened to Rogers.

He looked around again. The blackness seemed to be pressing in on him from all sides, squeezing him almost, pushing against his chest, making it hard to breathe. . . .

That did it. He grabbed the still-warm soldering gun and other materials, threw them into his satchel, and closed it up. Kneeling in the Crow's Nest, he unzipped a half circle of the protective tarp, exposing an opening to the inside of Red. Below was a vertical tube, lit infrequently by LEDs, into which the housing of the mast descended, like a pipe cleaner into a pipe. Slipping the satchel over one shoulder, he grabbed the rungs, descended past the tarp, paused to zip it closed again, then continued down. He climbed carefully—it was thirty feet to the bottom, and he sure as hell didn't want to fall.

Reaching the base of the mast, he fetched a deep breath, wiped his sweaty hands on his shirt. He'd go check out the low-frequency radio, make sure its gremlins had been exorcised. Then he'd look for Fontaine, no doubt grabbing himself an early dinner.

But as he prepared to leave the mast enclosure, Perlmutter paused. There were two hatches leading out of the enclosure. One led to the hallway containing the science labs and the communications room. The other led to Red's power substation. Fifteen minutes earlier, when he'd stepped into the mast enclosure, the substation hatch had been closed.

Now it was open.

He took a step forward, frowning. Normally the substation was a lights-out facility, operating without need of human intervention. The only time anybody would have to go in would be to make repairs. But if there was something wrong with the electrical system, he'd have been the first to know. He took another step forward.

"Hello?" he said into the darkness. "Anybody in there?"

Was he going crazy, or had he just seen a dim light deep within the substation extinguish itself?

He licked his lips, stepped through the hatch into the substation. What the hell—there was a puddle of water here. What was going on? Had some kind of a leak to the outside formed?

He took another step forward, simultaneously fumbling for the light switch. "Hello? Hell—"

And then his world exploded in a concussion of pain and furious, inviolable white.

25

At nine thirty the following morning, the internal phone in Logan's office rang.

He picked it up on the third ring. "Jeremy Logan here."

"Jeremy? It's Porter Stone. Am I interrupting anything?"

Logan sat up. "Nothing that can't wait."

"Then come to the Operations Center, if you would. There's something here I think you ought to see."

Logan saved the file he'd been working on—a write-up of his conversation with Hirshveldt the evening before—then stood up and stepped out of his office.

He had to stop and ask directions twice before he found his way. The people on the Station seemed jumpy this morning—and it was hardly surprising. The previous evening, a communications worker named Perlmutter had been badly, almost fatally, electrocuted. Logan had pieced together the story from various mutterings he'd overheard during breakfast: how the worker had stepped into a puddle of water in which a live electrical wire had been lying. "It was Fontaine, his boss, who found him," Logan had heard someone say. "Horrible. Like he was covered in soot, almost, blackened from the electrical burns."

Logan had been irresistibly reminded of the curse of Narmer. **His limbs will turn to ash.** Rather than mentioning this to anyone, he mentally shelved it for later consideration.

Unlike the previous tragedy at the generator, there had been no follow-up meeting to analyze this accident, to try to determine cause. Logan assumed that one had not yet been scheduled—or, perhaps, it had been confined to the very highest levels of management. He did know that Perlmutter was in serious condition and was being closely monitored by Ethan Rush.

The Operations Center, located deep within White, turned out to be the large, monitor-stuffed space he'd visited before. Once again, Cory Landau—the cherub with the Zapata mustache—was manning the futuristic central cockpit. On a nearby screen, Logan noticed the wireframe CAD image representing the extent of the dig mapping. Its extent had advanced dramatically since the first time he'd seen it.

Ranged around Landau were Porter Stone, Tina Romero, and Dr. March, all of whom were staring at one of the larger monitors that displayed what looked to Logan like a kind of greenish soup, punctuated by lines of static.

As he entered, Stone looked over. "Ah, Jeremy. Come take a look at this."

Logan joined them at the central cockpit. "What is it?"

"Skeletons," said Stone. He said the word with almost hushed reverence.

Logan peered at the screen with increased interest. "Where is this, exactly?"

"Grid square H five," murmured Stone. "Forty-five feet below the surface."

Logan glanced at Tina Romero, who was staring at the screen and playing idly with her yellow fountain pen. "And how far is this from the first skeleton?"

"Approximately sixty feet. In exactly the direction I suggested the divers concentrate on." She glanced over at March with a smug **I told you so** smile.

"Here's another," came a squawky voice over a microphone. Logan realized it was one of the divers, speaking from the muddy depths of the Sudd.

On the monitor, the figure of a diver in a black wet suit suddenly emerged out of the green soup. He was holding a bone in one hand.

Stone leaned toward a microphone. "How many is that so far?"

"Nine," the distant voice replied.

Now Stone turned toward Romero. "Ethan told me what you said during his examination of the initial skeleton. That you knew the death was a suicide and that you knew where the next cache of bones would be found. Care to enlighten us?"

If Romero had felt like remaining coy, this request from the boss dispelled it. "Sure," she said, pushing back a stray hair from her forehead with a finger. "First, we found one body. Now we've found several—I'd guess twelve in all. Next, we will find a huge cache of bones. It's because of the way Narmer would have been buried and the way his tomb was concealed. Recall this was before the days of pyramids—the earliest pharaohs were buried in shaft tombs and mastabas. We have to assume that Narmer's tomb, whatever it looks like, is unique in prefiguring later tombs to come. But unlike many kings who followed him, Narmer didn't want even the **location** of his tomb to be remembered. At the site of its construction, there would have been hundreds of workers doing the building, as well as members of Narmer's bodyguard. Once the work was done, all those workers—every last one—would have been killed. Their bodies would be left at the periphery of the tomb. Later, when Narmer himself was placed in the tomb, the priests and lesser guards who attended the ceremony would have been killed at a ritual distance from the tomb by Narmer's personal bodyguard. The bodyguard himself would then have moved out another respectful distance—and killed himself. All this to maintain the sanctity of Narmer's earthly remains. An army of the dead was to stand guard around the tomb for all eternity. Only one person, the god-king's personal scribe, walked out of the desert with these secrets in his hand. And once he had committed them to the ostracon, he would have instructed his personal guards to kill him, as well."

Stone nodded. "Hence the decreasing number of bodies found moving outward from the site of the tomb." He looked from Romero to the screen. "And the direction you instructed our divers to look—was it due north?"

"It was."

"And that's because the entrances to the king's chambers in the pyramids and other burial sites historically faced north?" Logan interjected.

Stone smiled. "Very good, Jeremy. My deduction as well." He glanced back at Romero. "And the large cache of skeletons, the builders—it will be due north of this point, as well?"

"I believe so," she replied. "Approximately sixty feet."

"And the tomb entrance . . . another sixty feet north of that?"

Romero did not answer. She did not need to. Stone turned toward the door. "I've got to see Valentino. We need to put triple dive crews on this right away."

The radio crackled. "And here's another skeleton. Completely buried in mud. Sir, what are we to do with them?"

March spoke up for the first time. "You know what to do. Get the evidence lockers and bring them back to the Station."

The smile quickly left Romero's face, replaced with a frown. "Wait a minute. We needed to bring up that first skeleton so we could analyze it, be sure of our direction. But these priests and retainers—we should leave them in peace."

Logan looked at her, noting the sudden urgency in her voice. He remembered what he'd heard about her ambivalence regarding grave goods.

"That's rubbish," March retorted. "If these really are the priests of the first Egyptian pharaoh, their remains are historically invaluable."

"We're here to learn the tomb's secrets," Romero snapped, "not to plunder the—"

"One moment," Stone interrupted. He was clearly eager to give new orders to Valentino and had no patience for an ideological argument. "We shall bring up six skeletons. One will go to Ethan Rush for his examination—although at the moment he is rather busy with another matter. Fenwick, you may analyze the other five. The surrounding matrix should be gridded and sieved for jewelry or the remains of clothing—although I doubt you'll find much. Once you have completed your examination, five of the six must be returned. We shall retain only one skeleton. Acceptable?"

After a moment, Romero nodded. March grudgingly followed suit.

"Very good. Landau, you'll convey the instructions?"

"Yes, Dr. Stone," Landau said.

"Thank you." And—after a glance at each of them in turn—Stone ducked out of the Operations Center.

Four hours later, when Logan peered in, the archaeology labs in Red were a scene of controlled chaos. A half-dozen gowned figures were standing over sinks and metal examination tables, gingerly probing and examining delicate brown bones with latex-gloved hands. A half-dozen others were tapping at keyboards, tagging artifacts with plastic labels, and taking evidence bins down from shelves and putting others back up in their place. Voices spoke over one another, competing with the sound of running water and the whine of microsaws. Fenwick March walked among them, the lord of the manor, now pausing to pluck an artifact from the hands of a worker, now peering into a microscope or speaking into the digital recorder he carried in one hand. The room smelled powerfully of the rotting vegetal muck of the Sudd—and something else even less pleasant.

"Don't **wash** it!" March barked at one of the gowned figures, who jumped at the sound. "You rinse it, **rinse** it, dribble by dribble!" He turned to another. "Dry that section, quickly, we have to stabilize it before there's any more flaking. Hurry, man, hurry!"

Another worker looked up from a scattered pile of hips and long bones. "Dr. March, these were brought up from the dive interface in no order at all, there's no way we can attempt a formal articulation—"

"We'll scan them later!" March said, rounding on her. "The important thing is to get them cleaned, tagged, and in the database. **Now,** not yesterday. We'll worry about the articulation later."

Maybe, Logan thought as he stepped forward, **March believes that—if he gets them all nicely cleaned and classified—Stone will let him keep them, after all**. It was at moments like this that a person's true interests came to the fore. March was an archaeologist, not an Egyptologist—to him, the bones came first and foremost.

March turned and noticed him for the first time. He frowned, as if disapproving of this violation of his domain. "Yes?" he said. "What do you want?"

Logan put on his most ingratiating smile. "I wonder," he said, nodding at a skull that was being carefully cleaned of mud in a nearby sink: "Could I borrow one of those?"

26

Logan sat at the computer in his small office, typing slowly and deliberately. It was late at night, and Maroon was quiet as the grave. He had finally gotten the chance to enter his remaining notes on his conversation with Hirshveldt and the various observations he'd made during their brief trip out into the Sudd. Now he closed that document and opened another, detailing the unexplained and ominous occurrences on the Station, and added entries on the generator fire

and the electrocution of the communications specialist, Mark Perlmutter. Despite a painstaking inquiry,
no good explanation had been found for the presence
of a live wire or the pool of water in the substation.
Perlmutter, slipping in and out of consciousness, had
said something about seeing a light, but there was
no way to tell if this was just delirious babbling. The
rumors flitting around the Station—of sabotage or of
the curse of Narmer making itself felt—had spiked
significantly. With the discovery of the cache of skeletons, and the near certainty that the tomb itself lay
close by, there seemed to be a strange mix of emotions
among the personnel: a charged sense of anticipation,
mingled with creeping dread.

Logan himself had examined Red's power substation and spoken to those few who might have had
any reason to enter the room that day. None of them
knew anything or had seen anything out of the ordi-
nary. Moreover, all had seemed straightforward and
honest—Logan had sensed nothing but sadness and
confusion from the group.

He closed the file and glanced at the small
blue evidence case beside his computer. Picking
it up, he removed the top and carefully took out a
cloth-wrapped bundle from within. Pulling away the
folds of cloth, he exposed an ancient skull the color
of tobacco.

Cradling it in the cloth, he turned it this way
and that, peering at it closely. March had clearly not
wanted to lend it to him, but—aware of the favor

Stone had conferred upon Logan—hadn't dared refuse. Nevertheless, the archaeologist had been careful to give Logan the least interesting, most damaged of the skulls, with strict orders to return it—in identical shape—before the end of the evening.

The skull had been relatively protected by the matrix of mud and silt that had surrounded it for some fifty centuries, and though it was pitted, cracked across its top, and missing its teeth, it was nevertheless in good condition, considering. It smelled strongly of the Sudd—the odor that permeated the Station and had begun to haunt Logan's dreams. Taking a jeweler's loupe from his satchel, he fixed it to his eye and made a careful survey of the entire surface of the skull. Despite the fact that the occipital bone was missing, there were no obvious indications of violence. It was badly scratched across the crown, as well as within the left eye socket, but these were no doubt the result of pebbles. He examined the ectocranial sutures in turn: coronal, sagittal, lambdoid. Judging from the size of the mastoid process and the rounded nature of the supraorbital margin, he felt confident the skull had belonged to a man rather than a woman—no big surprise there.

Now he put the cloth aside and, very gently, held the skull in his bare hands. Two eyes had once stared out from this cranium: What wonders had they seen? Had they viewed Narmer, overseeing in person the construction of his tomb? Had they perhaps witnessed the decisive battle in which Narmer had united all Egypt? At the very least, they had watched the line of other priests as they headed south into a foreign and hostile land, there to entomb their king's mortal remains as his **ka** went on to join the gods in the next world. Had this fellow guessed it was a journey from which he would never return?

Turning the skull over slowly in his hands, Logan emptied his mind, leaving it open to perception or suggestion. "What's it trying to tell me, Karen?" he asked his dead wife as he handled the skull. But there was nothing—the skull left him with no impressions save fragility and great antiquity. At last, with a sigh, he wrapped it back in its cloth and returned it to the evidence case.

If Tina Romero was right, they would soon find a vast cache of bones—the remains of the tomb builders—and, shortly after that, the tomb itself. And Porter Stone would have yet another coup to add to his record. And if the tomb contained the crown of unified Egypt, it would undoubtedly be the largest coup of Stone's career.

Logan sat back, still idly eyeing the box. Stone was an unusual man—most unusual. He was a person of almost limitless discipline, with passionate convictions—and yet he hired those who disagreed with him, perhaps even doubted his chances of success. He possessed an impeccable scientific background, and was a rationalist and empiricist almost to a fault—yet he was not afraid to surround himself with people whose specialties most conventional scientists would scoff at. Logan himself was the perfect example of this. He shook his head wonderingly. The fact was, Porter Stone would do anything, no matter how unorthodox or seemingly tangential, to guarantee success. After all, there was no other reason that he would include someone like Jennifer Rush on this dig, a woman who read Zener cards like a monkey juggled coconuts and who was able to . . .

All at once, Logan sat upright in his chair. "Of course," he murmured. "Of course." Then, slowly, he rose—tucked the evidence case under one arm—and walked thoughtfully out of the office.

27

The medical suite was quiet as Logan entered. The overhead lights were dimmed, and a single nurse sat at the front desk. From somewhere far back in the maze of rooms, the low bleating of instrumentation could be heard.

Ethan Rush came striding around a corner, speaking to an accompanying nurse. He stopped when he saw Logan. "Jeremy. Are you here to speak with Perlmutter? He's in rather a lot of pain, we've had to keep him sedated—" Rush stopped, peered more closely at Logan.

"It's not about Perlmutter," Logan said.

Rush turned to the nurse. "I'll speak with you later." Then he gestured toward Logan. "Come into my office."

Rush's office was a sterile-looking cubicle behind the nurse's station. He gestured Logan to a chair, poured himself a cup of coffee, took a seat himself. He looked bone tired.

"What's on your mind, Jeremy?" he asked.

"I know why your wife is here," Logan replied.

When Rush did not reply, he went on. "She's trying to contact the ancient dead, isn't she? She's trying to channel Narmer."

Still, Rush said nothing.

"It's the only thing that makes sense," Logan continued. "You told me yourself that many people who return from near-death experiences develop new-found psychic abilities. Some of them claim to speak to the dead. You also told me that your wife's particular gift was retrocognition. **Retrocognition.** That is, having knowledge of past events and people, beyond any normal understanding or inference."

He got up and helped himself to coffee. "It's a very rare form of parapsychology, but it has been documented. In 1901, two female British scholars, Anne Moberly and Eleanor Jourdain, were touring Versailles. They began to wander the grounds in search of the Petite Trianon, Marie Antoinette's château. In

the process, they encountered strangely dressed figures, including footmen speaking in antique voices
and a young woman sitting on a stool, sketching.
Moberly and Jourdain experienced a strangely oppressive gloom that did not lift until they abandoned
their search and walked away. Later, both women
became convinced they had entered telepathically
Marie Antoinette's own memories and visions at that
spot—and that the woman sketching had, in fact,
been the queen herself. In the years that followed,
Moberly and Jourdain conducted extensive research
on their experience, which they finally published in
1911 in a book titled **An Adventure**. I highly recommend it, by the way."

He sat down again, took a sip of coffee.

Finally, Rush stirred in his chair. "You know Porter Stone's kitchen-sink approach to his projects: he
would rather bring in ten specialists, each with a different discipline, at ten times the cost, than one gen-
eralist with almost the same skill set. For him, that
almost is the difference between success and failure."
He paused, looked away. "Early on, the big worry was
the tomb's location. Stone was convinced the tomb
was here. But the precise spot was unknown, and he
had a deadline. Anybody who could help find the
site, **anybody,** was considered."

Rush shook his head. "Somehow, he found out
about the Center, about my wife's . . . gift. Don't ask
me how—this is Porter Stone we're talking about.
He approached us. At first I refused point-blank. The

Sudd seemed such a desolate, hostile place. I'd have to go along, of course—after all, nobody else could manage her 'crossings'—and I simply had too much work to consider it. He offered us more money. I still refused—as I think I told you, the Center has plenty of wealthy patrons who have experienced NDEs. Then he offered me the post of expedition doctor, and so much money that it would have been fool-hardy to say no. Also"—here for a moment his voice dropped almost to a whisper—"I thought it might be beneficial for Jennifer."

"Beneficial?" Logan repeated.

"To give her a chance to use her gift in a positive way. Because, Jeremy, I'm not convinced she considers it a gift at all."

Logan thought back to his meeting with Jennifer Rush, to the private sorrow he'd sensed, to the still-unexplained storm of empathetic emotion he'd felt when he shook her hand. **No gift, indeed,** he told himself. Years before, he had known a deeply talented telepath. The man had fallen into increasing despondency, ultimately killing himself. Doctors had labeled him mentally deficient, had ascribed the voices in his head to schizophrenia. Logan knew differently. He himself knew the downside of possessing a gift you could not turn off. Now he felt like even more of an ass for the way he'd spoken to Jennifer Rush.

"So at first," Rush said, breaking Logan's train of thought, "Jen was brought here simply to get sensations—fleeting pictures or glimpses of past events that might help locate the tomb. But then Fenwick March and Tina Romero managed to pinpoint the site more precisely, and the original reason for her presence became less important. Besides, by that point . . ." Rush hesitated. "By that point, everything had changed."

"You mean, she'd made contact with an actual entity from the past," Logan said.

For a moment, Rush did not respond. Then he nodded, ever so slightly.

Logan felt a thrill course through him. Even he found it both incredibly exciting—and hard to believe. **My God, could it really be true?** "Does Stone know?" he asked.

Rush nodded again. "Of course."

"What does he think?"

"It's like I've told you—he'll do anything, try anything, to get what he wants. And Jen has demonstrated her psychic powers in enough ways that I know he wants to believe." Rush stared at him. "What about you? What do **you** think?"

Logan took a deep breath. "I think—no, I **know,** because I've sensed it myself—that certain very strong personalities, life forces if you will, can linger in a place long after the corporeal body has died. The stronger, the more violent, the personality and the will, the longer it will persist—needing only an unusually gifted mind to sense it."

Rush slowly ran his fingers through his hair. He glanced at Logan, looked away, glanced back. **This**

whole development has him agitated, Logan thought. **This isn't what he expected to happen—at all.**

"Who else knows about this?" he asked.

"March and Romero, for sure. One or two others, maybe . . . then again, maybe not. You know Stone. And this isn't exactly charted territory."

"And what does your wife think?"

"She doesn't like it. It's foreign and strange and, I think, frightening."

"Then why go on with it? If she was brought here to help find the tomb, and the tomb might be located any minute—why stay?"

"Porter Stone's express request," Rush replied, his voice still lower. "Two reasons, I think. First, we haven't yet found the tomb—and with his belt-and-suspenders mentality, he's not going to release a potential asset until he's certain it's been located."

He fell silent.

"That's one reason," Logan pressed.

It seemed a long time before Rush finally answered. "Her mission here was altered when we received . . . certain data."

"Data?" Logan asked.

Rush did not reply—he did not need to.

"You mean the curse," Logan said. Now he, too, was almost whispering. "What, exactly, has Narmer—or whoever it is—been saying through Jennifer?"

Rush shook his head. "Don't ask me, please. I'd rather not talk about that."

Logan thought for a moment. The feeling of excitement, of otherworldliness, hadn't left him. **So the curse is bothering Stone, too.** That was the only explanation he could think of for altering Jennifer Rush's assignment. **Stone doesn't know what he's going to find when he reaches the tomb. He wants to be as prepared as possible to meet any eventuality—and he'll accept any help he can get his hands on . . . even from beyond the grave.**

"Would you talk with her, please?" Rush suddenly asked.

For a moment, Logan did not understand. "I'm sorry?"

"Would you speak to Jen about all this—about these, um, crossings she's been doing, her feelings?"

"Why me?" Logan asked. "I've only met her once—and then only briefly."

"I know. She told me about it." Rush hesitated. "It sounds funny, but I think she would trust you, might even open up to you. Maybe it's your unusual line of work; maybe it's just something in your manner—you made a good impression." Again he hesitated. "You want to know something, Jeremy? Jen never, ever talks about her NDE. Everyone else won't shut up about going over, about what they've experienced. She never has—not even for data collection sessions at the Center. Oh, we talk about the sensitivity it's given her, we measure and try to codify her special gifts—but she never speaks of the experience itself. I was wondering if . . . well, if perhaps there was a way you could get her to share it with you."

"I'm not sure," Logan said. "I can try."

"I wish you would. I just don't want to push it any further myself." Rush plucked at his collar. "I put up a brave front, but the fact is, I worry about her. I can't pretend that things haven't been a bit strained between us since her accident, but I've tried to give her a lot of space. All I can tell you . . . All I can tell you is that we once had about as close a relationship as two people could have." He stopped. "We still love each other very much, of course, but she's had, um, a hard time interacting with the world in the way she used to. And since arriving on site—well, she wakes up sometimes in the middle of the night, trembling, bathed in sweat. When I ask her about it, she just brushes it off as a bad dream. And now, with these crossings Stone is insisting on . . ." He looked away.

"I'd be happy to do anything I can to help," Logan said.

For a minute, Rush didn't look back. Then, with a deep sigh, he met Logan's gaze, pressed his hand briefly, and gave a mute smile of thanks.

28

When Logan entered the cafeteria for his usual break-fast of poached egg and half an English muffin, he found Tina Romero sitting by herself in a far corner, hunched intently over an iPad.

"May I join you?" he asked.

She gave a grunt that might have been either yes or no. Logan sat down, then peered at her iPad. Romero was doing a **New York Times** crossword puzzle.

"What's a four-letter word meaning 'small box for holding scissors'?" she asked, eyes on the screen.

" 'Etui.' "

She entered the word, then looked up. "And just how the hell did you know that?"

"The **Times** crossword is one of my guilty pleasures. They use that one all the time."

"I'll remember that." She put down the iPad. "So. I heard you were doing your Hamlet imitation yesterday."

"What? Oh, you mean the skull."

Romero nodded. "I overheard March complaining about it to one of his minions. Get any bad vibes from the thing?"

"I didn't get any vibes at all." Logan cut into his egg. "But I was surprised at how good a shape the skull was in. Only some scoring across the top and in one of the eye sockets."

"Eye sockets?" Romero repeated.

"Yes."

"Which one?"

Logan thought a moment. "The left. Why?"

Romero shrugged.

Logan thought back to Dr. Rush's request the night before. "What did you think of Jennifer Rush's performance back in the staff lounge?"

"I've been thinking about that. Can those cards be faked?"

"Only if you've got a partner handling them."

"In that case, it was remarkable."

Logan nodded. "She seems to be a rather remarkable woman."

Romero took a sip of coffee. "I feel sorry for her."

Logan frowned. "Why?"

"Because it just isn't right—dragging her out here after all she's been through."

"You think she didn't want to come?"

Romero shrugged again. "I think she's too kind to deny **him** anything."

Him? Logan thought. Did she mean Porter Stone—or her husband?

Romero took another sip of coffee. "This kind of job can bring out the worst in anyone. I've seen people come to digs with the crappiest of motives." She lowered her voice. "I don't know. Maybe Ethan Rush is doing the greatest work in the world. But it sure seems to me that Jennifer is a guinea pig."

Logan stared at her. Was she actually implying Rush was exploiting his wife—using the terrible experience of hers for his own gain? The truth was, he knew very little about the Center for Transmortality Studies. And yet, Rush seemed to care deeply for his wife. **I put up a brave front,** he'd said just the night before, **but the fact is, I worry about her.** Was he worried for her—or for her importance to his Center?

There was the beep of a two-way radio. Romero reached into her bag, pulled her radio out, pressed the transmit button. "Romero here." She listened for a minute, her eyes widening. "Hot **damn**! I'll be right there."

She dumped the radio back into her bag and stood up, nearly knocking over her chair in the process. "That was Stone," she said as she scooped up her iPad and bag. "They've found the mother lode!"

"The cache of skeletons?" Logan asked.

"Yup. And you know what that means? We're practically sitting on top of the tomb entrance. Stone's put all the diving teams online. I'll bet you a round of drinks in Oasis that we find the tomb itself within ninety minutes." And with that she left the cafeteria, Logan practically running after her to keep up.

29

Tina Romero was off by seven minutes. It was just over an hour and a half later that dive team five reported finding what appeared to be a natural fissure at the bed of the Sudd—forty-three feet below surface level—that had been completely filled in with large boulders. Leaving a single archaeological dive team at the site of the skeletons, to be overseen by Fenwick March, Stone ordered all the other teams to five's location. From the Operations nerve center,

Logan watched the drama unfold on huge flat-panel monitors, their video feeds choreographed by Cory Landau, a phlegmatic figure even amid such palpable excitement.

The images from the videocams attached to the divers' headgear were grainy and distorted, but just staring at them made Logan's pulse race. Narrow flashlight beams, lancing through the black mud and silt of the Sudd, traced the opening in the igneous rock: some eight feet tall and four feet wide, shaped like a cat's pupil, packed solid with large rocks. Teams of divers had tried to dislodge the boulders but without luck: their weight, the gluelike muck of the Sudd, and the passage of years had fused them into a nearly solid mass.

"This is Tango Alpha," came the disembodied voice from forty feet below. "No joy."

"Tango Alpha, understood," came Porter Stone's voice from somewhere else on the Station. "Use the juice."

The radio crackled again. "Tango Alpha, roger that."

Logan turned to Romero, who was standing beside him, also glued to the screens. "Juice?" he asked.

"Nitroglycerin."

"Nitro?" Logan frowned. "Is that wise?"

"Don't leave home without it!" Romero cackled. "You'd be surprised how often Stone's had to employ nitro in his various digs. But not to worry—one of our divers is an ex-SEAL, an artist with the stuff. It'll be a surgical strike."

Logan continued listening to the radio chatter. As one of the divers at the tomb site released a marker buoy, Stone—apparently monitoring the action with Frank Valentino at the Staging Area—dispatched the diver with the nitro. Logan and Romero watched the screens as the man gingerly arranged the high explosive around the boulder-sealed entrance—four marble-sized pouches of black rubber, joined by lengths of det cord—then retreated to the rest of the divers, who were hanging well back.

"Charges in place," radioed the diver.

"Very well," came Porter Stone's voice. "Detonate."

There was a moment in which the entire Station seemed to hold its collective breath. Then came a low **whump** that made everything around Logan shudder slightly.

"Redfern here," came another voice over the radio. "I'm in the Crow's Nest. Marker buoy sighted."

"Can you get an exact fix?" Stone asked.

"Affirmative. One moment." There was a pause. "One hundred and twenty yards almost due east. Eight seven degrees relative."

Romero turned to Logan. "It's going to take some time for that shitstorm of mud down there to clear again," she said, indicating the monitors. "Come on. I think there's something you're going to want to see."

"What is it?" Logan asked.

"Another of Porter Stone's miracles."

She led the way out of White, through Red, and then, via the serpentine corridors of Maroon, to a hatch whose window overlooked the unbroken vista of the Sudd. Opening the hatch revealed a stairway that rose on stiltlike legs to a narrow wooden catwalk that circumscribed the entire outer extremity of Maroon's domelike tarp. Logan followed her up the stairway, and then—from that vantage point—paused to look around, first at the hellish tangle of the Sudd, then at the miniature city that housed their expedition. Rising above Red was a tall, narrow tube, topped by a small railed perch and a forest of antennae. A man stood on the perch, binoculars in one hand and a radio in the other. This, Logan realized, must be the Crow's Nest.

He turned back to Romero. "It's quite the view. What am I supposed to be looking at?"

She handed him a tube of bug dope. "Wait and see."

But even as she spoke, Logan heard the rumble of engines. Slowly, from the direction of Green, appeared both the large airboats, each eighty-foot vessel now equipped—bizarrely—with what looked like a combination of snowplow and cow-catcher. These had been fixed to the bows, each bristling with an arsenal of chain saws and long, hooked spikes that stretched forward like bowsprits. The two vessels were followed by a veritable armada of Jet Skis and small boats. As Logan watched, the large craft maneuvered into position directly in front of them. Men and women ran across their sterns, shouting instructions, as cables were attached to heavy cleats on Maroon, Red, and Blue.

Logan glanced over at one of the smaller boats. It was busily pulling in yet another cable from the depths of the Sudd, reeling it over a capstan. Sticks, plant tendrils, and thick muck clung to the cable like roots.

Logan nodded at the boat. "What's it doing?"

Romero smiled. "Raising anchor."

There was a flurry of shouted orders. All of a sudden the engines of the two big airboats roared in tandem, and they started slowly forward. For a moment, Logan was aware of an unusual sensation he couldn't immediately identify. Then he understood. They—the entire Station, with all its barges, pontoons, catwalks, methane scrubbers, and generators—were **moving**.

"My God," he murmured.

Now he realized the purpose of the strange devices on the bows of the airboats. They **were** plows in a very real sense: plows to push aside the near-impenetrable tangle of the Sudd. He could hear the spit and snarl of chain saws. The smaller boats began darting around and between the big airboats, removing stubborn bits of flotsam or helping cut away thick masses of rotting vegetation with hooks, prods, and gas-powered saws.

Slowly, inch by inch, the Station crept forward, making due east. Glancing over his shoulder, Logan saw the surface of the Sudd come together again in their wake, like a puddle following the tracing of a child's finger, leaving no hint of their passage.

"We're moving to the tomb," he said.

Romero nodded.

"But why? Now that we know where it is, why not just dive to it from our present position?"

"Because that's not the way Stone works. That would be inefficient, slow—and, if you think about it, impractical. Remember, the entrance to that tomb is forty feet below the surface, encased in thick muck. How would you enter? How would you preserve the artifacts within from the foulness of the Sudd?"

Logan looked at her. "I don't know," he said over the howl of the airboats and the whine of the buzz saws.

"You fit an air lock to the tomb entrance. Then you deploy the Umbilicus."

"Umbilicus?"

"A pressurized tube, six feet in diameter, with light and power, footholds and handholds. One end mates with the air lock. The other to the Maw. Any stray mud is forced from its interior, and the pressure is equalized. **Et voilà**—a nice, dry passage to and from Narmer's tomb."

Logan had to shake his head at the audacity of such a design. **Another of Porter Stone's miracles,** Tina had called it—and she wasn't far wrong.

"It'll be an hour before we're anchored over the tomb," she said. "That mud must have settled from the explosion by now. Shall we see what it is that's down there?"

Back in the Operations Center, Cory Landau obligingly scrolled through the video feeds from the divers' transmissions until Tina Romero told him to stop.

"That one," she said. "Who's that?"

Landau peered at the screen. "Delta Bravo," he said.

"Can you get me on radio to him?"

"Sure can." Landau reached over, dialed a knob, then handed her a radio.

"Delta Bravo," she said, speaking into it. "Delta Bravo, this is Dr. Romero. Do you read?"

"Five by five," came the response.

"Can you approach the entrance, pan across?"

"Roger."

They watched the video feed silently. The boulders had been either blasted or pulled away now, and Logan could just see beyond them into the cleft in the rock. In the divers' powerful lights, it appeared to be tightly sealed by courses of stone, creating a solid vertical face, as if workers had created a wall within the natural cavity of the rock.

"Closer, please," Romero almost whispered.

The video tightened in.

"My God," she said. "That looks like granite. Until

now, scholars thought that Netcherikhe was the first Egyptian king to have graduated from mud-brick walls."

"Narmer must have wanted it to last for all eternity," Logan replied.

Romero raised her radio again. "Delta Bravo, pan up, please."

The image rose slowly up the stone face.

"There!" she cried. "Stop. Pan in."

The muddy, grainy video feed tightened on something affixed to the granite and one side of the igneous rock: a lozenge-shaped disk imprinted with hieroglyphics.

"What is that?" Logan asked.

"It's a necropolis seal," Romero replied. "Amazing. Completely unheard-of on a tomb this old. And look—it's unbroken. No desecration, no spoiling."

She wiped her palms on her shirt, then took fresh hold of the radio. Logan noticed her hands were trembling slightly. "Delta Bravo. One more thing, please."

"Shoot."

"Pan down. Down toward the base of that wall."

"Roger. There's still some rock and debris we need to clear away."

They waited as the image slowly traveled down the face of dressed stone. Clouds of silt and muck occasionally blocked their view, and Romero asked the diver to backtrack. Then, quite suddenly, she told him to stop again.

"Right there!" she said. "Hold it!"

"I'm at the base of the wall," the diver replied.

"I know."

Logan found himself staring at another unbroken seal, this one larger than the first. There were two hieroglyphs carved into it.

"What is that?" he asked quietly.

Romero nodded. "It's a serekh. The earliest depiction of a royal name used in Egyptian iconography. Cartouches didn't become common until the time of Sneferu, father of Khufu."

"And the name in the serekh? Can you read the name?"

Romero licked her lips. "They're the symbols for the catfish and the chisel. The phonetic representation of Narmer's name."

30

"How long will it last?" Logan asked Ethan Rush. It was evening, and they were traversing the near-deserted corridors of Maroon.

"The productive period, you mean?" Rush replied. "Five minutes, if we're lucky. The lead-in period is much longer."

He stopped beside a closed, unmarked door, then turned back to Logan. "There are a few ground rules. Keep your voice low. Speak slowly and calmly. Make no sudden movements. Don't do anything to disturb or alter the ambient environment—no brightening or dimming lights, no moving chairs or equipment. Understand?"

"Perfectly."

Rush nodded his satisfaction. "At the Center, we've learned that crossings are most successful if triggered by the environment of an NDE."

"The environment? I'm not sure I understand."

"Simulating the actual experience. This is done via a medically induced coma—very light, of course. Along with psychomantetical techniques. You'll see what I mean."

Logan nodded. He knew that psychomanteums were rooms or booths, frequently mirrored and very dark, constructed in such a way as to induce a trance or state of psychical openness in the occupant, thus helping enable a portal, or conduit, to the spirit world. Psychomanteums had been developed by the ancient Greeks, and several still operated in the present day in America and around the world, helping—many believed—people contact the spirits of those who had moved on. Logan had thought about the mirror he'd seen in the testing chamber that first day, with Jennifer and Ethan Rush. It had been one of the things that led to his deduction of why Jennifer Rush was at the Station.

"Do you induce the Ganzfeld effect?" he asked.

Rush looked at him curiously. "The meds make that unnecessary. Now, please observe everything closely. Keep your comments to a minimum until we speak afterward. The more you know, the better equipped you'll be to—to help her."

Logan nodded.

"One other thing. Don't expect revelations. Don't even expect what you hear to make sense. Sometimes we need to analyze a transcript for some time afterward before we understand—if we ever do." With this, Rush opened the door and quietly stepped inside.

Logan followed. He recognized the room. There was the hospital bed, with its banks of medical and other instrumentation. There was the large mirror on the wall beyond the bed, polished to a brilliant gleam. The lighting was just as dim as it had been the first time he'd seen the room.

And, once again, Jennifer Rush lay on the bed, garbed in a hospital gown. EKG lines snaked away from her arms and chest; many more electroencephalograph leads were attached to her head. The red and gray stripes of the medical leads looked out of place against her cinnamon-colored hair. A peripheral IV line was fixed to the inside of one wrist. She glanced at Rush, glanced at Logan, smiled faintly. Her eyes had a vague look, as if she was sedated.

To Logan's surprise, Stone was standing at the head of the bed, one hand on Jennifer's shoulder. He gave it a reassuring pat, then stepped away. He nodded at Logan, turned to Rush.

"You'll ask her?" he said in a low voice. "About the gate?"

"Yes," Rush replied.

Stone looked at him a moment more, as if considering speaking further. Then he simply nodded his good-bye and quietly left the room.

Rush indicated for Logan to take a seat near the head of the bed. For perhaps five minutes Rush busied himself connecting various pieces of equipment, calibrating monitors, checking displays. Logan sat quietly, taking in everything. The room smelled faintly of sandalwood incense and myrrh.

At last, Rush approached the bed, hypodermic in hand. "Jen," he said softly, "I'm going to administer the propofol now."

There was no response. Rush inserted the needle into the connecting hub of the IV cannula. Jennifer went as still as death. Glancing at the instrumentation over the head of the bed, Logan saw her blood pressure dip, her respiration and pulse slow almost by half.

Rush carefully monitored her physical state from the devices at the foot of the bed. Neither man spoke a word. After several minutes, Jennifer stirred slightly; Rush immediately took two leads with cotton disks at their ends and affixed one to each of her temples.

Logan glanced at him in mute inquiry.

"Cortical stimulator," Rush replied. "Encourages pineal activity."

Logan nodded. He knew studies had demonstrated the pineal gland's neurochemical effects on previsualization and psychic activity.

Rush returned to the forest of monitoring devices at the foot of the bed. For another minute or two he watched as his wife slowly drifted back into semiconsciousness. Then he came forward again and inserted a second needle into the IV's connecting hub.

"More propofol?" Logan asked in a quiet voice.

Rush shook his head. "Versed. For its amnesiac effect."

Amnesiac effect? Logan wondered. **Why?**

Approaching the head of the bed, Rush slipped two items out of the pockets of his lab coat. One, Logan saw, was an ophthalmoscope. The other, to his surprise, was an ancient-looking amulet of untarnished silver, a small white candle set into its upper edge. Rush examined her pupils with the ophthalmoscope, then lit the candle and gently dangled the amulet from its chain, between Jennifer Rush's face and the mirror.

"I want you to stare at the amulet," Dr. Rush said, his voice a low, soothing murmur. "See nothing else. Visualize nothing else. **Think** of nothing else."

He continued murmuring instructions. Logan recognized this: a standard hypnosis tool known as an eye-fixation induction text. But then, the text changed.

"Now," Rush said, "breathe slowly, deeply. Let your limbs go limp. Relax your neck. Relax your shoulders. Relax your arms: first the fingers, then the wrists, then the lower arms, and then the upper. Relax your feet. Relax your legs."

For a minute, maybe two, there was no sound in the room save for Jennifer Rush's soft breathing.

"And now, relax your **mind**. Let it go free. Let your consciousness slip from your body. Leave it an empty shell, unpossessed."

In the sandalwood-fragrant room, Logan watched. After another minute, Rush blew out the candle and put the amulet aside. Quietly, he walked back to the foot of the bed, examined the instrumentation. Then he returned to her side, waiting.

Jennifer Rush's breathing grew louder, almost stertorous. The room seemed to darken, as if strange, antique mists were gathering.

All of a sudden, Logan became alarmed. He did not know why it was, not exactly—but for some reason his fight-or-flight instinct began to go off, five-alarm. It was all he could do not to leap to his feet and run from the room. He felt his heart hammering, struggled to get himself under control.

From the bed, her breathing grew more labored.

Rush turned on a digital voice recorder, which he placed on a nearby tray. Slowly, he bent over the bed. "Who am I speaking to?"

Jennifer's mouth worked, as if trying to form words. Logan saw her hands ball into fists, as if from the effort.

"Who am I speaking to?" Rush asked again.

A hissing sound emanated from Jennifer Rush. **"Nut,"** she said in a dry, distant voice. Or perhaps it was "Set"—Logan could not be sure. All he knew was that merely speaking this syllable clearly took enormous effort.

"Who am I speaking to?" Rush asked a third time.

Again, Jennifer's mouth worked. **"Mmm . . . mouthpiece . . . of Horus."**

Rush adjusted the recorder, seemingly encouraged.

But Logan did not feel encouraged. It wasn't only the chill sense of evil that had come over the room, all too similar to what he'd experienced the day of the generator fire. It was also the evident strain, both physical and emotional, that Jennifer was undergoing.

"Can you tell me about the seal?" Rush asked. "The first gate?"

"The . . . first . . . gate," she repeated.

"Yes," Rush replied. "What should we—"

Suddenly, Jennifer's eyes bulged, their whites a sickly green in the faint light of the instrumentation. The tendons of her neck stood out like cables. **"Infidels!"** she said. **"Enemies of Ra!"** Her head rose menacingly from the bed; a half dozen of the EEG leads popped loose and fell away. **"Leave this place. Or else He Whose Face Is Turned Backwards will feed upon thy blood and take the milk from the mouths of thy children. The foundations of thy house will be broken, and thou will die an endless death in the Outer Darkness!"**

Logan rose quickly from his chair. Her voice was infinitely more awful for being a mere hissing whisper. Instinctively, he put a hand out to calm her. But the moment his skin touched hers, he was staggered by a flash almost like lightning: he felt the presence again, implacable, violently angry, its hatred radiating toward them from the blackness of the abyss. With a groan of dismay he sank back into the chair.

As quickly as it began, the imprecation ceased. Jennifer Rush fell silent. Her head sank back to the pillow and lolled to one side.

"That's it," Rush said. He snapped off the recorder, returned to the monitors at the foot of the bed. He seemed oblivious to the brief but terrible drama Logan had experienced.

Logan passed a hand over his forehead. "Is that—typical?"

Rush shook his head. "The very first crossing—the first that made contact, I mean—was actually beneficial. It helped pinpoint the location of the tomb with greater accuracy by providing a point of triangulation. But after that . . ." Rush sighed. "It's almost as if the entity now understands who we are, why we're here."

Logan glanced at Jennifer Rush, supine on the bed. Now he felt even more like a fool: assuming such experiences had been pleasant for her, congratulating her on her abilities. He looked back at Rush. "Is all this trauma really . . . really necessary?"

Rush returned the look. "Most spiritual exchanges at the psychomanteums back at CTS are pleasant. But then, they usually involve loved ones who have recently passed over. This . . . this is a very different animal. Remember that Jennifer won't have much memory of the actual crossing. That's what the Versed is for. We'll try a few more crossings in the days to come. If they aren't of any additional help, then . . ." He shrugged.

Logan glanced back at the woman on the bed. He knew that some people, particularly March, thought she was faking, grandstanding—perhaps at the urging of her husband, who after all as head of CTS had something to gain. But after seeing this crossing in person, he felt absolutely sure there was no fakery. Something—someone—had been speaking to them through Jennifer Rush. Someone who was very angry indeed.

Rush made a few notes on a clipboard, snapped off some instrumentation. "She'll rest comfortably now," he said. "As you'll discover, she rebounds very quickly." He pointed at the equipment arrayed before him. "Jeremy, I want to input some of this data into the computer right away. Would you mind staying with her for a minute or two while I get the analysis started?"

"Of course." Logan watched as Rush picked up his digital recorder, then left the room.

For a minute, perhaps two, all was quiet. Logan, still shaken, tried to calm himself, tried to focus on evaluating and understanding what had just happened. Then there was a faint movement from the bed and he glanced over to see Jennifer Rush looking at him.

"How are you feeling?" he asked.

She just shook her head. Then, suddenly, she reached out and grasped his wrist, tightly, almost painfully. He tensed for a moment, fearing another explosion of sensation, but there was nothing.

"Dr. Logan," she said, her silky voice low and urgent, "when we spoke in the lounge, I told you I experienced what everyone else who 'goes over' does."

"Yes," he replied.

"And that's true. I did—at first. But then I saw things that were completely different. **Completely** different."

Her grasp grew even tighter, and her amber eyes held his own. There was something in those eyes, in that face, he couldn't read.

"Help me," she suddenly whispered, almost below the threshold of audibility. **"Help me."**

The door handle rattled. Immediately, Jennifer Rush released her hold on his wrist. She kept her gaze on him for another few seconds. Then, as the door opened and Rush stepped in, she slowly lay back on the bed—and passed out.

31

Logan sat at the desk of his small office in Maroon, looking at the laptop screen without really seeing it. It was very late—almost two in the morning—but he still felt too restless to sleep.

In his career as an enigmalogist, Logan had experienced many unusual and, at times, dangerous things. He had climbed the Himalayas in search of yeti. He'd descended to the bottom of Scottish lochs in a diving bell. For every half-dozen ghosts or spectral presences he'd debunked, there had been at least one other he'd been unable to explain away with science. He'd attended three exorcisms. But nothing in his wide experience had caused him quite the kind of unease as the invisible presence he'd felt beside Jennifer Rush's hospital bed that evening.

He stirred in his chair, picked up a transcript of the "crossing":

> **[Begins 21:04:30]**
> **Q:** Who am I speaking to?
> **Q:** Who am I speaking to?
> **R:** (Unintelligible reply)
> **Q:** Who am I speaking to?
> **R:** Mouthpiece of Horus.
> **Q:** Can you tell me about the seal? The first gate?
> **R:** The first gate.
> **Q:** What should we—
> **R:** Infidels! Enemies of Ra. Leave this place. Or else He Whose Face Is Turned Backwards will feed upon thy blood and take the milk from the mouths of thy children. The foundations of thy house will be broken, and thou will die an endless death in the Outer Darkness.
> **[Ends 21:07:15]**

The foundations of thy house will be broken. That was part of the curse of Narmer, as Tina Romero had translated it for him. Logan wondered how much, if anything, Jennifer Rush knew about the curse.

He put down the transcript. There was something else. He tried recalling what it was Romero had told him. **An'kavasht—He Whose Face is Turned Backwards. A god of nightmare and evil, who dwelled Outside, "in the endless night."**

Outside. The Sudd.

Over the past several days, Logan had done research—via a special computer in Stone's outer office with a satellite connection to the Internet—into the curses of ancient Egypt. They had a long and colorful history that extended far beyond the tabloid sensationalism of King Tut and Howard Carter. Logan had encountered curses before, of course: in Gibraltar, Estonia, New Orleans. In each case, there had been an anodyne, a counterspell: some method for deflecting or ameliorating the execration. Not so with the tombs of ancient Egypt. Despite all his reading, all his research, only one method for countering such curses seemed to exist: stay well away from them.

Irresistibly, his thoughts were drawn back to Jennifer Rush: to the almost desperate way she had grasped his wrist, to the look in her eyes when she asked for help. It was as if the scales had fallen from his own eyes, and he had seen her, and her terrible vulnerability, for the first time.

I thought it might be beneficial for Jennifer, Rush had said. **Give her a chance to use her gift in**

a positive way. But how could what he'd witnessed ever be considered beneficial?

There was a knock on his door. Logan turned to see—as if in response to his thoughts—Ethan Rush standing in the doorway.

"Come in," he said.

Rush entered. He nodded at Logan, but deferentially, almost like a schoolboy conscious of some misdeed. He sat down in the chair beside the desk.

"Thoughts?" Rush asked after a brief silence.

"I think your wife should be spared any future crossings."

Rush smiled slightly, then shrugged, as if to imply it was out of his hands. "I'm not happy about it, either. But Stone's a hard man to say no to. And Jennifer has always been game."

"And you've seen nothing like this before? In your studies at CTS?"

"Nothing of this magnitude. And nothing from such—such a temporal distance. As I told you, most of the experiences we've seen deal with recently deceased relatives or people—also recently deceased—who had lived in the vicinity of the crossing site. But, then again, Jen has a unique talent." Rush shook his head.

"You mention a temporal distance. So you think that whoever is speaking through her might be contemporaneous with the construction of the tomb?"

"I don't know." Rush seemed unsettled by the question—or perhaps by the concept itself. "It seems incredible. But what other spiritual force would be found in such a remote place?" He paused. "What do you think?"

For a minute, Logan did not respond. "Earlier, when I implied your wife was channeling Narmer, I was being facetious. Now I'm sorry I joked about it. In any case, whoever is speaking through Jennifer, I don't think it's Narmer. You see, the ancient Egyptians believed that after death, the soul persisted through eternity. As long as you knew the secret rituals, as long as you brought with you in your tomb all the possessions you needed for a physical, earthly life, your soul—**ba**—and its protective spirit—**ka**—would find their way to the next world." He thought a moment. "Clearly, Narmer would have done this, would have moved on to the next realm. So perhaps whoever is speaking through your wife is someone else, a restless soul, adrift in the spirit world yet somehow tied to this place."

"But a soul so ancient . . ." Rush stopped briefly for continuing. "How is such a thing possible? I mean, I, of all people, seeing what I've seen at the Center, am disposed to believe. I wouldn't have brought Jen all the way out here if I thought it was impossible. Our own studies have shown it's **theoretically** possible. But how . . ." He faltered into silence.

"There are numerous theories that might help explain," Logan said. "There's a belief that strong evil persists in spirit long after the physical body has perished. The greater the evil, the longer its influence lingers—not unlike the half-life of radioactive material. Your wife, with her unique sensitivities, may well be acting as a conduit for such an influence. You should think of her as a psychical weather vane—or, perhaps better, as an unwitting, and unwilling, lightning rod. A lightning rod does nothing on its own—it simply attracts."

"But attracts who?" Rush asked.

"Who's to say? One of the dead priests? Someone left to guard the tomb? Perhaps it might even be someone who died a hundred years ago, rather than five thousand."

"But during her first productive crossing, she made some specific references to the site that helped us."

"You mentioned that before." Logan shifted in his seat. "I'd like to see those transcripts, if I may."

"I'll see what I can arrange."

"I would also like a copy of your CTS records."

Rush looked at him. "Which records?"

"Whatever you can give me. Trial studies, doctor's reports, interviews with test subjects."

"Why is that important?"

"You asked me for help. The more I understand of your work—of what Jennifer and the others have undergone—the better prepared I'll be to help you."

Rush considered this a moment. Then he nodded slowly. "I'll burn a DVD for you. Anything else?"

"Yes. What's so important about the first gate?"

"The first gate?" Rush seemed surprised by this

non sequitur. "It's the sealed entrance to the tomb. Stone was looking for any assistance in how to safely breach it."

"Safely breach it," Logan repeated. "He's afraid of a trap."

Rush nodded. "Narmer went to incredible lengths to secure his tomb," he said. "It doesn't seem likely he'd hand over the keys without a fight."

32

Porter Stone's office looked as immaculate and minimalist as the first time Logan had entered it. The only difference he noted this time was that the lone calendar page of the current month had been removed, leaving the walls completely bare.

Stone, who had been speaking into a radio, snapped it off as Logan stepped in. "Jeremy. Please have a seat."

"Thank you."

Stone looked Logan up and down with his cool, appraising gaze. "So. What did you want to see me about?"

"I understand that things are proceeding very well."

"I'm extremely happy with our progress. The tomb interface—the air lock—has been permanently affixed to the surrounding rock. The Umbilicus has been run from the Maw to the air lock. It's now fully powered and pressurized. The link is stable—we've run numerous tests and diagnostics. We sent down a five hundred megahertz ground-penetrating radar, piloted remotely. It, along with sonic imaging tests, seems to detect three chambers beyond the first gate, one placed after the other in series."

Although he was talking about the find of his career, Stone's verbal delivery and body language remained calm and reserved. Only the hard glitter in his blue eyes suggested what he was really feeling. "Everything is in readiness," he continued. "It's time to break the seal and enter the tomb."

Logan ran a hand through his hair. "Who will be making the initial penetration?"

"Tina. Dr. March. Ethan Rush. A couple of Frank Valentino's boys for the heavy lifting. And myself, of course." He smiled. "One of the perks of funding this little expedition."

"I would recommend one other," Logan said.

Stone raised his eyebrows. "Oh? And who might that be?"

"Me."

Slowly, Stone's smile faded. "I'm afraid that won't be possible. Why should I bring you along on this first incursion?"

"There are lots of reasons. For one thing, it's part of my job description. You brought me here to investigate various strange phenomena: we both have a strong suspicion this tomb may in some way be responsible for them. I'm also uniquely qualified to document this event—and I know that such documentation will be important to you in the future."

"Yes. But why not wait until the tomb is stabilized?"

"Because if there is indeed an active curse—in whatever form it might manifest itself—I should be there from the beginning. Recall Narmer's opening words: 'Any man who dares enter my tomb.' Nobody has yet entered the tomb—but the Station already has been plagued with unexplained phenomena. There is a good chance that whatever else might happen may well start with this initial penetration."

"That's true," Stone said. "All the more argument for you to wait. There's no reason to expose you needlessly to danger."

"I've signed the liability waivers and indemnification documents, just like the others—Ethan Rush made sure of that." Logan sat forward in his chair. "And there's another argument for my presence, Dr. Stone. Nobody knows what lies on the far side of that gate. But of anyone on this Station, **I'm** the most prepared to deal with it. You've seen my résumé.

You know the kinds of—shall we say—**nonnatural** phenomena I've come up against in the past. I'm as inured to such things as anyone could claim to be. Frankly, I've seen things that might break a less experienced person. You need me **precisely because** we don't know what we're going to find."

Stone fixed him with a penetrating gaze. "You forget I'm not exactly a novice at this sort of thing. I've unsealed more than my share of tombs."

"Not one with a curse like this on it." Logan drew in a deep breath. "Let me do my job, Dr. Stone."

For a long moment, Stone continued to stare at him. Then his sly, almost private smile slowly returned. "Eight a.m. sharp," he said. "Don't be late."

33

The last time Logan saw the Staging Area was on the day of the dive accident. The huge, echoing room had been crowded then. It was even more crowded now. At least a dozen people were monitoring the wall of instrumentation, and a small army of assistants and technicians were massed in the center, crowding around the Maw, all talking animatedly.

Slowly, Logan approached them. The huge flat-panel monitor that had displayed the chessboard-like grid of the Sudd floor was now dark, its purpose fulfilled. Tall racks of sodium vapor lights were aimed into the Maw. As he drew close, he could make out Tina Romero in the crowd. She spotted him, detached herself from the group, and came over.

"I heard you invited yourself along," she said. "Stone must really dig you."

Logan shrugged. "What's not to dig?"

"You want a list?"

The banter was light, but Logan detected an edge in her voice. He knew what she was feeling, because he felt it himself. Great excitement to be here for this, perhaps the most important day in archaeology since Schliemann discovered Troy—but also deep and pervasive anxiety over what King Narmer might have in store for them.

Porter Stone was standing to one side with Frank Valentino. He glanced at his watch, then said something to Valentino, who immediately raised a bullhorn. "Attention!" the chief barked. "Break it up, please. Back to your stations."

Slowly, in ones and twos, the people drifted away from the Maw. Now Stone and Valentino approached, along with two burly roustabouts. Stone nodded at Tina and Logan in turn. "Ready?"

"Yes," they replied in tandem.

"This is how we'll proceed. Valentino's men will go first, followed by myself, Tina, Dr. March, Dr. Rush, and then Jeremy here. We've already lowered most of the equipment we'll need down to the air lock platform. Once we've established that the site is secure, we will perform a close examination of the gate itself, followed by a test core. Only then will we break the seal and enter. This first penetration of the tomb will be limited to a visual reconnaissance only—everything will be recorded on video, but nothing is to be touched, save samples taken for analysis by Tina and Ethan Rush. Is that understood?"

While he had been speaking, Ethan Rush and Fenwick March joined the group. Everyone nodded.

"Good. Then put on your respirators and gloves. We'll communicate via radio."

Following Tina's example, Logan stepped over to a small wheeled lab table, picked up a pair of latex gloves, and pulled them on. Then he took a respirator from among several lying on the table and snugged it over his mouth and nose. He attached the radio clip to his belt and turned it on.

All the others did the same. Valentino's men wore small backpacks, as did Ethan Rush. Tina hoisted a compact videocam.

And then they were ready. Stone looked at each in turn, then glanced at Valentino's men and gave them a thumbs-up. As the two stepped over to the Maw, Logan was surprised by a spontaneous burst of applause from the various technicians and assistants; instead of going back to their posts, as instructed, they had gathered near the industrial rolling ladder and were watching the seven as they prepared to descend to the tomb.

Logan hung back, watching, as—one after the other—Valentino's two men walked to the Maw, grasped the metal railing, swung their legs over, and slowly descended out of sight. Next went Stone, then Romero, then March, then Rush.

And then it was his turn. With a deep breath, he stepped to the edge of the Maw, grasped the railing, and peered over its edge.

The last time he'd done that, the Maw had been merely a portal to the Sudd below. Black, evil-smelling muck had filled it to the rim. Now, however, he found himself staring down a long, gently sloping yellow tunnel, made of some heavy, flexible material. At least a dozen cables of various colors and thicknesses ran down into its flanks, like veins. The tunnel—the Umbilicus, as it was called—was slightly narrower than the Maw itself. It was stiffened against the external pressure of the Sudd by wooden bracings, set in an overlapping hexagonal pattern, each support structure placed about two feet from the next. A pulley system of some kind ran down the left flank, apparently for bringing heavier items down to or up from the tomb. A series of lozenge-shaped LEDs was arrayed down the upper edge of the tube in an unbroken line, bathing the Umbilicus in cool light. Heavy foot- and handholds were set down its length. Below him, he could see the others, descending hand under hand toward what they had termed the Lock.

Taking another deep breath, he took hold of the

railing, swung himself over, made sure his footing was secure, then began to descend.

"Stone here," the voice crackled over his radio. "I've reached the outer air lock platform."

Logan descended, careful to keep his breathing regular. The Umbilicus was spotless: there was no trace of mud along its inner walls. The air that came through his respirator had only the faintest scent of rotting vegetation. And yet he found himself unable to forget, even for a moment, the vile ooze that pressed in on them from all sides of the tube.

The descent itself was easy enough. He'd assumed that the Station would be anchored directly over the tomb and that they would need to climb straight down, ladder-style. But Porter Stone, always thinking ahead, had positioned the Station at a sufficient distance to give the Umbilicus a forty-five-degree angle from vertical, allowing for relatively easy journeys up and down. As Logan descended, he noticed that the pieces of wooden bracing became thicker, no doubt compensating for the increased pressure from outside.

Within three minutes he had joined the group on the air lock platform. He looked around curiously. The platform was actually formed out of the base of the Umbilicus: a metal catwalk, roughly ten feet on each side. Beneath it, four thick metal supports pierced the yellow material of the tube and disappeared below, presumably anchored to the bed of the Sudd. The spots where the supports exited the base of the tube were composed of metal sleeves, their edges thickly sealed with latex, rubber, and narrow bands of steel.

In one corner of the platform, several large evidence lockers had been carefully stacked. Beside them were various archaeological tools and equipment for examining, stabilizing, and even field curation of ancient artifacts.

Three of the walls of the platform resembled the rest of the Umbilicus: hexagonally braced and thickly veined with cabling. The fourth wall, however, held a heavy circular door of an opaque material, as round as a bank vault's and seemingly as impregnable.

With all seven of them standing on the platform, there was precious little room to spare. For a moment, nobody spoke, looking instead at the others through their respirators. There was a tension in the air no one seemed eager to break. Finally, Stone pressed the Transmit button of his radio.

"Stone here," he said. "We're proceeding."

"Roger that," came the voice from the control station above.

Then—with Tina Romero videotaping—Stone moved toward the heavy door. "I'm opening the Lock," he said. He carefully unscrewed four large bolts in the circular panel, one at each point of the compass. Then, taking hold of a thick handle at its center, he pulled the door free of its enclosing hatch.

It swung open on silent hinges. Just beyond, Logan could see the face of dressed granite that sealed the entrance to Narmer's tomb. The boulders and mud that had helped keep it from the elements had been completely removed, leaving nothing but the courses of granite and the surrounding igneous matrix that formed the mouth of the volcanic cavity. The polished granite wall gleamed in the reflected light of the Umbilicus. Aside from the two seals, the rock contained no markings whatsoever. What had seemed so far away in the video feeds of the divers, so remote and unearthly, now stood directly before him, mere feet away.

Logan was aware that his heart was beating faster now, almost painfully so. The air lock itself had been fixed to the irregular surface of igneous rock by thick rubber gaskets, made airtight by some kind of compound and held in place by the same kind of metal rods that anchored the outer platform to the bottom of the Sudd.

Now Stone and Fenwick March came forward, each carrying magnifying glasses and powerful flashlights. As the others watched, the two examined every inch of the granite surface, probing and pressing gently with gloved hands. The process took almost fifteen minutes. Satisfied at last, they stepped back out onto the platform.

"Tina?" Stone said over the radio. "Would you examine the seals, please?"

Tina took the magnifying glass and flashlight from March and stepped forward. Peering closely, she examined first the upper necropolis seal, then—getting down on her knees—the royal seal at the base of the granite courses. Each was fixed in place by two bronze pikes, one at either end, with thin bronze wires wound between them in curls that reminded Logan of a hangman's noose. On the right-hand end of each seal was a fist-sized piece of reddish pottery, encasing both the wire and the spike. Into this had been set the actual hieroglyphic impressions.

"Well?" Stone asked.

"They're completely intact," she said. Logan could hear a faint tremor in her voice. "But this serekh—there's something unusual about it. It's of a form unknown to me."

"But it's definitely Narmer's seal?"

"The hieroglyphs are that of the catfish and the chisel—the rebus for Narmer's name."

"Very good. Get ready, please."

Romero rose to her feet. As she ran the video camera, both March and Stone again stepped up beside her. Stone held a small evidence box, its bottom lined with cotton; March held a scalpel and forceps. While the rest waited in anxious silence, March very cautiously brought the scalpel up against the necropolis seal. With a slow, methodical motion, he brought the scalpel down across the seal, cutting it in two. Then, with equally cautious movements, he used the scalpel and the forceps to tease the seal away from the granite and place the pieces into Stone's box.

Logan realized he was holding his breath. Quite consciously he expelled it, took in fresh air. Despite the high tension of the moment, he could not help but be impressed by the care Stone and his team were taking not only to record the entire event but to carefully conserve the elements of the tomb. Stone was no treasure hunter: he was a careful archaeologist, bent on preserving the past rather than destroying it.

Now the three had moved to the larger, royal seal. March placed his scalpel at the top of the seal. Then he paused. A minute went by, then two.

The tension in the Lock became almost palpable. This was it: once the royal seal was broken, the tomb would be in a state of desecration. Logan swallowed. **Any man who dares enter my tomb will meet an end certain and swift. I, Narmer the Everliving, will torment him and his, by day and by night, waking and sleeping, until madness and death become his eternal temple.**

"Fenwick?" Stone's mild voice sounded over the radio.

The archaeologist started. Then he bent closer over the seal, and—with a slow, slicing movement—drew the scalpel down through it, cutting it in two.

There was a general exhalation of breath from the assembled group that needed no radio to be heard. "Now we've done it," Tina said very quietly.

March took the two pieces of the seal and placed them into Stone's box. Then Stone, March, and Romero all stepped away from the granite wall. Every move seemed so carefully choreographed it was almost like a ballet.

Stone turned to Dr. Rush. "Go ahead, Doctor."

Reaching into his backpack, Rush removed a battery-powered drill and a thick bit about twelve inches long. Fixing the bit to the chuck, the doctor approached the granite face, chose a spot directly in the center, placed the bit against the stone, and fired up the drill.

Stone urged the others to keep back as the drill whined. After about sixty seconds, Logan heard the pitch of the drill abruptly drop; Rush was through. There was a low, faint whistling sound as air escaped through the drill hole.

The doctor pressed a plastic plug into the hole he'd made, then put the drill to one side. "The granite's not particularly thick," he said over the radio. "Perhaps four inches." Reaching into his backpack again, he withdrew a strange-looking instrument: a long clear tube, fixed to a plastic housing containing an LED readout. A rubber bladder hung from one side of the housing. Removing the plug from the hole he'd made, Rush threaded the clear tube through the borehole, then pushed a button on the housing. There was a whirring sound as the bladder inflated. Rush pressed additional buttons, then examined the LED display.

"Dust," he said over the radio. "Particulate matter. High levels of CO_2. But no pathogenic bacteria."

Logan now understood the purpose of the device. It was the high-tech equivalent of Howard Carter holding a candle up to the air exhaling from King Tutankhamen's tomb.

"Any fungal concentrations?" Stone asked.

"A full biological study will have to wait until I get back to the medical suite," Rush replied, "but nothing stands out in a field analysis. There's a marked absence of fungi, in fact. The tomb microclimate shows no anaerobic bacteria and acceptable levels of aerobic bacteria."

"In that case, we will proceed. Just to be sure, however, we'll move decontamination showers into the Staging Area and use them when we exit the Umbilicus."

As Rush returned his equipment to the backpack, Stone approached the borehole. He had removed something from the boxes at the rear of the air lock: a SWAT-style fiber-optic camera, a light at its tip, its long flexible cable attached to goggles. Fitting the goggles over his bulky respirator, he aimed the tip of the camera at the hole, then threaded it through. For a long moment he stood silently, peering through the goggles into the interior. Then, quite abruptly, he stiffened and gasped.

"God," he said in a broken whisper. "My God."

He withdrew the camera from the borehole, slowly pulled the goggles from his head. Then he turned to face the others. Logan was shocked. Stone's carefully studied nonchalance, his unflappable poise, seemed to have deserted him. Even with his face half covered by a respirator, he looked like someone who had . . . Logan, heart still beating fast, found it difficult to describe the expression. Like someone, perhaps, who had just gazed upon the face of heaven. Or, perhaps, hell.

Wordlessly, Stone motioned to the two roustabouts. They came forward, one equipped with a small power chisel, the other with a vacuum cleaner attached to a long hose. They numbered each granite slab with a wax pencil, then the first roustabout began clearing away the plaster between the slabs while the other used the vacuum cleaner to suck up the resulting dust. Logan assumed this precaution was taken in the event that the plaster had been laced with poison.

Once the first slab was out, the work proceeded quickly. Before twenty minutes had passed, several of the granite slabs had been stacked to one side of the air lock and a hole large enough to admit a person had been made in the tomb entrance.

Logan glanced at that hole, at the blackness that lay beyond. As if by unspoken consent, nobody had yet shone a light into the tomb, waiting instead until they could enter it.

Now Stone glanced around at the assembled company. He had recovered his voice and at least some of his self-possession. He located Tina Romero, then extended his gloved hand toward the dark opening in the granite wall.

"Tina?" he said over the radio. "Ladies first."

34

Romero nodded. She gripped her flashlight, then took a step forward, swinging her light up into the black void of the tomb entrance.

Immediately, she staggered backward. "Holy **shit**!" she said. A collective gasp sounded from the rest of the group.

Inside the tomb, mere inches from the opening, stood a terrifying limestone statue: a creature, nearly seven feet tall, with the head of a serpent, the body of a lion, and the arms of a man. It was crouched, its muscles tensed as if ready to spring through the opening toward them. It had been painted in amazingly lifelike colors, still vibrant after five thousand years in the dark. Its eyes had been inlaid with carnelians, which glittered menacingly in the gleam of their torches.

"Whew," Romero said, recovering. "Some guardian."

She moved forward again, letting the light play over the disturbing statue. At its feet lay a human skeleton. The tattered remains of what had once been rich vestments still clung to the bones.

"Necropolis guard," Romero muttered over the radio.

She very carefully made her way around the statue and moved deeper into the chamber. Each footfall raised tiny clouds of dust. After a pause, Stone followed; then March; and then Rush, holding his monitoring equipment forward. The roustabouts remained on the platform. Last to enter was Logan. He stepped past the granite seal, slid around the guardian figure and the skeleton at its base, and entered the tomb proper.

The chamber was not large, perhaps fifteen feet deep by ten feet wide, narrowing slightly as it went back. Their flashlight beams cast long, eerie trails in the rising dust. The walls were completely lined in turquoise-colored tile that Logan realized must be faience. Their surfaces were busy with primitive

hieroglyphs and painted images. The air felt remarkably cool and dry.

The tomb was filled with neatly organized grave
goods: intricately carved and painted chairs; a massive, canopied bed of gilded wood; numerous ushabti;
beautiful wheel-turned pottery; an open, gold-lined
box full of amulets, beads, and jewelry. Tina Romero
moved slowly around the room, capturing everything
on the video camera. March followed in her wake,
examining objects with the gentle touch of a gloved
finger. Rush was monitoring his handheld sensor.
Stone hung back, taking in everything. When people
spoke, it was in hushed, almost reverential voices. It
was as if, only now, the realization was taking hold:
We've entered King Narmer's tomb.

Logan stood back with Stone, watching the pro-
ceedings. Despite his insistence on accompanying
the group, he had nevertheless been dreading this
moment, fearing that the malignance, the malevo-
lence, he had sensed before would be even stronger
here. But there was nothing. No, that wasn't quite
right: there **did** seem to be some presence—but it
was almost as if the tomb itself was watching them,
waiting, biding its time for . . .

For what? Logan wasn't sure.

March placed his hand on the turquoise-colored
wall in an almost caressing gesture. "This lava tube
would have been formed of extrusive igneous rock,
very rough and sharp. Now the surface is as smooth

as glass. Think of the man-hours involved in polishing it with the rude tools of the day."

Tina had stopped before a long row of tall jars of reddish clay, perfectly formed, their rims dark. "These black-topped jars were common around the time of unification," she said. "They'll be useful for dating."

"I'll take samples for thermoluminescence tests on our next descent," said March.

There was a moment of silence as the group continued taking it all in.

"There's no sarcophagus," Logan said, glancing around.

"This outer room would normally hold household items, perhaps some business details," Stone replied, "things the king would need in the next life. The sarcophagus would be deeper within the tomb, most likely in the final chamber beyond the third gate. That's what the pharaoh would be most concerned about preserving in an unspoiled state."

Tina knelt before a large chest of painted wood, edged in gold. With slow, delicate motions, she swept the dust from its top, then freed the lid and gently raised it. The glow of her flashlight revealed dozens and dozens of papyri within, rolled tight, in perfect, unspoiled condition. Beside them were stacked two tall rows of carved tablets.

"My God," she breathed. "Think of the history these contain."

Stone had moved toward the gilded, canopied bed. It was beautiful, shimmering with an almost unearthly glow in the beams of their flashlights. Its various intricately worked pieces were held together by huge bolts of what appeared to be solid gold. "Notice the canopy," he said, pointing. "That gilded piece of wood must weigh a thousand pounds. Yet everything's perfectly preserved. It could have been fashioned yesterday."

"This is odd," said March. He was peering at an image painted on one of the walls: a depiction of two strange-looking objects. One was box shaped, topped by a kind of rod that was surrounded by a copper-colored crest or banner. The other was a white, bowl-like artifact, with long wisps of gold trailing from its edges. They were surrounded by a blizzard of hieroglyphics.

"What do you make of it?" Stone asked.

Tina shook her head. "Unique. I've never seen anything like these before. Anything **remotely** like them. They look like tools. Implements of some sort. But I can't imagine what they might be used for."

"And the glyphs surrounding them?"

There was a pause as Romero striped her flashlight across them. "They seem to be warnings. Imprecations." A pause. "I'll have to examine them more closely in the lab." She stepped back, panned over the images with her camera.

"It might be unique," Logan said, "but it's not the only one in here." And he pointed at a nearby wall relief, the largest in the chamber. It depicted a seated male figure, shown in side view, left leg forward, as was common with all ancient Egyptian art. He was wearing fine clothes, clearly a personage of great importance. And yet—bizarrely—the same two objects had been placed on his head, the bowl-shaped one below, the box with the rod atop. He was surrounded by what appeared to be high priests.

"I'll be damned," March murmured.

"What do you suppose they are?" Stone asked. "They can't be crowns."

"Perhaps it's a punishment of some kind," Logan said.

"Yes, but look at that." Tina pointed to an embossed detail below the relief. "It's a serekh—meaning the figure in the picture is royal."

"Is it the serekh of Narmer?" Stone asked.

"Yes. But it's been altered, defaced somehow."

Slowly, the group began to gravitate toward the rear wall. Their flashlight beams played over its surface: another face of polished granite, the slabs mortared in place. Again, the necropolis seal and the royal seal were both intact, untouched. Unlike the first doorway, however, this one was outlined in what appeared to be solid gold.

"The second gate," said March almost reverentially.

They stared at it for a moment before Stone broke the silence. "We'll return to the Station, analyze our findings. We'll have an engineering team come down to examine this chamber, ensure it's structurally sound. And then"—he paused, his voice trembling ever so slightly—"we'll proceed."

35

The setting looked the same: the same dimly lit lab, with its single bed and array of medical instrumentation. There was the same mingled scent of sandalwood and myrrh; the same bleating of monitoring devices. The same large, carefully polished mirror reflected the tiny, winking lights. Jennifer Rush lay on the bed, breathing shallowly, once again under the influence of propofol.

The only difference, Logan thought, was that—

this morning—they had violated the tomb of King Narmer.

He watched as Rush fixed the leads to her temples, administered the Versed, went through the hypnotic induction. He was aware of feeling a great tension, of a deep unwillingness in himself to reexperience the trauma of the first crossing. And yet this time, the malignant influence he'd felt before—while still present—seemed remote, even faint.

The door opened on silent hinges and Tina Romero entered. She nodded at Rush, smiled at Logan, and quietly stepped over to stand beside him.

Rush waited until his wife stirred slightly and her breathing grew labored. Then he snapped on the digital voice recorder. "Who am I speaking to?" he asked.

This time, the reply was immediate. **"Mouthpiece of Horus."**

"What is your name?"

"One . . . who is not to be named."

Tina leaned in close to Logan, whispered in his ear. "Scholars speculate that Narmer—when he became the god-king—wouldn't allow his royal name to be spoken aloud upon pain of death."

Rush bent closer to the supine figure of his wife, spoke softly. "Who was that figure—that figure guarding the tomb?"

"Thou . . . hast defiled me." The voice was not angry this time. Instead, it seemed sorrowful, almost dolorous. **"Thou hast desecrated my sacred house."**

"Who is the guardian?" Rush asked again.

"The eater . . . of souls. He who dwells in the tenth region of night. Tasker of Ra."

"But who—"

"He will come for thou, the defilers. The unbelievers. Thy limbs shall . . . be rent from thy body, and thy line broken. Geb will place his foot upon thy head . . . and Horus will smite thee. . . ."

"What was that image in the tomb painting?" Rush asked, careful to keep his voice neutral. "The, ah, ornament on the man's head?"

A brief silence. **"That which brings life to the dead . . . and death to the living."**

Rush lowered his voice still further. "What can you tell me about the second gate?"

"Despair . . . thine end comes quickly, on . . . taloned feet." And with this Jennifer Rush let out a long, low sigh, turned her face to the wall, and went utterly still.

Rush turned off the recorder, slipped it into his pocket, then gave his wife a careful examination. Frowning, he turned to study the monitoring equipment at her feet.

"What is it?" Logan asked.

"I'm not sure," Rush said, peering at the indicators of her vitals. "Give me a minute."

"'Geb will place his foot upon thy head,'" Tina repeated. "Sounds like a paraphrase of the Pyramid Texts. Utterance three fifty-four or three fifty-six, I believe. Now, how would she know about those?"

"The Pyramid Texts?" Logan asked.

"The oldest religious documents in the world. They were Old Kingdom spells and invocations that could only be spoken by royalty."

"Narmer," Logan muttered.

"If so, if they date back as far as Narmer's time, then the Texts are even older than scholars believe—by at least seven hundred years."

"What were the Texts about?"

"Reanimating the pharaoh's body after his death, protecting his corpse from despoliation, seeing the pharaoh safely into the next world—all the things that concerned the ancient Egyptian kings."

Logan realized they were whispering. "What was that she said about the ornament depicted on the wall?"

"That it brought life to the dead and death to the living," Tina replied.

"What do you suppose that means?"

"Perhaps gibberish. On the other hand, the Egyptian pharaohs were in fact fascinated by near-death experience, what they called the 'second region of night.'"

"The second region of night," Logan murmured. "Jennifer mentioned a region of night, too."

Rush had looked up from his instrumentation and was glancing their way. "Tina," he said, "I wonder if you would mind excusing Jeremy and me for a minute."

Tina shrugged and began to walk toward the door. With her hand on the knob, she turned back.

"I hope this is the last time you put her through this," she said. Then she left, closing the door quietly behind her.

In the silence that followed, Logan turned to Rush. "What is it?"

"It's taking her longer to snap back this time," he said. "I'm not sure why."

"How long does it normally take?"

"Usually it's almost immediate. But that last crossing, the one you witnessed—it took her almost ten minutes to rouse completely. That's uncommon."

"Is there something you can give her?"

"I'd rather not try. We've never had to administer anything at the Center. Propofol is such a short-acting hypnotic, she should have been fully conscious for some time already."

There was a moment of silence. Then Rush started, as if remembering something, and plucked a disk from the pocket of his lab coat.

"As you requested," he said. "The patient records, clinical trials, and test results from our work at the Center. Please treat them as absolutely confidential."

"I will. Thanks."

Rush glanced back toward his wife. As if with one thought, the two men moved to the head of the bed.

"I think I'll have a session with her myself," Logan said. "Tomorrow, if that's okay with you."

"The sooner the better," Rush replied.

36

The communications room was deep within Red, down the hall from the power substation where Perlmutter had received his near-fatal shock just days before. It was a relatively small space, crowded with arcane electronic equipment whose purpose Logan couldn't even begin to guess at.

Jerry Fontaine, the communications chief, was a heavyset man in faded khakis and a pink short-sleeved shirt. The white cotton handkerchief in his right hand was never permitted to rest: either it was nervously being squeezed in Fontaine's bearlike paw, or it was being wiped across his forehead, onto which beads of sweat kept reappearing.

"How's Perlmutter?" Logan asked as he opened a notebook and took a seat in the room's only unoccupied chair.

"The doctor says he can come back to work tomorrow," Fontaine replied. "Thank God."

Logan pulled a folder from his duffel and opened it. "Tell me about these phenomena you've observed."

More dabbing of the handkerchief. "It's happened twice now. Always late at night. I hear equipment coming to life, beeping and blinking, when everything should be turned off. The comm room is a daytime operation only, see."

"Why is that?" Logan asked.

"Because there's just me and Perlmutter manning it. And we operate it almost like a telegraph office—Stone's orders. Any requests for Internet searches, for calls back to the main office, have to go through us. No night operation except in emergencies."

Stone and his habitual secrecy, Logan thought. "Which machines are, ah, waking up, exactly?"

"One of the sat phones."

"**One** of the sat phones? You mean, there's more than one?"

Fontaine nodded. "We've got two. An NNR GlobalEye, for the geosynchronous satellite, and then the LEO."

"LEO?"

"Low earth orbit satellite. Terrastar. Good for the high-bandwidth stuff."

Logan scribbled in his notebook. "Which one was it you heard?"

"The one linked to the LEO."

Logan gazed around at the incomprehensible, knob-encrusted facades of equipment. "Can you show it to me?"

Fontaine pointed to a rack-mounted device at his side. It was of brushed gray metal, with an embedded keypad and an attached headset. Logan reached into his duffel, pulled out the air-ion counter, held it before the sat phone, then examined the readout.

"What are you doing?" Fontaine said.

"Checking something." The reading was normal; Logan put the counter away.

He glanced back at Fontaine. "Give me the details, please."

Another swipe of the handkerchief. "The first time was—let me see—almost two weeks ago. I'd forgotten something in the communications room and I came back here to get it just before going to bed. There was a beeping, then a bunch of electronic noise from the LEO."

"What time was this?"

"One thirty in the morning."

Logan made a notation. "Go on."

"The second time was the night before last. With Perlmutter in Medical, I had to do everything myself. There was a backlog of jobs, so I came here after dinner to finish up. It took me longer than I expected. I was just doing the final log entries when there was that beeping again, and the LEO woke up. Scared the dickens out of me, I can tell you."

"And what time was this?"

Fontaine thought a moment. "One thirty. Like the first time."

Awfully punctual for a mechanical gremlin, Logan thought. "How does the phone work, exactly?"

"Pretty straightforward. You establish the satellite link, check the upstream and downstream numbers. From there, it depends on what you're transmitting. You know, analogue or digital, voice, URL page, e-mail, and so forth."

"And I assume, from what you're telling me, the phone has no built-in timer—it can't wake itself to send or receive a message."

Fontaine nodded.

"Do you maintain a log of all sat phone use?"

"Sure do. Dr. Stone insists on logs of everything— who made the request, where the transmission was sent, what was included." He patted a row of thick black binders that resided on a shelf behind him.

"Does the phone maintain an internal log as well?"

"Yes. In flash RAM. You have to manually erase it from the front panel."

"When was the log last erased?"

"It hasn't been. Not since the site's been live. To do so requires a password." Fontaine frowned. "You don't think . . ." His voice trailed off.

"I think," Logan said quietly, "that we should take a look at that internal log. Right now."

37

When Logan was called to a meeting in Conference Room A to review the previous day's initial penetration of the tomb, he assumed the group would be as large as the first conference he'd attended, when they'd assembled to discuss the generator accident. Instead, he found the big room to be relatively empty. There were Fenwick March with one of his assistants, Tina Romero, Ethan Rush, Valentino, one or two others he didn't recognize.

Looking around at the small group, Logan decided that perhaps he could bring up his discovery, after all.

Stone entered, his personal secretary following in his wake. Closing the door, he walked past the two circles of chairs to the front of the room and took up position before the whiteboard.

"Let's begin," he said briskly. "Please keep your reports brief and to the point. Fenwick, I'll start with you."

The archaeologist shuffled some papers, cleared his throat. "We've already begun to put together an inventory, based on the video analysis of chamber one. Our epigrapher has begun recording the inscriptions. And once Dr. Rush has given the okay, we'll send the surveyor down to begin making a detailed survey of the room's dimensions and contents."

Stone nodded.

"Our art historian has been analyzing the paintings. Her opinion—based for now only on the video evidence, of course—is that they are among the oldest known of Egyptian tomb paintings, almost as old as those at Painted Tomb One Hundred at Hierakonpolis."

"Very good," said Stone.

"While on visual inspection the artifacts appear to be in excellent shape, considering their age, there were several that could clearly benefit from careful stabilization and restoration. The black-topped jars and some of the beaded amulets, for example. When can we begin the process of tagging and removal?"

This prompted an angry chirrup from Romero.

"First things first, Fenwick," Stone told him. "The chamber needs to be gridded, mapped, and pronounced safe. Then we can proceed to the actual artifacts."

"I don't need to remind you that our time is growing short," March said.

"No, you don't. That's why we're going to press on with all speed. But we are not going to rush things, risk either the tomb or ourselves with undue haste." Stone turned to Romero. "Tina?"

Romero stirred. "It's a little early to get into specifics. And of course I still need to examine the tablets and papyri more closely. But what I've found so far is somewhat confusing."

Stone frowned. "Explain."

"Well . . ." Romero hesitated. "Some of the inscriptions seem to have been carved and painted a little crudely—as if they were rushed."

"You forget we're dealing with the archaic period," March sniffed. "The First Dynasty. Egypt's skill with the decorative arts was still in its infancy."

Romero shrugged, clearly unconvinced. "In any case, many of the items and inscriptions are unique to Egyptian history. They speak of gods, practices, rituals, and even beliefs that are at odds with the conventional wisdom; with what followed in later periods—the Intermediate Periods, the New Kingdom."

"I don't follow," Stone said.

"It's difficult to describe, because everything's so new and unfamiliar, and I've just begun to analyze it. But it's almost as if . . ." She paused again. "When I first looked at the inscriptions, at the names of the gods evoked, gender, sequence of ritual, that sort of thing, it almost seemed as if . . . Narmer got it wrong. But then of course I realized that was impossible. Narmer was the first: this is clearly the oldest tomb of an Egyptian pharaoh ever found. So I can only assume that, well, the transfer of Narmer's beliefs and practices to future generations was faulty. It's as if his descendants **didn't understand** what Narmer was trying to do, and so they aped it, ritually, without fully fathoming it. See, there are certain things about ancient Egyptian ritual that we still don't comprehend, that seem self-contradictory. It's entirely possible that—if we reexamine these now, in light of the Narmer 'original'—we'll be able to pinpoint the differences and articulate them. I'll know more once I've analyzed things further. Any way you look at it, though, this is going to turn Egyptology on its head."

Stone rubbed his jaw. "Fascinating. Any thoughts as to the—the tomb guardian?"

"At first I thought it was a representation of Ammut—the Swallowing Monster—who—in later Egyptian belief systems, anyway—sends unworthy souls to the Devourer of the Dead. But then I realized the morphology was wrong. It's only conjecture, but I think it may be a very rough and primitive rendering of the god that, in the Middle Kingdom, would come to be known as Aapep. In later years he would be depicted as a crocodile, or a serpent. This is in keeping with the figure we saw. Aapep was the god of darkness, chaos, the eater of souls, the personification of everything evil. Interesting choice of babysitter." She paused. "We may be seeing an extremely early version of this god, before Amemit and Aapep developed fully individual identities."

Logan saw Rush catch his gaze. **The eater of souls,** Logan thought. This was the god Jennifer had referred to, as well. **How could she have known that,** he wondered, **unless a voice from the ancient past told her?** The doctor looked tired—and Logan wasn't surprised. It had taken Jennifer almost two hours to revive from the previous day's crossing.

"Of course," Romero went on, "we don't yet know exactly how this god figures in Narmer's theogony—or what he represented at such an early period."

"What about the primary tomb painting?" Stone asked. "The one that appears to represent a punishment of some sort?"

"I don't know any more than I did yesterday. Sorry. It's completely foreign to my experience."

"And the second gate?"

"From what I can tell by visual inspection, the royal seal appears to be similar to the first."

"Thank you." Stone turned to Dr. Rush. "And you, Ethan?"

Rush shifted in his seat, cleared his throat. "My analysis of the atmosphere, dust from tomb surfaces, and grit from the plaster is complete. Everything appears to be inert. There's a relatively high concentration of mold spores and pollen, but nothing to be alarmed about if exposure times are kept limited. A careful cleaning, of course, will take care of that. I found no evidence of harmful bacteria, viruses, or fungi. Until the decontamination process is complete, I'd recommend N-ninety-five facepiece respirators be worn for particulate filtering, along with latex gloves, but you would mandate that as standard procedure, anyway."

"Poison?" Stone asked.

"Nothing came up on my tests."

Stone nodded his satisfaction, then turned to one of the others. "GPR report?"

A thin, nervous-looking young man sat forward and pushed his glasses up the bridge of his nose. "Ground-penetrating radar, targeting the second chamber, shows a very large mass—apparently a single object—approximate dimensions four meters in length and two in height. Arranged before it are four smaller, identical objects."

There was a brief silence.

"A sarcophagus," March murmured.

"And its four canopic jars," Romero added.

"Perhaps." Stone frowned. "But in the second chamber—not the third?"

"There appear to be several other objects," the young man said, "but the back-scatter makes them difficult to distinguish effectively."

"Very well." Stone thought for a moment. "We'll spend the rest of the day securing, stabilizing, and decontaminating chamber one. Then, first thing tomorrow, we'll proceed to the second gate. Meanwhile, if in your analysis any of you discover anything particularly unusual, let me know at once."

He turned to Logan. "Speaking of that, is there anything you'd like to add, Jeremy?"

"Yes. Last evening, I spoke with Fontaine. He'd reported that one of the electronic devices under his care had been acting strangely—turning on at unexpected times, working when it wasn't supposed to, operating by itself."

Very softly, Romero whistled the **Twilight Zone** theme.

"The machine in question was one of the satellite phones. When I learned that both these incidents had occurred at one thirty a.m., I asked Fontaine to check the flash memory of the sat phone."

"And?" Stone said.

"Its internal log showed a total of four unauthorized satellite uplinks, each made at precisely 1:34 a.m. local time. The uplinks were encrypted e-mails, each sent to an Internet remailing service, rendering them untraceable."

The room fell into a shocked silence.

Stone had gone ashen. "How is that possible? Nobody has access to the sat phones; they can only be used by the communications officers."

"Further examination of the phone showed it had

been tricked out with a hand-built internal circuit board. Fontaine is examining the board with an oscilloscope and signal generator, but its function appears to be to receive wireless text messages from the Station's WAN, encrypt them, and send them out to the satellite at a very late hour when the communications room would be unoccupied. The satellite then forwards the messages to their destination."

Another, longer silence. Logan noticed the assembled group glancing around at one another uncomfortably.

"Who knows about this?" Stone asked.

"Fontaine, myself, and—now—those in this room."

Stone licked his lips. "This is to go no farther. Understood? Nobody else is to know." He shook his head. "Good Christ. A spy."

"Or a saboteur," said Romero.

"Or both," Logan added.

38

Tina Romero made her way down the Umbilicus, hand under hand, following Porter Stone. She wore no respirator on this descent, just an N-95 mask, and the air both smelled and tasted faintly of vegetative rot. As she descended, it grew cooler, until by the time she had reached the air lock platform there were goose pimples on her arms.

A guard on the platform greeted them with a nod.

Since Logan's discovery of the unauthorized transmissions, Stone—obsessive about secrecy at the best
of times—had doubled the usual security. In addition to a twenty-four-hour guard stationed at the
Maw, there was also the guard here on the platform.
In addition, video cameras had been installed, monitored by Corey Landau and the other tech weenies in
the Operations Center.

Tina smiled a little grimly to herself. Despite
Stone's imprecations, threats, and demands for abso-
lute silence, word of the saboteur—or corporate spy—
had leaked out to the Station at large. It was a little ironic: while there was of course consternation,
there was also a guarded sense of relief. She herself had wondered: If there was a saboteur in their
midst, might that not account for the inexplicable
happenings?

There was a clatter overhead, and then Fenwick
March joined them on the platform. He was followed
by two of Valentino's roustabouts. Each man carried
pieces of a stainless-steel hoist under their arms.

Stone glanced around at the group. "Right," he
said through his mask. "Let's get started."

The security guard picked up a battery-powered
winch from the metal grating, and the group of six
approached the tomb interface. Tina noted that the
rest of the granite facing had been carefully removed,
and the first gate was now completely open. She
hoisted the video camera she carried. This was only
her second trip down. March had already been down

several times; Stone had been down twice more, to supervise the unsealing of the second gate.

As she stepped into chamber one, she noticed that supportive bracing had been placed longitudinally from one wall of the tomb to the other, as a precaution. The guardian statue of Aapep had been covered by a tarp, and Tina found herself glad of it: the figure had been so lifelike, so violent in appearance, that—despite its incalculable importance—she hadn't been looking forward to seeing it again.

The chamber that before had been so dim was now brightly lit by high-pressure sodium vapor lights, and she was surprised afresh by the beauty and remarkable condition of the artifacts. She also noticed—to her irritation—that many of the most interesting and important had already been removed, archival labels put temporarily in their place. No doubt that was the work of March, she thought: the bastard could never wait to get his grubby hands all over the antiquities. If he had his way, every dig site would be completely gutted, with nothing left in situ to show how it had once looked. Her own philosophy was the polar opposite: examine, stabilize, analyze, describe, document—and then, once curated, leave everything exactly where it had been found.

The rear wall of chamber one had been obscured by plastic sheeting. Beyond it, the darkness was complete. The second gate, she knew, had already been fully removed, but chamber two had not yet been entered. They would be the first to do so.

Wordlessly, Stone nodded to the two roustabouts. They came forward and—with great care—removed the plastic sheeting, folded it, and placed it to one side. A rectangle of black space lay beyond.

Stone stepped up to the second gate. Tina followed, with March right behind. Here, at the very entrance to chamber two, Tina could make out vague shapes within. Her mouth went dry.

"Bring one of those lights over here," Stone said.

One of the roustabouts wheeled the powerful light up to the group. As he did so, the room beyond burst into sudden brilliance.

It was as if somebody had just turned on the sun. The gleam of the chamber beyond was so bright, Tina had to turn away.

"God," Stone muttered in a strangled voice. Once again, his veneer of detached reserve had fallen away under the spell of Narmer's tomb.

As her eyes adjusted, Tina was able to make out the details of chamber two. She raised the video camera and began recording. Every surface—walls, floor, ceiling—had been covered in what appeared to be solid gold. This accounted for the incredibly bright sheen. Although the room was just slightly smaller than chamber one, it held far fewer objects. There were indeed four canopic jars, made of calcite, to hold the viscera of the mummified king. Before each jar was a small box, apparently also of solid gold. On one wall was a large painting, depicting what looked like Narmer's victory over the king of upper Egypt.

Another painting showed Narmer, lying on a dais, seemingly already in his tomb, being attended to by a mortuary priest. There were two shrines, set against the opposing walls of chamber two. Each bore a serekh, in sunk relief, of Narmer, using his coronation name, **niswt-biti,** king of upper and lower Egypt. It was funny, she thought—while Egyptologists could read the language, its pronunciation remained a mystery. Although most uses of this phrase, she knew, were the phonetic spelling **nzw,** as found in the Pyramid Texts, here the feminine ending **t** remained. Odd. But then, so much of what she had observed about Narmer and his tomb was odd. There was so much here that was surprisingly **modern**—in ancient Egyptian terms. The tomb burial, the royal seals, the grave goods, the hieroglyphic messages so reminiscent of the Book of the Dead—they were of the Middle Kingdom and New Kingdom, not the Archaic Period, the First Dynasty of the earliest pharaohs. It was as if Narmer had been many centuries ahead of his time, and his knowledge, practices, discoveries, and epiphanies had died with him, not to be resurrected until the pyramid builders of a thousand years later. . . .

She shook these thoughts away and busied herself with the video camera. Atop the two shrines were various offerings: amulets, beautifully knapped flint knives, figures of alabaster, ivory, ebony. But the most remarkable object of all lay in the center of the room. It was a huge sarcophagus, of a most unusual pale blue granite, unpainted—also most unusual—and in absolutely perfect shape; far better, for example, than that of the cracked outer shell of King Tutankhamen's coffin. The granite had been worked into tracery relief of the most detailed and painstaking kind. At the head of the sarcophagus stood the figure of a giant falcon, its wings spread wide, the stylized feet thrust out like the hands of a clock at five and seven, ceremonially standing watch over the body of the king.

The others had been silent, seemingly struck dumb by the splendor of the sight. Now Stone stepped forward. He walked a little stiffly, as if on wooden legs. He made a brief inspection of the chamber, and then he approached the row of four small gold chests.

"These chests, arranged before the canopic jars," he said, absently, more to himself than to the others. "That's something I've never heard of." He knelt before the closest, examining it carefully, touching it gently here and there with a latex-gloved hand. Then, ever so carefully, he lifted its lid. Tina caught her breath. Sparkling back at them from inside the box was an overflowing abundance of gemstones: opals, jade, diamonds, emeralds, pearls, rubies, sapphires, cat's eyes—an almost obscene riot of treasure.

"Good lord," March murmured.

Tina had lowered the video camera to take a closer look. "Half those gemstones weren't even known to the ancient Egyptians," she said. "At least, not so early."

"Narmer must have established trade routes that collapsed after his rule ended," Stone replied, still in a quiet voice.

Tina licked dry lips. The splendor was so overwhelming she realized she was in denial. It was physically impossible to take it all in.

Stone glanced at Tina. "What about those two shrines? I've never seen quite such configurations before."

"I'd have to examine them more closely. But I think perhaps they form a double function. Not only are they shrines, but they are symbolic of the greatest test Narmer would face in his passage through the Underworld: the Hall of Two Truths—assuming that belief system had been developed in such an early era. But then again, they seem unique—such a dual purpose must have been lost in the dynasties following Narmer's."

"Symbolic, you say?" Stone repeated.

"Almost as if they were to be used in a **simulation** of the Hall of Two Truths. A dry run, so to speak."

"But that's unheard-of," said March.

Tina waved a hand around the tomb, as if to say, **Isn't that true of everything here?**

The roustabouts were now busy assembling the stainless-steel hoist. The security guard attached the winch to it, and then—at a nod from Stone—fired up the motor. A roar filled the room before settling back to a low grumble. The roustabouts fixed the hoists' grappling hooks to the edges of the sarcophagus lid, then—moving at a snail's pace—they raised the lid from the coffin, swung it to the side, and placed it gingerly on the floor.

The security guard killed the motor and everyone—even the roustabouts—drew closer. Inside the sarcophagus was a shroud made of unknown material, woven into a complex design. Stone reached out a hand to touch it. As his glove made contact with the shroud, it crumbled away, disintegrating into gray dust.

A low murmur of dismay rose from the group, quickly changing to gasps of surprise. Through the dust, a coffin was visible within the sarcophagus—a coffin of solid gold, its face carved into the effigy of a splendidly robed king.

Without a word, Stone and March picked up the inner coffin lid by its handles and pulled it aside. Within lay a mummy, thickly covered in winding sheets. Lotus petals were strewn across its upper surface. Over the face lay a golden mask, beaten into the shape of the god-king's commanding, almost forbidding visage.

A faint smell of dust and decay rose from the mummy, but Tina did not notice it. She bent in closer, filming, heart beating fast.

"Narmer," Stone whispered.

39

"Ethan tells me that you never talk about your near-death experience," Logan said.

Jennifer Rush nodded. They were seated across from each other in Logan's office. It was very late at night, and Maroon—in fact, the entire Station—seemed intensely silent. He had skipped the descent into chamber two in order to prepare for this meeting. Something inside him sensed that, in the short term, it was more important for his work—and, perhaps, for Jennifer Rush's well-being.

"I'm sure you of all people realize how unusual that is," he went on. "Most who've undergone an NDE like to discuss it. Your husband's research, in fact, is built on that willingness to talk."

Still Jennifer did not speak. She lifted her eyes to his briefly, then looked away.

"Listen," Logan said in a gentle voice, "I'm sorry for the things I said to you earlier. I'd assumed your abilities were—well, that they were a gift. That was a naive assumption."

"It's all right," she replied at last. "Everyone else assumes the same thing. It's all they talk about at the Center—what a revelation they've had, how indescribably wonderful it was, how the experience made them appreciate God, how it changed their lives."

"Your life has changed, too—but, I sense, not in the way theirs have."

"They hold me up as some kind of poster child," she said, the faintest hint of bitterness in her voice. "I'm the wife of the Center's founder, I experienced the longest NDE of anybody ever tested, my psychic abilities are the strongest. I know how important this work is to Ethan, I want to help him any way I can. It's just that . . ."

"It's just that—if you spoke of **your** experience—you fear it might have a negative impact on the Center."

She looked at him again, and Logan could read anxiety, even a kind of desperation, in her amber-colored eyes. "Ethan's told me of—of your work," she said. "The kind of things you've done in the past. Somehow I thought you'd understand. You'd believe. I've just never had anyone else I could speak to about this. Ethan . . . I don't think he'd **want** to hear it. It's so counter to everything he's—" She stopped.

"I'll do whatever I can to help."

When she didn't respond, Logan continued. "I know it's difficult, but I think the best thing would be for you to tell me, in as much detail as you can, exactly what you experienced, that day three years ago."

Jennifer shook her head. "I don't think I can do that."

"Share it with me. If you bring it out in the open, it may lose its ability to disturb you."

"Disturb," she repeated mirthlessly.

"Look, Jennifer—may I call you Jennifer? I'm an empath—I'll experience it, too, at least in part. I'll be there every step of the way. If things get too difficult, we'll stop."

She looked at him. "You promise that?"

"Yes."

"And you really think this might help?"

"The more you can confront it, the easier it will be for you to deal with."

She was silent for a moment. Then she nodded slowly. "All right."

Logan reached for his duffel, rummaged around

inside it, found his digital timer, and placed it on his desk. "I'll turn out the lights. I want you to sit back in your chair, get as comfortable as you can."

He stood up, shut the door of his office, turned off the lights. Now the room was illuminated only by the timer and the glow of his laptop screen. He returned to his chair and took her hands in his.

"Now just relax. There's no hurry. Think back to what you remember happening, during and after the car accident. Start when you're ready. Relate the experience to me in real time, if possible. Use the clock as a guide."

He sat forward and fell silent. For a long time, he heard nothing but Jennifer's regular breathing. So much time passed, in fact, that he wondered if she had fallen asleep. Then—out of the darkness—she spoke.

"I was in my car," she began. "I was driving down Ship Street, near Brown University. All of a sudden this SUV—it was blue, with a big black push bar on the front grille—swerved out of the oncoming lane and hit me."

She swallowed, took a deep breath, then continued. "There was this terrible impact, a crashing noise, an instant of pain, a flash of white. Then, for a long, long moment—nothing."

Logan reached over, set the timer to fourteen minutes—the amount of time Jennifer Rush had been clinically dead.

"The next thing I remember was my head feeling

uncomfortably . . . well, **full**. I don't really know how else to describe it. Then there was this buzzing noise. It started very softly and slowly grew louder. It frightened me. And then all of a sudden it stopped, and I found myself moving very quickly down a dark passageway. I wasn't walking or running—I remember I was being pulled. And then there was another flash of white. For a moment, nothing more. And then I was . . . I was hovering over a hospital bed, looking down at myself, lying on a gurney. It was odd, that hovering: I wasn't exactly still; I was moving slightly, up and down, as if floating in a swimming pool. Doctors and nurses were standing around. Ethan was there. He—he had defib paddles in his hands. They were all talking."

"Do you remember what they were saying?" Logan asked.

Jennifer thought for a moment. "One of them said: 'Hypovolemic shock. We never had a chance.'"

"Go on," Logan urged.

"For a moment I felt this terrible need to get back into my body. But I was helpless; there was nothing I could do. So I just watched them. Very quickly, the feeling of need went away. After that, I felt nothing—no pain, no fear, nothing. And then—slowly—my body, the doctors, everything, faded away. And I began to feel this immense sense of peace."

"Describe it to me," Logan said.

"I'd never felt anything like it before. It was as if my entire being, my very essence, was suffused with well-being. At that moment I **knew** nothing could go wrong ever again."

Logan closed his eyes. He sensed it, too—as if from a great distance. "As if you were surrounded by love."

"Yes. Exactly." She paused. "I seemed to feel that way for a long time."

She went silent. Logan waited, holding her hands in his as the time ticked down. Over six minutes had elapsed—already, longer than most NDEs.

"I was in blackness, but I sensed that I was moving again. Then, ahead in the distance, I saw something. It was a golden border, or barrier, of some sort. There seemed to be nothing beyond it. And someone . . . something . . . was standing before it."

"A being," Logan said. "A Being of Light."

"Yes. I couldn't see its face—not clearly, anyway— the light was too bright. I thought it might be an angel, but it had no wings. I sensed somehow that it was smiling at me."

"Yes," Logan whispered. He could make it out, too, barely: a shimmering, spectral vision of unearthly beauty. It was from this being that the boundless love seemed to be streaming in endless waves.

"I sensed it was speaking to me. Not out loud but in my head. It was asking me a question."

"Can you tell me what the question was?" Logan asked—but already he could guess the answer.

"It was asking me whether I was content with what I'd done with my life. If I had done enough."

Logan nodded. So far, everything Jennifer had mentioned—the out-of-body experience, the dark tunnel, the Being of Light, the borderland, the "life review"—was consistent with other NDEs. He glanced at the timer. Over ten minutes had passed. This was longer—he knew from a cursory examination of the CTS documents—than any other near-death experience recorded at the Center.

"The Being asked the question again," she said. "As it did, I saw my life—from early childhood, things I hadn't thought about or even remembered for decades—flash before me. And then . . ." She swallowed again. "And then it started."

Logan took tighter grasp of her hands. "Tell me."

Even in the dark room, he could see the beautiful lines of her oval face become strained. "The Being said a single word: 'Insufficient.' And then it . . . **changed**."

Her breathing grew a little labored.

"Just relax," Logan said. "Describe it to me. How did the Being change?"

"At first, it was just a sensation I had. I felt the inexpressible, endless love begin to die away. So did the warmth, the well-being, the joy. It was so slow, so subtle, I didn't realize it at first. But when I did realize it, I suddenly felt . . . exposed. And then the Being . . . grew dark. The bright light dimmed. And now I could see its face."

For a moment, an image appeared in Logan's mind: a face, leering, hirsute, goatish.

Jennifer's breathing grew more rapid. "Suddenly, the border ahead of me . . . began to change, too. It was no longer golden. It wavered, become wet somehow. It looked like a curtain of blood. Then . . . and then it melted away." Her voice began to tremble. "And beyond . . . **beyond** . . ."

"Go on," Logan barely whispered.

"Beyond lay . . . lay the screaming dark. I tried to run, to get away. But I was being pulled in, I couldn't fight. And then it was too late. There was no light, there was no air. I couldn't breathe. There were . . . bodies, all around me, invisible, slippery, sliding past me. Screaming, always screaming. I was hemmed in by the bodies, I couldn't move. I felt . . ." She was gasping now. "I felt a terrible pressure. A pressure inside me. As if the very essence of my being was getting sucked away . . . And always **he** was laughing. . . . And then I felt the edge of the—the . . . oh, **God**!"

And suddenly, Logan sensed **it** again: the malignant, demonic presence; the endless enmity and hatred and rage. It was a tangible thing that almost pushed him back in his chair.

"**Jesus!**" he said, jerking violently, breaking contact with Jennifer.

She gasped. For a moment, the office was quiet. And then she dissolved into racking sobs.

Logan embraced her gently. "It's all right," he said. "It's going to be all right."

But she only continued to weep.

40

Robert Carmody stood in the dust-scented confines of chamber one, moodily playing with the focus ring on the lens of his digital camera. Nearby, Payne Whistler was kneeling on the newly cleaned floor, holding a carved tablet in a gloved hand.

"Item A three forty-nine," Whistler murmured into a pocket recorder. "Tablet. Polished limestone." He pulled out a ruler, measured the object carefully. "Seven centimeters by nine and a half centimeters." He scrutinized the tablet's face for a minute. "It appears to be an invocation for the pharaoh's safe journey to the next kingdom."

He made a few additional remarks, then gently placed the tablet on a white linen cloth that lay nearby. "All right, Bob," he said.

With a sigh, Carmody wheeled over a freestanding light, then leaned in, focused his camera on the tablet, snapped a dozen shots from different angles, bracketing the exposures. Then he straightened up and reviewed his work on the camera's LED screen. "Another masterpiece."

Whistler nodded, then picked up the tablet, tagged it, carefully wrapped it in a fresh cloth, and placed it in a plastic evidence locker. Carmody jotted down the photo reference numbers in a small notebook.

"Jesus," he said, flipping the notebook closed. "We've been here—what—three hours already? And not one interesting damn piece."

Whistler glanced at him. "You kidding? **All** this stuff is interesting. More than interesting—these are the grave goods of the first pharaoh of unified Egypt."

Carmody scoffed. "Listen to you. You're starting to sound like Romero."

Whistler stood up, brushed his pants back into place. "You have to be patient. If you wanted instant gratification, you picked the wrong profession."

"What profession? You're the archaeologist."

"Surveyor," Whistler corrected.

"I'm a photographer. I've been here three weeks

now. Can't call home, can't order in a pizza, can't even go for a damn jog."

"There's all the pizza you could ever eat in the mess. And the exercise room has plenty of treadmills."

"Can't get HBO. Can't play World of Warcraft. Can't get laid."

"Well, that's your problem." Whistler set the evidence locker aside.

"I mean, I'm not stupid. I knew what I was getting into when I signed the nondisclosure forms. But I thought I'd get to shoot pictures of, you know, mummies. Golden masks. That kind of thing. Stuff that would look good on the résumé, later, when I could talk about it. But **he's** picked this place clean, cleared out everything sexy. He's keeping all the good stuff for himself. I mean, look at that." And Carmody gestured toward the rear of the chamber, where a locked partition sealed off the entrance to chamber two.

"What did you expect? March is the head archaeologist. Stop grousing—you're getting well paid. I mean, you could have it a lot worse. You could be doing **his** job." And Whistler jerked a finger out toward the Umbilicus platform, where a security guard stood, monitoring their progress.

"I didn't sign on to be a door shaker. I'm an artist at what I do. I don't just point my camera and fire away. I've had my work in five different shows."

"Sell anything?" Whistler grinned wickedly.

"That's not the point."

"Let's get on with it." Whistler turned and carefully removed another object from the gilt-edged wooden box that sat nearby. He turned it over in his hands, peered at it closely. "Item A three fifty. Tablet. Polished limestone." He measured it. "Six and a half centimeters by nine centimeters." He glanced at its inscription. "It appears to be an itemized list of the gifts Narmer's wife, Niethotep, was given on her thirtieth birthday." He nodded to himself. "Now this is interesting."

"Yeah. As interesting as watching paint dry. How do you say 'fuck you' in hieroglyphics?"

Whistler raised his middle finger. Then he placed the tablet on the linen cloth. "Do your thing."

With a huge sigh, Carmody raised his camera, took the obligatory shots. He made some notations in his book, then watched sourly as Whistler put the tablet carefully away for curation and documentation.

"I just want a little fun," he said as Whistler reached again into the gilded box. "I mean, stuck out in the ass end of nowhere for three weeks—I'm going crazy here."

"Take a walk out in the swamp. Then come back and count the mosquito bites. That'll give you something to do." Whistler shook his head. "Last tomb I worked on was a Neolithic sand pit burial. Compared to that, this is heaven."

"You know what? You need to get out more."

"Maybe." Whistler pulled another object from the box, examined it. "Item A three fifty-one. Tablet. Polished limestone."

"Not another one," Carmody groaned. "Somebody shoot me. Just shoot me, please, and get it over with."

Out on the metal grating, the guard's radio crackled into life. "Maw Base to Eppers, come in."

The guard raised the radio to his lips. "Eppers here."

"Sensors are picking up a pressure spike in the Umbilicus, at waypoint nineteen. We'd like you to climb up and do a visual before we send a repair team down."

"Copy that." The guard snugged his radio into his belt, then turned toward the metal rungs and climbed out of sight.

Carmody watched him disappear. Then he looked around the chamber. As he'd already pointed out, it had been cleared of most of the easily transportable items. Beyond the gilt box and a scattering of grave goods, only the furniture and the huge guardian statue, covered by a tarp, remained.

His eye settled on one of the chairs: intricately carved, decorated with gold filigree. "Watch this," he said. He walked over to the chair and sat down in it with an air of mock gravity.

Whistler looked at him with a mixture of surprise and horror. "What the hell are you doing? Get out of there! It hasn't been fully curated—you could damage it!"

"No way. This stuff is solid as a rock." He folded his hands over his chest. "King Narmer speaking. Bring me the virgin du jour."

Whistler looked worriedly up at the security camera. "They're going to see you. Stone's going to have your ass."

"Calm down. Paxton's manning the desk this afternoon—he's a buddy of mine." Carmody got out of the chair, looked around to make sure the guard was still out of sight, then walked over to the massively constructed royal bed. While the legs, posts, and canopy were dense with inlay and gold leaf, the bed surface itself was of plain, unornamented wood. He tested it with his fingers, pressing, and then—satisfied—lay down on it.

"Carmody, you've gone frigging stir-crazy," Whistler said, his voice low and serious. "Get out of there before the guard sees you."

"I'll just take a quick forty winks first," Carmody replied. He raised his head, made a show of looking around the chamber. "Hey, Cleopatra, get your ass over here, I've got a royal scepter that needs polishing—"

There was a sudden, sharp cracking noise; the entire frame of the bed vibrated, then gave a violent shear. Before Carmody could move, there was a little puff of displaced air and—with a second, even louder crack—the massive wooden canopy overhead broke loose from its anchors and hurtled down onto his prostrate form.

A flash of brilliant white—a moment of unspeakable, crushing pain—and then nothing at all.

41

When Logan entered the forensic bay of the Station's medical suite, Dr. Rush was just pulling a green shroud over Robert Carmody's crushed and broken body. Hearing footsteps, the doctor looked over, caught sight of Logan, and shook his head.

"I've never seen a body so thoroughly destroyed as this one," he said.

"They've finished the preliminary investigation," Logan told him. "The gold bolts holding the can-

302 • LINCOLN CHILD

opy bed together appear to have been deliberately loosened."

Rush frowned. "Loosened? You mean, as in sabotage?"

"Perhaps. Or perhaps in preparation for being pocketed by somebody. They're solid gold, after all, each one as big as a railroad spike."

Rush was silent a moment. "What's the mood?"

"More or less what you'd imagine. Shock. Grief. And anxiety. Talk of the curse has spiked again."

Rush nodded absently. He looked pale, and there were dark patches beneath his eyes. Logan recalled what the doctor had told him on the plane: **I trained as an ER specialist. But somehow, I could never get used to the death. Oh, I could handle natural causes all right. But sudden, violent death . . .** He wondered if this was the right time to talk to Rush; decided there wasn't likely to be a better.

"Do you have a moment?" he asked quietly.

Rush glanced at him. "Let me just finish up here, make a few notes. You can wait in my office if you like."

Ten minutes later, Rush came into the office. He appeared to be more composed, and the color had come back into his face. "Sorry for the delay," he said as he took a seat behind his desk. "What's up, Jeremy?"

"I've spoken with Jennifer," Logan said.

Rush sat forward. "Really? Did she tell you about her NDE?"

"We basically relived it together."

Rush looked at him for a moment. "She's never spoken of it in detail at CTS. It's rather awkward, really, given my position there."

"I think she needed to speak about it to somebody who was completely objective," he said. "Somebody with experience dealing with—the unusual."

Rush nodded. "What can you tell me?"

"I suppose I should get her permission before I go into details with anyone—even you. I can tell you that the first part of the experience was relatively textbook. But the last part—where she was 'over' longer than anyone else in your database—was the opposite of textbook." Logan paused. "It was . . . horrible. Terrifying. It's no wonder she doesn't want to speak of it to anybody—let alone relive it."

"Terrifying? Really? I suspected there was some unpleasant aspect, given her unwillingness to confront it, but I had no idea . . ." Rush's voice trailed off for a moment. "Poor Jen."

For a moment, the office fell into silence. It was on the tip of Logan's tongue to say: **There's something else. I can't say why—but Jennifer's description of her NDE, of the horror near its conclusion, reminds me strongly of King Narmer's curse.** But he could not explain why; it was just a feeling, like the seed between one's teeth that wouldn't go away. Nothing would be helped by mentioning it. But maybe . . . maybe . . . there was another way he could help.

He cleared his throat. "I strongly recommend that she have no more channeling sessions. They're upsetting her and may even be psychically damaging."

"I mentioned as much to Stone," Rush said. "He's agreed to dial back the number of future sessions to just one or two more. He wants me to ask her about the third gate and what lies beyond. Also, what she meant about that odd tomb painting: 'That which brings life to the dead, and death to the living.'"

"It's a bad idea," Logan replied. "And the sessions I've witnessed haven't provided you with anything material."

"Actually, the last session did. Tina Romero's been studying some of the utterances—and she finds them to be very intriguing, given the context of what's known about the stability of ancient Egyptian texts."

"You asked me to see Jennifer—and I'm giving you my recommendation." Logan took a DVD case out of his pocket, placed it on the desk, and tapped it with a finger. "Here's the data you provided me with from your CTS files. I've been going over it."

"And?"

"And I want you to answer a question—please answer it honestly. Has Jennifer been acting differently since her NDE? Is she in any way a changed person?"

Rush looked at Logan but did not respond.

"I'm no expert in such matters. But based on what I've read in these files, from what you've already told me about your changed relationship with your wife, and from what she's said herself—not only was Jennifer's NDE very different from other people's, but I believe her **behavior** in its wake has been different from the others you've studied at the Center."

For a long moment, Rush remained silent. Then, at last, he sighed. "I haven't wanted to admit it—even to myself. But it's true. More than just our relationship has changed."

"Can you qualify the change for me?"

"It's subtle. At times I think it's more me than her, seeing things that aren't there. But she seems . . . remote. Detached. She was always so warm, so spontaneous. I don't sense that as much in her these days."

"That doesn't necessarily have to do with her near-death experience," Logan said. "Those could be manifestations of depression, as well."

"Jennifer was never a depressive personality. And it's not just that. She . . ." Rush paused. "I don't know how to put it. She seems to have less of a—a moral center than she used to. Here's a stupid example. She was always a sucker for sappy movies. Toss in a little melodrama, and she'd be crying like a baby. But not anymore. One of the first nights here on the Station, they screened the old tearjerker **Dark Victory** for the crew. Even some of the toughest roustabouts were choked up by the end. But Jennifer remained stone-faced throughout. It was as if the emotion . . . well, as if it no longer penetrated."

When Logan next spoke, it was slowly, thoughtfully. "You know, Ethan, there are cultures on earth who believe that—under the right circumstances—a person can be separated from their inner spirit."

"Inner spirit?" Rush repeated.

"I mean the intangible life force that links us from this world to the next. The Byzantines, the Incans, certain Native American tribes, Enlightenment-era Rosicrucians, all had variant belief structures regarding such a thing—there were, and are, many others."

Rush looked at him but did not speak.

"At the end of her NDE, Jennifer mentioned feeling a terrible pressure. She felt as if—let me try to recall her exact words—'as if the very essence of my being was getting sucked away.'"

"What is it you're saying, exactly?"

"I'm not saying anything. I'm just speculating. Is it possible that your wife was clinically dead for so long that she . . . well, that she lost an integral part of her human spirit?"

Rush let out a short, explosive laugh. "Her **spirit**? Jeremy, that's crazy."

"Is it? I plan to research it further. But one could argue that such phenomena might explain the need for one of the rites of the Catholic Church itself."

"Oh? And what rite is that?"

"The rite of exorcism."

A sudden, freezing silence fell over the office.

"What is it you're implying?" Rush asked after a minute. "That Narmer isn't just speaking **through** Jennifer? That in those crossings she's being—**possessed** by Narmer?"

"I don't know what's happening during those crossings," Logan replied. "I don't think anybody can know, exactly. I only know it might be dangerous."

Rush fetched a deep sigh. "Just one last crossing. To ask about the third gate. Then I'll refuse to authorize any more."

42

Logan stepped into the brilliantly lit Staging Area, notebook in hand. Somewhere here—amid the bustle, noise, and ceaseless activity—was the workman who had reported hearing strange, ominous whisperings in the night. He was next on Logan's list to interview . . . if he could manage to find him.

He glanced around, then stopped short. Something was happening at the Maw. Numerous people were gathered around it—technicians, roustabouts, a scientist or two. Porter Stone and Fenwick March were among them, speaking earnestly together. Logan stepped closer, curious. Industrial-grade mesh netting of blue plastic had been lowered into the Maw, suspended from a heavy winch, looking like the strings of some monstrous marionette.

Even as he watched, the winch motor started up; with a clanking of gears, the netting began to rise. Stone was leaning over the mouth of the Maw now, staring down intently, as he gestured with an upraised palm for the winch operator to keep hoisting.

Logan looked on as the netting spooled up around a capstan set just below the winch. A minute later, Stone gave the operator a signal to slow. And then Logan saw a large stainless-steel box, held in place by the netting, emerge into the light. It was about seven feet by three feet long, and it looked to Logan almost like a coffin.

At that moment, he realized it **was** a coffin. There was only one thing it could possibly contain: the mummy of Narmer.

With exquisite care, two technicians pulled the netting-enclosed coffin over to a waiting medical gurney, lowered it onto the gurney, then pulled the netting free. This operation was supervised by March, who flitted around the technicians like an angry insect, barking orders. Stone looked on, arms folded, his face expressionless.

All of a sudden, Logan caught movement in his peripheral vision. He turned to see Tina Romero, framed in the entrance of the Staging Area. She glanced around for a moment, then caught sight of the coffin and the gurney. For a second, she froze. Then her eyes narrowed. She stalked forward, stopping directly before March. Logan heard a low, angry exchange. Then, quite abruptly, Romero exploded.

"You selfish, arrogant **prick**!" she shouted, grasping his shirt, bunching it in her fist, then physically pushing him backward. "You keep your hands off him!"

There was a brief, shocked silence. Then Porter Stone quickly inserted himself between the two, put an arm around Romero's shoulder, and half walked, half propelled her away from the group, all the time talking to her in a gentle but urgent voice. March, his face red as a beet, tucked in his shirt, passed a hand through his thinning hair, and turned back to the gurney.

Logan stepped a bit closer to Stone and Romero. ". . . only being removed for the CT scan," he heard Stone say before his voice dropped even further.

After a few more minutes of quiet talk, Stone squeezed Romero's shoulder, looked at her intently for a moment, then turned away and rejoined the group by the Maw. Romero stood where Stone left her, breathing heavily, her mouth set in a grim line. Then she, too, turned away and quickly left the Staging Area.

Logan hurried after her down the catwalk leading out of Yellow. "Tina!" he called.

She turned, saw him, and continued walking.

"What's the problem?" he said as he caught up with her.

"That **bastard** March," she said without stopping. "Before the expedition began, we set down ground rules about how the artifacts would be curated. Everything would be studied in situ, carefully documented and stabilized. Anything to be removed would be agreed upon first by a committee of the team leaders. But that scumbag has gone behind my back. Already he's managed to remove just about everything of value from the tomb that hasn't been nailed down. It's all being tagged and labeled by those pack rats of his. All I have are the frigging videos." Her voice trembled slightly as she spoke. "Now, to get access to anything, I have to fill out requisition forms. I can't believe Stone went along with this bullshit. And now, for Christ's sake, he's even got Narmer's **mummy. . . .**" She shook her head. "It's times like this that I wish this whole goddamned Station would just sink to the bottom of the swamp."

They walked for a moment in silence.

"Porter Stone has always been known for his non-invasive touch," Logan said.

"I know. He's famous for it. But he's also superparanoid about how tight our schedule's become. The Af'ayalah Dam is well ahead of schedule—this whole place could be underwater, flooded out, in weeks rather than months. March has been using that fact to goad Stone into speeding things up. He keeps pointing out how this is the greatest find of Stone's career, preying on his ego. And now that the artifacts are out of the tomb, up here . . . well, it's going to be hard as hell convincing those two to ever put any of them back." She shook her head in bitter resignation.

They had reached the hallways of Red. Logan followed the Egyptologist into her office and they took seats on either side of her artifact- and notebook-covered desk.

"I was curious," Logan said, "if you'd made any progress. On the aspects of the tomb that have you so puzzled, I mean."

"The whole damn thing's a puzzle," she growled. Her mood was still dark but she seemed to be calming down.

"You said there were inscriptions that didn't make sense. Unusual serekhs. Items that don't jibe with the pharaohs and the traditions that followed later."

She nodded. "Riddles within riddles."

"I was wondering—do you think what we'll find in the third chamber might clear any of that up?"

"It's possible. Normally, the final chamber of a tomb is where the most valuable, important objects are. That's why we were surprised to find Narmer, and his precious grave goods, in chamber two." She shrugged. "Yet another mystery."

Logan paused. "What do you think we'll find? Beyond the third gate, I mean."

She thought for a moment. Then she looked at him. "I'm one of the top Egyptologists in the world.

That's why Stone chose me. I've studied just about every royal tomb, sand burial, pyramid, cult temple, and mastaba ever discovered and documented. Nobody knows more about this stuff than I do. And you want to hear something, Mr. Ghost Hunter?" She leaned forward, piercing him with her gaze. "I don't have **the faintest idea** what we're going to find when we unseal that third gate."

43

When Logan stepped into the testing chamber, Dr. Rush was leaning over the figure of his wife, who was lying on the examination table, dressed—as with the previous crossings—in a hospital gown. "Last time, honey," he was saying as he caressed her cheek.

She looked up at him, smiled briefly. Then she glanced over at Logan as he approached the bed. He nodded, took her hand, gave it a brief squeeze. He could not read the look on her face—apprehension?

resignation?—and this time the touch of her hand told him nothing.

He stepped back as Rush consulted the instrumentation, prepared to administer the sedative. Five minutes passed, then ten, as the doctor lit the incense; inserted first one needle, then another, into the IV's connecting hub; applied the amulet and the candle; and went through the modified hypnosis text. Finally, he picked up the digital recorder and approached the head of the bed.

"Who am I speaking to?" he asked.

The only reply was Jennifer's labored breathing.

"Who am I speaking to?" he asked again.

No response.

"That's odd," Rush said. "I've never had a problem with the induction process before." He examined the instruments again, gently raised one of his wife's eyelids, peered at the eye with his ophthalmoscope. "I'll up the propofol, deepen the sedation slightly. And I'll give the cortical stimulation an extra notch."

Logan waited, without speaking, as the doctor busied himself around the table, then went through the hypnosis text again. This time, Jennifer's breathing became shallower, more rapid.

"Relax your mind," Rush told his wife in a calm, almost cooing tone. "Let it go free. Let your consciousness slip from your body. Leave it an empty shell, unpossessed."

An empty shell. Without knowing exactly why, Logan suddenly grew alarmed. He took a step forward, instinctively, as if to stop the procedure, before managing to get himself under control.

Rush picked up the recorder again. "Who am I speaking to?"

No reply.

Rush bent closer. "Who am I speaking to?"

Jennifer's mouth moved. **"Mouthpiece . . . of Horus."**

"And do you know who I am?"

"The defiler. The . . . unbeliever."

"Tell me more about the ornament in the wall painting. The one the pharaoh, or high priest, was wearing."

"No . . . priest. Only for . . . child of Ra."

Child of Ra. The pharaoh. Logan frowned. But that epithet hadn't become common until at least the fourth or fifth dynasty, hundreds of years after Narmer's time. Could this be more evidence of what Tina Romero had speculated about—a historical anachronism, a kind of collective amnesia of ritual and religion in the wake of Narmer's death?

Rush held the digital recorder close to Jennifer's lips. "You called it 'that which brings life to the dead, and death to the living.' What did you mean?"

"The . . . great secret . . . Gift of Ra . . . It must not be . . . polluted . . . by the touch of the infidel."

Jennifer's breathing was growing still more rapid and shallow.

"Keep this short," Logan told Rush in a low voice.

"What lies beyond the third gate?" Rush asked.

Jennifer's face grew contorted. **"Swift death. Thy limbs shall be . . . scattered to the corners of the earth. Thou . . . all of thee . . . will find madness and death to be thy share. . . ."**

The curse of Narmer, Logan thought.

Suddenly, to his inexpressible horror, he saw Jennifer—still under the influence of the drug—slowly sit up on the table. But her movements seemed strange, wrong somehow—it was as if she was being **pulled** into a sitting position by some invisible force.

Abruptly, her eyes opened, but they were staring, sightless. **"Madness and death!"** she cried in a terrible voice. And then her eyes closed and she crumpled back onto the bed. As she did so, the instrumentation started to bleat.

"What is it?" Logan asked sharply. But Rush did not answer, instead busying himself with the medical equipment. He moved to Jennifer's side, gave her a quick examination. After several minutes, he straightened up again.

"She seems to have suffered a brief seizure of some kind," he said. "I can't tell without further tests. But she's resting comfortably now. I'll keep the propofol going another few minutes, then bring her around."

Logan frowned. This procedure had gone far beyond his comfort factor. "That's the last one—right?"

"Right. After this, I'd never ask her to do another—not even if Stone demanded it."

"I'm glad to hear it. Because having seen this, I

have to tell you, Ethan, that in my opinion, such treatment of her—given my earlier recommendation—is indefensible. Especially considering her past."

Rush glanced at him. "What past is that?"

"The past I just uncovered in those CTS documents you gave me. Her psychological history."

Rush continued to look at him, his face hardening. When he did not reply, Logan continued. "I'm talking about her diagnosis of schizoaffective disorder."

"You're **talking** about a twenty-year-old diagnosis," Rush said, his tone turning defensive. "And a misdiagnosis, at that. Jen didn't suffer from schizoaffective disorder—it was just a bout of teenage acting out."

Logan didn't reply.

"At the very most, it was a mood disorder. Mild, and temporary, and it went away with the onset of adulthood."

"Even so—given that, how could you put her through this? How could you allow her to be so traumatized?"

Rush frowned, opened his mouth to retort. Then he paused, took a deep breath. "It was important to Stone. It was important to **me**. I thought this was a chance to further our CTS research, to apply our findings in the field. And as I told you before, I thought it would be a good thing for Jen as well. I didn't expect she would find it so difficult. Had I known—well, let's just say it will never happen again."

There was a brief silence. Then the two stepped

away from the table, but both kept their eyes on Jennifer's still form.

"I've been thinking about what you said," Rush murmured in a quiet voice. "That Jen was brain-dead for so long—that her NDE was so protracted—that, in essence, she might have lost her . . . her soul."

"That's not what I said," Logan replied.

"It's what you implied. That she was a kind of empty vessel. And that if King Narmer's spirit was still intact, in this place, that it could . . . well . . . take temporary possession of her."

"Since we last talked, I've done more research into that myself. In theory, what you say is possible. However, that's not the case here."

"I'm relieved to hear it. But how can you be sure?"

Logan's gaze was still on Jennifer. "Two reasons. I do believe it's possible for the life force of one whose **physical** form is dead to take residence in a living body whose soul had been—compromised. However, such intimate physical possession is rare. I've studied the literature, and there are only half a dozen cases, all poorly documented. However, there is something they all agree on. The spirit of that dead person cannot take possession of the body of someone **of the opposite sex**."

"So it isn't King Narmer," Rush said, with evident relief.

"Not if what I'm postulating is really the case here."

Rush nodded slowly. "You mentioned two reasons."

"I've mentioned the other before. Recall that the primary purpose of burying a pharaoh in his tomb is to facilitate his journey to the next world. With no actual mummy, the **ka**—the spiritual essence—would have no place to go and would remain restless, basically haunting the tomb forever. But with a physical body—such as Narmer has in the tomb—his **ka** could make the journey through the underworld with his **ba,** which is the part of the soul more mobile and able to travel. Everything we've seen in the tomb has served to prepare Narmer, to make the journey successful."

"And since we found Narmer's mummy intact, that means his **ka** would no longer be here," Rush said.

"So it would seem."

"But if it isn't King Narmer"—Rush hesitated— "then who have we been communicating with?"

Logan didn't answer.

44

At two in the morning, the Station slept restlessly under a bloated yellow moon. A few technicians were at work in Operations, preparing for the morning's mission to break the final seals and pass the third gate; guards were stationed at the Maw, at the base of the Umbilicus, and at the communications center. Otherwise, all was quiet.

A lone figure strode down the deserted corridors of Red. Dressed in a white lab coat, it looked much like the many others who inhabited the science labs during the day. Only its movements were different. It was wary, almost stealthy; it hesitated at each intersection, satisfying itself it was entirely alone before proceeding.

The figure drew up to the main door of the archaeology lab. It was locked, but the figure had long before procured a skeleton key and opened the door with silent fingers. It glanced down the hallway again, paused a moment to listen, then slipped inside and closed the door quietly behind.

Without turning on the lights, it slipped through the rooms full of lab tables, artifact lockers, and preservation and curatorial equipment, until it reached the storage facility at the rear of the laboratory. The figure opened the heavy door and stepped into the chill interior. Only now did it switch on a small flashlight. The beam licked over the surfaces of the small room, coming to rest at last on a wall containing a half-dozen large drawers, like the corpse lockers of a morgue.

More quickly now, the figure came forward, slid the fingers of one hand down the drawers, then seized the handle of one and—as quietly as possible—drew it out. The smell of the room, dust and mold and chemicals and the faint rot of the swamp outside—became freighted with another smell: the smell of death.

Inside the locker lay the mummy of King Narmer.

The figure drew the locker out to its full length. It

shone the flashlight beam over the pharaoh's corpse. It was remarkably well preserved for its five-thousand-year entombment. Remarkable, too, how the mummy had been wrapped, or—indeed—that it had been wrapped at all: such a mummy would not be seen again until perhaps the New Kingdom, a millennium and a half later. Amazing, how much had been forgotten—and relearned, much later—more than a thousand years after Narmer's death. Was this in part because of the pains the pharaoh had taken to delude all by creating a false tomb; by having his corpse buried at such a distance from his own lands?

At the moment, however, the figure was not interested in theoretical questions. It was interested in the mummy's bandages—and what they contained.

The mummy's body cloth had been removed and the linen wrappings were now exposed, glistening faintly with ancient unguent. The figure reached into the pockets of the lab coat and removed several evidence bags and a heavy scalpel. Working quickly, it cut away the bands that fixed the papyrus scroll—with its spells for a safe passage through the underworld—from the mummy's hands and placed the papyrus aside. It then cut the black scarab lying on the mummy's chest—placed over the heart and inscribed with its own magical spells—away from its golden necklace and placed both necklace and scarab into one of the evidence bags. Next, the figure began removing the individual strips of linen wrapped around the mummy's fingers. As it did so, artifacts began coming to light: golden rings, gems, and beads, all winking dully in the gleam of the flashlight.

The figure laughed delightedly under its breath at these finds and quickly slipped them into the evidence bag.

Now it moved toward the mummy's head and—working even more quickly—freed the outermost bandage from its resin bonds and began unwrapping it. More items appeared: a falcon collar fashioned out of gold, another of faience. These, like everything else secreted within the mummy's bandages, were meant as magical protections to help speed the king from this world to the next. Tearing them roughly away from the bandages, the figure placed them in the evidence bag. After all these years, they were still thickly smeared with unguent—a different type of unguent, it seemed, than that which protected the mummy's outer wraps. No doubt some primitive preservative, lacking the refined preparation of later dynasties.

The figure continued unwrapping the head bandages. More objects appeared: a resin scarab, a beautiful diadem inlaid with gems. Both went into the bag.

The first evidence bag was full now, and the figure sealed it and placed it back into the pocket of the lab coat. Time was critical, and the intruder dared not dally much longer. Already it had harvested a dozen items from within the mummy's wrappings—a dozen more and it would leave.

It moved back down to the mummy's chest. A painting of Osiris had still been faintly visible on the body cloth—given such a wildly anachronistic find, was it possible the pharaoh's crook and flail might also lie buried beneath the layers of linen? If so, it would be a princely discovery indeed.

The intruder picked up the scalpel—fingers now sticky with unguent, its movements feeling a little heavy and slow—and, no longer showing the least reverence for the long-departed king, sliced deeply into the wrappings that covered the chest. The smell of death grew stronger. Immediately, twinklings of gold peeped out through the cut layers of bandages. The figure identified a dagger, a golden chain, several protective amulets of the most ornate design. And—what was that, barely visible beneath the lowest layers of bandages? Was it possible, remotely possible, it was a large, golden **ba**-bird, its wings studded with countless gemstones . . . ?

Working feverishly now, the figure dug into the bandages, feeling around, plucking out the amulets one after another and depositing them in the second bag. These, too, were thickly smeared with a primitive unguent, the color of earth—disgusting, but there would be plenty of time to clean up later.

The figure wiped its hands together, wiped the stickiness off onto its lab coat. Then, picking up the scalpel again, it bent over the mummy, preparing to slice away the final bandages.

But wait . . . something was wrong. What was this

strange sensation of prickly heat that seemed to rise from within? What was this horrible smell—of sulfur, or something worse, that grew and grew until it filled the entire room?

The figure stepped back in alarm. But even as it did so, the feeling of heat turned to one of flame, of roiling smoke. The figure opened its mouth to gasp—but the gasp turned into an escalating shriek, rising in pitch and volume, as the pain quickly spread, wrapping the tomb robber in a vise of intolerable pain.

45

This time, when Jeremy Logan descended to the air lock platform at the bottom of the Umbilicus, it was so crowded there was almost no room for him to stand. He counted ten others, including Tina Romero, Ethan Rush, Stone, Valentino—in person, for a change—two of March's archaeologists, two roustabouts, and two security guards. He nodded at the assembled group. Several—Rush, Stone, the archaeologists—looked rather drawn and ashen. The mood was serious, tense, with little of the fraught anticipation he'd noticed during his first descent to the tomb.

Logan understood why Rush would look upset—Jennifer was still comatose, having slipped into some kind of hypnotic trance from which she could not be immediately wakened—but not the others.

"Where's Dr. March?" he asked, looking around. Nobody answered.

"Are we ready?" Stone asked after another minute. There was a scattering of nods, murmured assents.

"Then let's get started." As he spoke, Stone took Logan by the arm and went on ahead of the others, moving into chamber one. When they were several steps inside, he leaned in close to Logan. "March is dead," he muttered.

Logan looked at him, shocked. "Dead?"

Stone nodded. His lips were pressed together so tightly they were barely visible. "He snuck into the archaeology lab late last night and violated Narmer's mummy. Unwrapped the bandages, started looting the corpse of the treasures bound into its windings. There was a small explosion, a fire . . ."

"An explosion?" Logan repeated.

"Two different chemicals were secreted in the strata of Narmer's bandages. I've been informed that, separately, they are inert, but when mixed together—well, they act like an ancient version of napalm."

"You mean, a booby trap? What kind of chemicals? How could it still be effective after all these centuries?"

"My people are still analyzing things, but clearly the compounds were highly stable. Some kind of potassium derivative, it seems, with a primitive form of glycerol or glycol as the antagonist." Stone glanced back at the others, who were approaching. "Look, Jeremy—only a few know about this. We're keeping it quiet, for reasons of morale, and . . . other things."

"Any idea what his motive was?" Logan asked. "Surely it wasn't simple venality."

"It's too early to tell. But it just might be as depressingly simple as that. I've started conducting some inquiries back in the States. It seems March had run up staggering debts over the last year, living far beyond his means. He might have been in the employ of one of my rivals, trying to spook our workers, faking up elements of the curse. Or maybe he was just hoping to line his pockets with as much gold and jewels as possible." He sighed. "I should have had him vetted again, like everybody else. But I'd worked with him so often before. I trusted him."

Logan nodded toward the tomb that stretched ahead of them. "Are you sure you don't want to postpone this?"

Another, brusquer shake of the head. "We can't. With the dam so far ahead of schedule, we can expect an official delegation to visit any day now to discuss the termination of our stay here—and we're too advanced in our work for any more dissembling. We have to remove what grave goods we can and leave before it's too late."

Remove what grave goods we can. Logan glanced in the direction of Tina Romero. It seemed that, even from beyond the grave, March's acquisitiveness had rubbed off on Stone. Logan wondered what the Egyptologist would think of this.

As the others assembled around them, Logan glanced over chamber one. His eyes stopped at the heavy, ornamental bed, now in ruins, its canopy collapsed onto the sleeping platform. There were still a few dried bloodstains marking the spot where the luckless Robert Carmody had met his end. The heavy gold bolts holding the canopy in place had been deliberately loosened—had that been March's handiwork, too—prepping them for later removal?

The hand that touches my immortal form will burn with unquenchable fire—Narmer's words, once again. And, once again, the curse seemed to be coming true. Ironic, he thought—if March **had** been giving Narmer's curse a boost of his own here and there, it had ultimately played out in a way the archaeologist would never, ever have desired.

Silently, the group made their way toward the opened gate in the rear that led to the next chamber. Chamber two was also almost completely empty; the only things remaining were the two shrines, physically built into the structure of the chamber, and the immense blue granite sarcophagus at the center.

Logan glanced again at Tina Romero. Her expression was set, unreadable.

Rush came up and Logan turned to him. "How's Jennifer?"

The doctor looked as if he hadn't slept in a long time. "We've moved her to the medical suite. Her vitals are strong, and she's stable. I'm uncertain why she hasn't regained consciousness."

"Do you think it could be a reaction to the stress of that last crossing? Some kind of hysteric catatonia?"

"I sincerely doubt it. She's never shown any indications of that before."

Logan looked around. "I assume it was you who pronounced March—right?"

Rush's bleak look grew bleaker still. "My God. What a thing."

Stone had moved ahead to the golden wall at the rear of chamber two. It looked the same as the other three walls, save the large seals placed along one edge and the design embossed in the gold. As Logan drew closer, he was able to make out the image: a huge, leering face that—disconcertingly, unlike the normal profiles seen in Egyptian art—was staring directly at them, seemingly half jackal, half human. The rest of the wall, Logan now noticed, was covered with very faint hieroglyphics, beautifully and cunningly embossed in the precious metal.

"Tina?" Stone murmured. "Can you make out the message in those glyphs?"

Romero drew closer. "It's the final part of the

curse, repeated over and over," she said after a brief examination. **"'Should any in their temerity pass the third gate, then the black god of the deepest pit will seize him, and his limbs will be scattered to the uttermost corners of the earth. And I, Narmer the Everliving, will torment him and his, by day and by night, waking and sleeping, until madness and death become his eternal temple.'"**

A brief silence settled over the collective company.

"And that image?" Stone asked. "That god-face?"

"I've never seen anything like it," Romero answered.

"What about the seals?"

"Royal seals. Like the others we've seen, only much larger and more ornate. Serekhs, with echoes of the curse woven in among the primitive symbols for the pharaoh's name."

Super seals, Logan thought to himself.

"The ground-penetrating radar readings for the room beyond were anomalous," Stone said. "According to the scans, it's as if there's nothing in there—which, of course, can't be right." He stared at the wall for a moment, lost in thought. Then he recovered himself. "All right," he said, turning to Rush. "Go ahead, Ethan."

The group waited in silence as the doctor drilled a test hole in the gold, inserted his instruments, sampled the air beyond, and pronounced it safe. Then Stone himself stepped up to the seals, and—with Romero standing by with an artifact storage container—carefully cut through first the upper necropolis seal and then the lower, more ornate royal seal. As he carefully pried them away from the gold sheeting, there was a loud click, followed by a sighing, grinding sound, and to Logan's surprise the entire rear wall pivoted inward about two feet, like a door moving on hinges. The group stepped back in unison, and there were gasps of consternation. But when nothing else occurred, Stone stepped forward once again—a little gingerly—and shone his light into the blackness of chamber three. After a moment, he glanced back at the roustabouts.

"Stabilize this entrance," he told them. "Then we're going in."

46

Once again, Stone went in first, barely waiting for the roustabouts to complete testing the integrity of the entranceway. His movements were quick, even brusque, as if the recent troubles—and the ticking clock—had given him an unseemly sense of haste. He ducked past the workers and through the narrow opening, disappearing beyond the wall of the third gate. For a moment, all was silent; the only indication anyone was in chamber three was the reflected glow of

Stone's flashlight, lancing here and there through the darkness. Then Logan heard Stone clear his throat.

"Tina? Ethan? Dr. Logan? Valentino?" he called in a strange voice. "Please come in."

Logan followed the others through the gap in the wall and into the final chamber. At first, he thought his flashlight was malfunctioning—it didn't seem to provide any illumination. And then he realized: the entire chamber was clad in what appeared to be onyx, walls and floor and ceiling, black and unreflective. The stone seemed to soak up their flashlight beams, pulling the light from them and leaving the small chamber so dim that its contents could barely be made out.

"Jesus," Tina said, shivering. "How creepy."

"Is that your professional opinion, Tina?" Stone asked.

"Kowinsky," Valentino called out through the gap in the third gate. "Bring up one of those sodium vapor lamps."

For a moment, everyone fell quiet, examining the chamber. To Logan, it did seem remarkably bare, compared to the opulent rooms that had come before. There was a single ornamental table placed along the left wall, enameled in gold, containing a dozen papyri, each carefully rolled and set in a line. In the rear of the chamber was what looked like a small bed, quite narrow, that had once been covered by some kind of linen coverlet and a pillow, both now sadly decomposed. Across from the table, placed along the floor by the opposing wall, were three small boxes—apparently of solid gold—along with a single urn.

But everyone's attention quickly turned to the artifact sitting in the center of the room. It was a large chest, about four feet square, fashioned of some black stone—perhaps onyx again—and set upon a fantastically carved plinth of dark, dense wood. Its edges were lined in strips of gold. On its sides were reproductions of several of the designs they had already seen in chamber one—the box-shaped artifact topped by an iron rod; the bowl-like object trailing wisps of gold from its edges. But this time, the images were fashioned out of a multitude of brilliantly colored gemstones, set into the surface of the chest. Across its top was an elaborately fashioned serekh.

"Tina?" Stone said, pointing at the serekh, his voice almost a whisper. "That's the rebus for Narmer's name. Right?"

Tina nodded slowly. "Yes. I think so."

Stone turned to her. "You think so?"

She had set down her video camera, the room being too dark to film, and was peering more closely at the chest. "The glyphs match, all right. But these scratches, here, through the head of the catfish . . . I don't know. It's most unusual. But it's **all** unusual. That cotlike structure in the rear, the shrines in chamber two, the strange emptiness of this room . . ." She paused again. "It's like I said once before. It's almost as if this entire tomb was used as a **rehearsal** for

Narmer's death, for his passage to the next world, the Field of Offerings."

"Have you come across anything like this before?" Stone asked.

"No." She looked around the dim space for a minute, brow furrowed in confusion. "It's almost as if . . . but, no, it couldn't be." She peered again at the chest. "If only I could get a better look at this."

"Kowinsky!" Valentino bawled. "What's up with those lights?"

"Not enough room to get them through this opening, sir," came the disembodied voice of Kowinsky.

"You might want to take a look at those papyri," Stone said to Tina. "Maybe they can shed some light on things."

She nodded, moved away with her light.

Now Stone, followed by Dr. Rush, moved over to the series of small golden boxes set along the right-hand wall. Stone crouched down and began to carefully remove the top of the first with latex-gloved hands.

Logan watched, hugging himself against the chill and a feeling of growing dismay. Ever since entering the chamber, he had been aware of the malignant presence. It sensed them—he was sure of that—but the overpowering evil he had felt several times before was being held in check for the time being. It was almost as if it was watching, waiting . . . and biding its time. He reached into his duffel, pulled out the air ion counter, and swept it slowly around. The air in here was significantly more ionized than normal—in fact, the air had grown increasingly ionized as they'd penetrated deeper into the tomb. What this meant he wasn't certain.

Stone had removed the top of the box. Reaching in, he gingerly pulled something out: a curl of metal, beaten very thin. "It appears to be native copper," he said. "There are at least half a dozen small sheets of it in here." Moving on to the next box, he removed its lid, peered inside, then pulled out something that in the faint light looked almost like a small bayonet, brownish and badly corroded. "Looks like iron," he said.

"If so, it's probably meteoric iron," Tina said, drawn back from the papypri. "And it would be the earliest known use of iron among the Egyptians by at least a few hundred years."

But Stone had already moved on to the third box. He opened it, placed a hand inside, then removed it again. In his cupped palm he held dozens of thin filaments of beaten gold, tangled together like Christmas tinsel.

"What the **hell**?" he muttered.

Tina Romero stepped over to the black-edged urn. She carefully lifted it, shone her flashlight inside. "Empty," she said. Then she raised it to her nose, took a gingerly sniff. "Odd. It smells sour, like—like vinegar."

Stone came over, took it from her, smelled it also. "You're right." He handed it back.

"Bands of copper, iron spikes, filaments of gold," Logan said. "What could this all mean?"

"I don't know," Stone said. "But **that** will answer all your questions—and more." He pointed at the onyx-colored chest that stood in the center of the chamber. "That will be what makes all our careers—and puts me in the history books as the greatest archaeologist of all time."

"You think . . ." Rush paused. "You think the crowns of Egypt are in that chest?"

"I **know** they are. It's the only answer. It's the final secret of the final chamber of Narmer's tomb." Stone turned to Valentino. "Frank? Have your men give me a hand with this."

Slowly—as if possessed by a single thought—the group drew together, forming a silent ring around the ebony chest.

47

Amanda Richards walked into the forensic archaeology lab and turned on the overhead lights with a flick of her fingers. She stood in the doorway a moment, taking in the racks of instrumentation, the carefully scrubbed lab desks and work surfaces. Then she stepped over to a table in one corner. The room smelled faintly of formaldehyde and other chemical preservatives—and, more chillingly, of sulfur.

Taking a seat at the table, she plucked a folder from beneath her arm and opened it. For several minutes, she examined the sheets within: X-ray fluorescence reports, the all-important CT scans, radiographies, and a brief summary analysis by Christina Romero, all pertaining to the same subject: the mummy of King Narmer.

Closing the folder, Richards sat still a moment, going through a mental checklist. Then she stood up and began assembling the tools she would need: scalpels, archival-quality linen thread, forceps, Teflon needles, fiberglass trays, scraps of ancient flaxen bandages taken from mummified remains too badly decayed or damaged to merit forensic intervention. With her tools assembled, she walked over to the corpse locker in the adjoining wall, grasped its handle, and—gingerly—drew out the mummified remains of King Narmer.

The corpse locker was similar to the ones in the storage area, where Fenwick March had been killed during his attempt to loot Narmer's mummy, with a single difference: this locker was equipped with an atmosphere of inert gas, nitrogen. Since March had violated the mummy so roughly, tearing the bandages and disturbing its internal microclimate, every attempt had to be made to prevent further decay or decomposition. That, in fact, was the reason Richards was here—to repair, as best she could, the damage March had caused and prepare the mummy for shipment, until a more careful and extensive restoration could be done at Porter Stone's lab complex outside London.

She swung down the stabilizing leg from beneath the locker, fixing its end to the floor. Then, pulling on latex gloves and a surgical mask, she carefully examined the mummy. Earlier in the day, technicians had removed the compounds in the mummy's windings that formed the ancient booby trap by exposing the mummy to a negative airflow chamber. Nevertheless, Richards handled the corpse with the utmost caution.

She continued examining the mummy, taking note of the damage to the bandaged hands, head, and—most extensively—the chest. She found herself still struggling with the idea that Fenwick March—one of the most revered archaeologists in the world—could have done something like this: not only robbing a mummy, but in such a crude, unprofessional manner. It was amazing, the deadly lure of ancient treasure. March had been studying it, handling it, all his life. Perhaps this find—the Pharaoh Narmer—had finally been too much for him. It was the straw, the golden straw, that broke the camel's back.

She swung a UV light into place over the mummy. It might be callous to think so, but a part of her was relieved March was out of the way. He had always been a tyrannical presence in the archaeology labs, micromanaging everything and everybody, insisting things be done his way, blustering and bullying and complaining. This was the second time Amanda Richards had worked with him, and he'd been much worse this time out. Perhaps it was all of a piece with whatever mind-set had prompted him to loot the mummy. She shrugged. All she knew for sure was that—had he lived, had somebody else been the one to violate Narmer's corpse—March would have been looking over her shoulder right now, scowling, second-guessing her every move and telling her how she was doing it all wrong.

As it was, the forensic archaeology lab was delightfully calm and silent.

She moved the UV light slowly over the mummy. Remains of mummy varnish fluoresced a pale gold under the light. Dark patches, where the technicians had stabilized the sticky glycerol with an inert compound to render it harmless, were scattered here and there throughout the upper layers of bandages, torn open by March in his feverish search for grave goods.

Richards snapped off the light and put it aside. Narmer's chest was the most badly damaged area—she would begin her restoration work there.

Wheeling over a powerful surgical lamp, she aimed it at the chest and began examining the damage with a jeweler's loupe. March had sliced right through the bandages, exposing numerous layers after the fashion of geologic strata. The anepigraphic scarab had been removed by March, but numerous other, smaller treasures peeped out from the layers of wrappings: beads and faience amulets and golden trinkets and the other items forming the "magic armor" that served to protect Narmer in his journey to the next world.

She shook her head, tut-tutting under her breath. March had made such a hash of the bandages covering Narmer's chest that she would have to unwrap still more of them before she could even think of putting them back into any sort of order.

Using the forceps, she carefully pulled back the edges of the disturbed wrappings, exposing the deeper layers, tangled and somewhat shredded from the effects of Narmer's booby trap. Putting aside the forceps and taking up the scalpel, she cut away first one, then a second wrapping, freeing them from the tangle and pulling them away. She hated to do it, but there was no other way to restore the damage. Narmer's body had been so carefully wrapped, and March had been so hasty and reckless in tearing at those wrappings, that it was like trying to realign the rubber bands around the core of a golf ball.

Taking a fresh grip on the scalpel, she sliced through yet another layer of the linen bandages. Now Narmer's actual flesh was exposed to the light, covered by a thin cloth and a golden chest piece, which itself had become dislodged, probably by the chemical reaction. That was not good—it might be pressing improperly against the flesh, perhaps damaging it further. She would need to reseat it upon Narmer's chest. Then she could begin the work of sewing back the layers of bandages with linen thread, and—in places where the original wrappings had decayed or become too brittle—replacing them with her supply of ancient flax wrappings. Then she could move on to the head and the hands, where the work should go much faster. In three hours—four at the most—Narmer's mummy would again be whole and stabilized for transfer to England.

Putting down the scalpel, she very carefully reached through the layers of cut bandages and gently grasped the edges of the golden chest piece. The surrounding tissue, she noted with approval, was in excellent condition given its great age: gray and desiccated, with no sign of deliquescence. The chest piece, however, was difficult to budge, and she was forced to apply additional pressure. Finally, it shifted, coming free of Narmer's body with a dry snick.

Richards lifted it slightly, preparing to reseat it properly and sew the bandages over it. But then she stopped abruptly, rooted in place by surprise and shock.

With the chest piece freed from its original position, the flesh of Narmer's chest was laid bare. And as Richards looked down at the body, she saw—in the pitiless fluorescent light of the laboratory—a wrinkled, shrunken, desiccated, and yet unmistakable **female breast**.

48

As the rest of the group watched in rapt silence, Stone stepped up to the large onyx chest. Valentino's roust-abouts came up to stand on either side of him. Stone hesitated briefly, then knelt before the plinth and let one latex-gloved hand brush gently across the upper surface of the chest. His shoulders trembled visibly. He pulled the gloves from his hands—Rush, Logan noted, made no protest at this—and caressed the chest once again. Despite what he'd implied about the chest holding the answer to all Narmer's secrets, Stone seemed to be in no hurry to open it.

Standing back in the darkness, watching, Logan understood. He remembered the speech Stone had given to the assembled troops, describing his first archaeological discovery: the Native American settlement everyone else had missed. He remembered the gleam in Stone's eye when he'd first met him, disguised as an elderly local researcher, that day in the Cairo museum when he'd said: **work quickly.** Over his illustrious career, Stone had uncovered almost incontrovertible evidence of the existence of Camelot. He'd recovered traces of Hippolyta, queen of the Amazons, whom historians had always consigned to myth. And yet in discovering the tomb of Narmer, he had outdone even himself. Logan knew that Stone held Flinders Petrie, father of modern archaeology, with a respect that bordered on reverence. And yet now Stone had accomplished what had eluded even Petrie. With the discovery of Narmer's crown, he would take his place in the highest circle of his profession—a circle reserved for one. His detractors would be forever silenced. Stone would become, for all time, the world's greatest archaeologist.

Silently, Stone ran his hands around the top of the chest, then along its sides, his spidery fingers moving this way and that, almost like a phrenologist analyzing a skull. "Tina," he said at last, his voice breaking the silence, "a scalpel, please."

Tina moved forward and handed Stone the thin,

straight blade. He nodded his thanks, then gently applied the scalpel to the strips of gold that lined the chest. Logan had assumed these strips to be mere inlaid decoration; instead, they appeared to be bands of precious metal holding the chest closed by ritual seals. Having cut through them, Stone peeled the bands away from the chest, then laid them carefully aside. A single band of gold remained, holding the elaborately bejeweled serekh in place on the chest's upper surface; another careful notch of the scalpel cut through this as well, and Stone gently placed both it and its attached serekh by the base of the plinth. Then he rose and nodded to the roustabouts. The two positioned themselves on each side of the chest. At Stone's direction, each grasped an edge of the lid and began to lift it. Although the lid could not have been more than two inches thick, the roustabouts could barely budge it from its position; Valentino and one of the security guards came forward to lend a hand. With great effort, the four raised the lid from the chest, moved it to an uncluttered area of the tomb, and—with a chorus of grunts—laid it on the floor. It hit the black surface with a dull thud that reverberated throughout chamber three.

Inside the large onyx chest was a black cloth shot through with threads the color of gold. Stone touched it gingerly but—as before—the moment his fingers made contact, the cloth disappeared into a mist of fine dust, its corporeal form preserved five millennia only through a caprice of nature.

Below lay a sheet of beaten gold, covered with primitive hieroglyphs.

"Tina?" Stone asked, angling one of the lights toward the sheet of gold. "What do you make of these?"

Romero came forward, examined the glyphs. "They seem to refer to those papyri, laid out on the table," she said after a moment. "I'd only begun to study them. It's almost as if they were . . ."

"Were what?" Rush prompted.

"Invocations. But not of the usual type."

"**What** type?" Stone said, an edge of impatience in his voice.

She shrugged. "Almost like—instructions."

"Why is that unusual?" Stone asked. "The entire New Kingdom's Book of the Dead could be seen as an instruction manual."

Romero didn't answer.

Stone turned back to the chest. Nodding for Valentino's men to remove the sheet of beaten gold, he eagerly glanced beneath, angling the light in closer for a better look. Stepping forward, Logan could see another sheet of precious metal—this one edged with faience and precious gems, its surface dense with hieroglyphs—once again covering the entire upper surface of the chest. Stone gestured for the roustabouts to remove it as well.

"Over here, please," Romero said. She instructed Valentino's men to place both inserts on the floor near the table with the papyri.

With the second sheet of gold removed, a rough, uneven surface greeted their eyes. To Logan, looking down into the chest through the dim light, the chest appeared to be filled with a superfluity of small, thin, desiccated bones, all jumbled about and knotted together in a crazy quilt of disarray.

Stone grunted in surprise. He reached forward; thought better of it; donned another latex glove, and then dipped a hand into the material.

"What is all that?" Logan asked.

"I'll be damned," Stone replied after a minute. "It's hemp."

Rush leaned forward, plucked a piece from the jumble with a pair of forceps, examined it with his flashlight. "You're right."

Nodding to Valentino's men, Stone began removing handfuls of the ancient plant stalks from the chest—first gingerly, then in larger and larger amounts, until it littered the floor of chamber three. As the material was disturbed, thin clouds of organic dust rose, and an odd scent—like that of a five-thousand-year-old harvest—rose to Logan's nostrils.

Embedded within the bundles of hemp were two bags, each slightly larger than a basketball, formed from strands of gold so tightly and expertly woven that they were as pliable as silk. Gently—gently—Stone freed them from the surrounding hemp and placed them on the floor before the plinth.

Once again, without speaking, the group closed in. Logan looked at the two roundish objects gleaming in the beams of a half-dozen flashlights. In his mind's eye, he saw within them the twin crowns of Egypt: the white, conical crown of upper Egypt, spotless and gleaming; the red crown of lower Egypt, high peaked and aggressive. What were they made of? Painted gold? Some unknown or unexpected alloy? What magic did they wield? He felt almost beside himself with eagerness to see what was inside those soft folds of woven gold. **Two** bundles. There was no longer any question: these were the double crowns of the first pharaoh of Egypt. What else would Narmer have guarded so jealously, so carefully, and at such great cost—not only to himself but to his legacy?

Stone appeared seized with a similar urgency. He picked up one of the golden bags, loosened its end, and—with a brief look around at the others—reached in and gently pulled out its contents.

What emerged was not a crown but something very different: a bowl-shaped implement, made apparently of white marble, trailing long gold filaments from its edge.

There was a murmur of surprise and dismay from the onlookers.

Stone frowned. He stared at the thing for a moment, uncomprehending, and then placed it aside atop its golden bag and—more quickly this time—thrust his hand into the second.

What he pulled out of this bag was even stranger: a construction of red enamel, topped by an iron rod that itself was surrounded by a curled sheet of copper. Logan, stunned, leaned forward, peering closely. The iron rod leading away from the enamel construction was sealed with a stopper of what appeared to be bitumen. They looked precisely like the images in the wall painting in chamber one.

These were not crowns. These could be called nothing else but—**devices**.

Stone stared blankly at the red-colored thing in his right hand. Then he picked up the white marble object in his left. As the group watched in silence, he looked from one, to the other, and then back again.

"What the **hell**?" he croaked.

49

In the rearmost of the three examination rooms of the Station's small medical suite, Jennifer Rush moved restlessly on the bed where she'd been placed for observation. The room was dimly lit, and the lone nurse who had been monitoring her had sneaked out of the suite—Jennifer's vitals had fallen into normal REM sleep, and the nurse was unwilling to miss a hairdressing reservation. All was still except for the

low, infrequent blinking and bleating of the surrounding medical instruments.

Jennifer stirred again. She took in a deep, shuddering breath. For a moment, she fell still. And then—for
the first time in more than thirty hours—her eyes
fluttered open. She looked at the ceiling, her gaze
vague, unfocused. Then—after another minute—she
struggled to sit up.

"Ethan?" she called out, her voice hoarse.

In the low light, with the surrounding forest of
tiny lights and digital readouts, the room seemed
strange, almost exotic: a mosaic of red and yellow and
green, as if the gods had laid a skein of jewels across
a night sky, transforming normally white stars into
brilliant colors. Jennifer blinked, then blinked again,
uncomprehending. And then her gaze fell on something familiar: the ancient silver amulet, left hanging
by Ethan Rush on its chain from a nearby monitor.

Jennifer's brow furrowed.

The amulet showed a crude depiction of one of
the most famous scenes of Egyptian mythology:
Isis, having assembled the fragments of the dead and
butchered Osiris, reanimating his body through a
magical spell and transforming him into the god of
the underworld.

The amulet gleamed fitfully in the lambent light
of the instrumentation. As she stared, Jennifer's body
grew increasing rigid. Her breathing slowly became
more shallow and ragged. Suddenly—with a faint
expelling sigh, like air escaping from a bellows—her

jaw sagged, her pupils rolled up into her head, and she collapsed back onto the bed.

Ten, or perhaps fifteen, minutes passed in which the examination room remained silent. And then Jennifer Rush sat up again. She took a shallow, exploratory breath, followed by a deeper one. She closed her eyes, opened them again. Then she licked her lips gently, almost experimentally.

And then—with a single, mechanical motion—she swung her legs over the side of the bed and let her feet slip to the cold, tiled floor.

She took a step forward, hesitated, stepped forward again. The pulse-oximeter clamp brushed against the nearest bank of instruments and fell away from her little finger. She reached up, felt the network of leads attached to her neck and forehead, and pulled them away like so many cobwebs. Then she looked around. Her eyes were cloudy but nevertheless focused.

The door lay ahead. She made for it, then stopped, her progress once again arrested. This time the culprit was the intravenous line, running from the saline bag to the catheter. Jennifer tried walking forward again, watched the saline rack tip forward; glanced along the IV line to her wrist; then grasped the catheter and pulled it roughly from her vein.

This time, when she moved toward the exit, there were no further difficulties.

Leaving the medical suite and stepping into the central hallway of Red, she glanced first left, then right. The corridor was empty: most off-duty personnel were either in their quarters or in the public rooms, eagerly awaiting word from chamber three.

Jennifer hesitated in the doorway for a moment, perhaps getting her bearings, perhaps simply regaining her equilibrium. Then she turned left and proceeded down the hall. At the first intersection, she turned right. Her eyes remained cloudy, and her gait was halting—like somebody who had been off her feet for a long, long time—but as she walked her gait improved, her breathing became more and more regular.

She stopped at a door marked HAZARDOUS MATERIALS STORAGE. EXPLOSIVE AND HIGHLY VOLATILE—ACCESS RESTRICTED. She turned the knob, found it locked. But the identity card around her neck—so crisp, so light, such a shiny shade of blue—slid easily through the reader beside the door; the lock sprang open; and she slipped into the room and out of sight.

50

Chamber three had fallen into a shocked, confused silence. As Logan watched, Porter Stone slowly sank to his knees before the large onyx chest—whether from weariness or disappointment, or some other emotion, he couldn't be sure. Wordlessly, Stone let the two objects slip to the floor.

Logan peered around the chamber, its black surfaces gleaming dimly in the reflected glow of the flashlights. He glanced at the bundles of ancient hemp, scattered around the floor in a corona of disarray. He glanced at the low bed at the rear of the chamber, almost too faint to make out, with its once-beautiful coverlet and pillow. He glanced at the gold-framed table, covered with carefully arranged papyri. He glanced at the small golden boxes, once sealed but now spilling their contents: curlings of copper, a spike of meteoric iron, filaments of gold. Finally, his eye came to rest on the two devices—he could think of no other word for them—that sat beside Stone: the white, bowl-like implement and the concave apparatus covered in red enamel. They rested upon the bags of woven gold that had held them: five-thousand-year-old enigmas, practically daring the onlookers to parse their secrets.

It all seemed impossibly strange.

From the beginning, everything about Narmer's tomb had been unusual. It had been similar to those of the kings who had followed him centuries later—and yet, in many ways, so very unlike. His mummy had been found in the second, not the third, chamber: reason dictated the final chamber would contain something even more critical, even more important, for the afterlife. And yet, as Logan glanced around at the scrolls and bits of metal, he could not begin to imagine what it was.

He stared down again at the two devices. One red, and one white—just like the old crowns of upper and lower Egypt.

"Crowns," he murmured.

His was the first voice to break the silence. A

half-dozen heads swiveled toward him. Stone's was not among them.

"Yes?" Stone murmured, his back to Logan.

"Those two devices. We know that, whatever they are, they're meant to be worn on the head. After all, that's the depiction in the painting, back in chamber one."

Stone didn't answer. He merely shook his head.

"There's nothing else they can be but crowns," Logan went on. "They're red and white—the proper colors. They even vaguely resemble the elements of the double crown, based on the depictions we've all seen."

"These aren't crowns," Stone said. His voice was low, distant. "These are the tinkerings of a mad king, indulged by his priests: toys, nothing more. No wonder his descendants broke with his ways."

"They're bizarre, I admit," Logan said. "They're not crowns in any decorative or stylized sense. But they **must** have value—and great value, at that. Otherwise, why place them in the most holy chamber of the tomb? Why seal them in enclosures of such magnificence? Why set such a terrible curse upon them?"

"Because Narmer went insane," Stone said bitterly. "I should have guessed it. Why else would he have himself buried out here, in this godforsaken place, many miles from his own kingdom? Why break with a tradition that would endure for a thousand years?"

"Narmer **was** the tradition," Dr. Rush said quietly. "It was those who followed that broke with him—not the other way around."

During this exchange, Tina Romero had returned to the gold-framed table and was again glancing from one papyrus to another with rapt concentration. All at once she straightened, turned back to the group. "I think I understand," she said.

All eyes swiveled toward her.

"I've said before that the ancient Egyptian pharaohs were interested in near-death experience," she went on. "What they called the 'second region of night.' But if I understand these texts, they were more than just interested. It seems they—or at least Narmer—practiced them as well."

"What are you saying?" Stone asked. "How can you **practice** a near-death experience?"

"I'm simply telling you what the scrolls tell me," she replied, lifting a papyrus as if to hammer home her point. "Again and again, **ib** is mentioned here. **Ib**—the ancient Egyptian word for heart. The Egyptians believed it was the heart, not the brain, that was the seat of knowledge, emotion, thought. The heart was the key to the soul, critical to surviving into the afterlife. But **ib,** as written in these texts, isn't being discussed in religious terms. It's described in more like . . ." She hesitated, searching for the right word. "More like **clinical** terms." She put down the scroll. "I said before these read more like instructions than incantations."

"Instructions?" Stone said, his voice dripping with skepticism. "Instructions for what?"

This was met by a brief silence.

"It sounds like a paradox." Logan turned to Romero. "You say the ancient Egyptians believed the heart was critical for surviving in the next world."

Romero nodded. "Once in the netherworld, the pharaoh's heart would have been inspected, tested by Anubis, in a ceremony known as the Weighing of the Heart. At least, that was the belief of later Egyptians."

"But death occurs when the heart **stops**. How could a stopped heart be of any use to Narmer in the next—" Logan paused abruptly. "Wait. What was it you said earlier? You said that this entire tomb seemed to be almost a rehearsal for Narmer's death, for his passage to the next world. A dry run, so to speak. Right?"

Romero nodded.

Logan looked from her, to the contents of the tomb, and then back to her again. All of a sudden—with a flash like a thunderstroke—he understood.

"Oh, my God," he whispered. "The Baghdad Battery."

For a moment, nobody moved. Then—as slowly as he had dropped to his knees—Stone stood up again, turned, and faced Logan.

"Just before the Second World War," Logan continued, "some artifacts were found in a village just outside Baghdad. The artifacts were very old, and their purpose was unclear. A terracotta pot; a copper sheet in the shape of a cylinder, topped by an iron rod. A few others. They were ignored until the director of Iraq's National Museum stumbled onto them in the museum's collections. He published a paper theorizing that these artifacts—when properly filled with citric acid, or vinegar, or some other liquid capable of generating electrolytic voltage—originally functioned as a primitive galvanic cell. A **battery**."

Everyone remained silent, all eyes on Logan.

"I've heard of all this," Stone said. "That battery was small, weak, perhaps used for the ceremonial electroplating of objects."

"True," Logan said. "It was weak. But it didn't **have** to be."

"Jesus." Romero pointed to the objects sitting at Stone's feet. "Are you implying—"

Carefully, Logan picked up the red-enameled object, topped by the iron rod and the curled piece of copper. Next, he picked up the bowl-shaped marble object, the long filaments of gold trailing. Very gingerly, he placed the red device atop the white one. They fit together perfectly.

"The double crown," Romero said.

"Exactly," Logan said. "But a 'crown' with a very special—even divine—purpose. Note the elements it is composed of. Copper. Iron. Gold. Add lemon juice or vinegar, and you'd have a battery—but potentially much stronger than the one found buried in Mesopotamia."

"That urn in the corner," Romero said. "It smelled like vinegar."

"And those gold filaments," Dr. Rush added. "You're guessing they could serve as . . . electrodes?"

"Yes," Logan said. "Properly placed on the chest, they could be used to stop the heart."

"Stop the heart," Stone repeated. "A dress rehearsal for death."

"Perhaps more than one rehearsal," Logan said. "Look at the extra materials stored in those golden boxes."

Stone held out his hands. Logan carefully passed over the crown apparatus.

"A dress rehearsal for death," Stone repeated. He gave the crown a brief, almost loving caress.

"It might be even more than that," Romero said. "Remember the tremendous importance the ancient Egyptians placed on the heart. By stopping the heart—and then restarting it—it might not only be a preparation for King Narmer, but a validation of his divinity as well."

"Of course," said Stone. "A way to establish, prove, his divinity—and the divinity of his line."

Logan looked at the expedition director. Over the last few minutes, Stone's voice had grown a little more excited, his movements a little more animated. True, this discovery was no jewel-encrusted crown—but in some ways it was even more remarkable.

"And that would explain why the 'crowns' were kept here," Romero said. "In the most sacred and secret place in the tomb, the holy of holies. It explains why such a dreadful curse was placed on the third gate. Narmer must have feared that, if anyone else were to get his hands on the crown—if anyone else were to experiment with making the journey to the next world—he might gain his power, perhaps even supplant him . . . both in this world and the next."

Logan stared at the double crown in Stone's hands. What was it Jennifer had said, during her final crossings? **That which brings life to the dead . . . and death to the living.**

How could she possibly have known about that?

He cleared his throat. Something had just occurred to him—something he almost did not want to mention.

Stone glanced toward him, his hands still grasping the double crown. "Jeremy?"

Logan shrugged. "I can't help but wonder. If this device was an invention of Narmer's, for the pharaoh to use as a trial run for what he'd experience after the death of the physical body, a way of preparing himself for the next world . . ." He stopped. All eyes were on him.

"Given the beliefs of the ancient Egyptians," he went on. "About the nature of the soul, I mean . . . might they not have believed that such a device could release the soul, the life force, from the body—and in so doing, achieve instant immortality?"

The silence that followed this was interrupted by a harsh squawk. One of the security guards plucked a radio from his belt; spoke into it for a moment; listened to the reply, awash in static. Then he held the radio out toward Stone.

"Dr. Stone?" he said. "A message from the surface. They say it's important."

51

Cory Landau sat in the Operations Center, feet up on one of the consoles, swigging from a twenty-four-ounce plastic bottle of Jolt Wild Grape. He'd recently finished reading **The House on the Borderland** and was now well and truly freaked out. His shift wouldn't end for another four hours; he'd brought nothing else to read; and the still, tomblike atmosphere of Operations was getting on his nerves. As a distraction, he'd begun running through video feeds from various locations around the Station, but things were depressingly quiet. There was a lot of activity at the Staging Area, but it consisted mostly of people monitoring various consoles or standing around the Maw. As for the tomb itself, the cameras had been turned off in chamber two—apparently at Porter Stone's request—so there was nothing to see down there, either. A few minutes earlier, there had been some excitement around the archaeology labs in Red, but that seemed to have settled down as well. Basically, the entire Station felt as if it was in a holding pattern, awaiting word from the party that had recently entered chamber three of the tomb.

He took another deep swig, sighed, twirled his Zapata mustache, and cycled through a fresh set of video feeds as if channel-surfing a television. He did not notice Jennifer Rush silently enter the Operations Center. He did not notice as she slowly approached a bank of consoles, then hesitated several moments, seemingly studying them. He did not notice when she lifted a red plastic protective shield on one of the consoles, then snapped the toggle switch beneath it from the on to the off position. He grew aware of her presence only when she turned from the console and, walking away, stumbled into a rack of diagnostic equipment, knocking some loose cabling to the floor.

"Whoa!" Landau said as he wheeled around, Jolt sloshing over his hand. Then he smiled as he recognized Jennifer, the doctor's wife. She was, he'd already discovered, a real babe, but standoffish, with a reserve that had always completely intimidated him. Oddly enough, she was dressed in a hospital gown, but Landau didn't mind—it was, he noticed, quite revealing.

"Hi, there," he said. "Your husband's down with the expedition team, isn't he? You here to watch the return of the conquering heroes? I've got the best seats in the house." And he gestured at an empty chair not far from his, overlooking the central bank of monitors.

Jennifer Rush didn't answer. Instead, she walked toward him, then past him, and then out the far door. She was cradling something in one of her hands.

At first, Landau assumed she was preoccupied, or just plain rude—he'd rarely seen her talk to anybody—rarely seen her, period. Then he'd noticed her opaque, cloudy eyes; her strange, shambling, almost robotic gait, as if the act of walking itself was a novelty.

As her form disappeared down the corridor, he nodded knowingly to himself. "Plastered," he murmured. Not that he blamed her—being stuck out here at the ass end of nowhere was enough to start anybody drinking.

Jennifer Rush continued on slowly, a little unsteadily, past a series of conference rooms, until she stood before the barrier that gave onto the pontoon-supported access tube leading to Maroon. She turned and opened the final door before the barrier, a heavy hatch with a label that read POWER SUBSTATION—WHITE.

The interior was cramped, a forest of thick tubing and small, blinking lights. Along the far wall were rows of dials and gauges, and a technician stood before them, peering curiously at a few, while making notations on a clipboard. At the sound of the hatch opening, he turned. The light was dim, but the technician recognized the woman standing in the hatchway.

"Oh. Hello, Mrs. Rush," he said. "Can I help you with something?"

Instead of answering, Jennifer Rush took a step inside. The faint lighting made her features indistinct.

"I'll be with you in a jiffy," the technician said. "Just let me finish inspecting these controls. It's my duty shift in Methane Processing, and a few seconds ago I started to get some weird error messages." He turned back to the gauges. "Almost as if the safety protocols had been disengaged. But that's impossible, you'd have to deliberately—"

Hearing another sound behind him, he turned back once again. Immediately, the smile on his face vanished, his expression turning to surprise and concern. Jennifer Rush had placed the items she was carrying on the floor, knelt over a bank of heavy valves, and was—once again, movements slow and awkward, but deliberate—turning one of them.

"Hey!" the technician said. "You can't do that— you're opening the emergency relief valve!"

Dropping his clipboard, he hurried over. Jennifer Rush did not protest when he gently propelled her to one side.

"You don't want to be doing that," he said, grasping the valve and preparing to close it again. "Open this, and we'd start venting concentrated methane throughout the crawl space beneath this wing. It would only be a matter of minutes until—"

An explosive impact against the base of his neck—a sudden wave of pain—and then a concussive burst of light that filled his field of vision before giving way to oblivion.

Jennifer Rush watched as the technician crumpled to the metal floor of the substation. Then she dropped the wrench she'd picked up, bent over the relief valve, and once again began to slowly open it wide, turning, turning, turning. . . .

52

Logan watched as Porter Stone handed the radio back to the guard. The conversation had been brief; Stone himself had said fewer than a half-dozen words. As he'd listened to the voice on the radio, his face had initially gone deathly pale. But now—as he looked at each of the expedition members in turn—his face went dark, almost purple. His pupils retreated to mere glittering pinpoints. His gaze fastened at last on Tina Romero.

Suddenly, he stepped forward. **"Bitch!"** he snapped, throwing one hand back in preparation for striking her. Immediately, Dr. Rush and Valentino rushed forward, restraining him.

"Idiot!" he cried, struggling to free himself. Romero took an instinctual step back.

Logan looked on in shock. It was as if all the setbacks and vicissitudes of this expedition—capped just now by the discovery that Narmer's crown was, in fact, completely unexpected and bizarre—had caused the normally dispassionate Stone to snap, to lash out in frustration and anger.

"Incompetent!" Stone shouted at the Egyptologist. "Thanks to you, all my effort, all my money—wasted! And now, there's no time. . . . **No time**!"

Logan came forward. "Dr. Stone, calm down," he said. "Just what exactly has happened?"

With an effort, Stone mastered himself. He freed himself from Rush and Valentino, who nevertheless stayed close.

"I'll tell you what's happened," he said, his breathing loud and ragged. "That was Amanda Richards on the horn. She was repairing the damage to Narmer's mummy—when she learned it **wasn't** Narmer, after all."

There was a moment of shocked silence.

"What do you mean—not Narmer?" Dr. Rush asked.

"That mummy **was a woman**. All this time, we've been working the wrong damned tomb." He looked back at Romero. "No wonder nothing's as it should be. You've led us to the wrong spot—a subsidiary tomb, for his queen, or—or a concubine! My **God**!" His hands balled into fists, and he seemed about to lash out once again. Rush and Valentino moved in still closer.

"Just a minute," Logan said. "There can't be any mistake. The seals, the inscriptions, the treasure—even the curse—everything indicates the resting place of a pharaoh. This **has** to be Narmer's tomb."

For a moment, nobody spoke. Stone struggled to get his breathing under control. "If this is Narmer's tomb," he said, "then where the hell's his mummy?"

"Wait a minute," said Logan. "Just hold on a minute. Don't be so hasty—let's think this through." He turned to Tina Romero. "Haven't you said, all along, that there have been things in this tomb that didn't add up—that didn't make sense?"

She nodded. "Little things, mostly. I ascribed them to the fact this was the tomb of the first pharaoh; it was only natural that we'd find the unexpected. The later tradition hadn't yet been fully established."

"Excuses," Stone said. "Mere excuses, nothing more. You're just trying to explain away your stupidity."

Ignoring this, Romero turned toward Logan. "It first started when you mentioned that skull to me. The one you examined, the skull of one of Narmer's priests, ritually killed to protect the secrecy and sanctity of Narmer's tomb. Do you remember telling me that one of the eye sockets—the left—had scratches?"

Logan nodded.

"And that was just the first sign that something was amiss. The rest of the signs are right here, among us. The serekhs we found in the tomb's royal seals—the glyphs are Narmer's, but they aren't quite right. They have unusual features, like the feminine ending of **niswt-biti**. Then there are those inscriptions in chamber one, with the ritual sequences reversed, the gender wrong. And the glyphs on this chest, here, with the head of the catfish, Narmer's symbol, scratched out."

"You said it had been altered," Logan added. "Defaced."

"What are you getting at?" Stone growled.

"That mark in the eye socket of the priest's skull," Romero said. "I'd assumed it was just decay, damage over time. But the fact is, that was the ritual way a priest or priestess of a **queen** would be killed—a knife through the eye into the brain. That way, symbolically, the queen would not be viewed in death. At the tomb burial of a king, the priests were killed by a knife blow to the base of a skull, severing the spinal column."

"So this is the tomb of Narmer's queen," Stone said. "Niethotep. That's my whole damn point! It's the **wrong tomb**!"

"No, no, you don't understand," Romero replied, a new urgency in her voice. "The evidence is conflicting. Everything about this tomb implies it was built for Narmer, following his royal instructions—except for those particular rituals **that would be carried out after death**. That's where the evidence becomes self-contradictory. The royal seals with the feminine flourishes. The final, ritualistic inscriptions—recall how I said they looked rude? And the mummy itself—I only got the briefest of chances to study it, but I noticed that the cut over the mouth was imprecise, incomplete."

"As if the actual burial ritual was rushed," Logan said.

A faint rumble, almost below the level of audibility, echoed through the chamber. The guards and several of the roustabouts glanced uneasily around at the supporting structure. But the sound appeared to have come from the surface, down to them via the Umbilicus, and after a moment the debate resumed.

"You're not making sense," Stone told her. "All this is hypothetical. Inconclusive."

"I'm not so sure," Logan said. He spoke slowly, thinking through what Tina Romero was saying. "You need to look at all this from another angle. If the crown we found here in chamber three could be used to simulate, **practice** death—in effect, to render a pharaoh immortal, ensure his divinity . . . wouldn't a queen desire that as much as a king? Especially a queen as powerful, as headstrong, as Niethotep was?"

There was a silence.

"You're saying . . ." Stone began. "You're saying

that Niethotep, Narmer's queen—**took Narmer's place** in the tomb?"

"It's the only thing that makes sense," Romero said. "Nothing else explains the conflicting evidence I've laid out for you."

"And it may also help explain why future generations misinterpreted Narmer's symbols and practices," Logan added. "It **wasn't** Narmer in the tomb, he **wasn't** buried in the proper manner. The wife would have substituted herself—and seemingly hastily, even prematurely."

"Then what happened to Narmer?" Dr. Rush asked.

"Who knows?" Romero replied. "Poison. A dagger to the throat, late at night in the conjugal bed. Perhaps killed with his concubines. You know the legends of Niethotep, of how strong-willed, blood-thirsty, and selfish she was. This would have been just her game. Can't you picture it? She may have even waited him out, let him die a natural death. Then she would have accompanied his body here, with their twin sets of retinues, to be present at the rituals of his interment—and then, by a prearranged plan, her guards overpowered his . . . and now his skeleton is lying in the muck of the Sudd, entangled with all the others, and her mummy took his rightful place."

Stone stared at the Egyptologist. The anger, the ferocity, had slowly left his face. "But if you're right about the—the crown," he said, "then only one person could be allowed to use it. If you were Narmer, once you had passed over into the netherworld, you wouldn't want another to take your place, to compromise your life force, your immortality. The crown would be linked to the soul of the person who wielded it."

"Which is exactly what Niethotep must have done," said Romero. "She tricked Narmer, had him killed, used the crown in his place. And then, believing herself immortal, she had herself buried in his tomb, which was hastily converted—the seals, the inscriptions—into her own."

"Is that even possible?" Logan asked. "Isn't a pharaoh's tomb designed to be the resting place for a specific monarch, and only that monarch?"

"That's just the problem," Romero said. "We need much more time to examine the evidence. Maybe she thought the gamble—eternal life as a supreme deity—was worth the risk."

"But why the haste?" Stone asked. "With Narmer out of the way, she could have taken all the time she wanted."

Romero thought for a moment. "I can think of several reasons. Maybe Narmer's main priests, with their private army, were still on the way to the tomb—and they wouldn't have taken kindly to what they found. She had to retrofit the tomb as best she could, seal it up before they arrived. Another possibility is that she and her retinue were unfamiliar with the operation of the battery—the double crown. They may have been . . . overzealous."

"What was supposed to be a near-death experience turned into a deadly one," Logan said.

Romero nodded. "If that was the case—the queen dying unexpectedly—they would have had to rush to get her mummified and entombed. Even to the point of cutting corners in the death rituals. As we've seen in some of the carvings here—the carvings that deal with those specific rituals."

"And if the queen had herself entombed without sufficient preparation?" Rush asked. "Sufficient rites?"

"Impossible to say. I mentioned the imperfect cut in the mummy's mouth. That's an important part of the Egyptian funerary magic: the Opening of the Mouth ceremony. It allows the **ba** to leave the dead body, reunite with the **ka** in the next life. It frees the mouth to accept food and drink so the soul can receive nourishment—in essence, survive—in the afterlife."

"Go on," said Stone.

"If such an important ritual as the Opening of the Mouth was rushed, it implies great urgency involved in the final stages of her entombment. Who knows what other critical steps for the journey of Niethotep's soul into the next world might have been abbreviated—or even skipped?"

"This Opening of the Mouth ceremony," Logan said. "If the queen's soul could not receive nourishment in the next world—what would happen?"

Romero thought a minute. "From the ancient texts, I would guess that her vital spark—the soul that leaves the body after death—would be trapped here."

Rush shook his head. "If she really committed this atrocity—killed her husband or at the very least usurped his place in the next world—I'd think at least a part of her **ka** would want to remain here. To guard the crown, safeguard her immortality, make sure nobody did to her what she did to Narmer."

"The curse," Romero murmured.

Her soul would be trapped here. . . . To guard the crown; to make sure nobody did to her what she did to Narmer . . . All of a sudden, a terrible thought struck Logan.

"Oh, my God," he said aloud.

Suddenly, there was another rumble from above, stronger than before. The papyrus sheets on the table trembled, as if from a gust of wind.

"What the hell is that?" Stone asked.

Valentino turned to two of the roustabouts. "Kowinsky. Dugan. Go out to the platform, see what's going on."

As the two headed back through the tomb, Logan took Rush aside. "We've been forgetting something," he said in a low voice, out of earshot of the others.

The doctor looked at him. "What? What is it?"

"Remember our earlier talk? Where we speculated that Jennifer was brain-dead for so long—that she went over for so protracted a period—that she might have, in essence, lost her soul? Your phrase, not mine."

The doctor frowned, nodded.

"I told you that I believe it possible for the life force of one who has already passed on to take residence in a living being—**if** that being's own life force, own soul, has been compromised. But that in all documented cases, the dead person's spirit can only take possession of someone of the same sex."

"I remember," Dr. Rush said. "That's how we knew Narmer, or some shade of Narmer's, could not be speaking through—could not be within—Jennifer."

"Exactly. But if it isn't Narmer's life force that's here at this site . . . if, rather, it's the life force **of a woman** . . ."

"Queen Niethotep." Slowly, Rush raised a hand to his mouth. "Oh, Jesus . . ."

At that moment, the two roustabouts, Kowinsky and Dugan, came running back. Both had their radios out.

"There's an emergency topside," Kowinksy said. "The emergency relief valves of the high-pressure methane system have been opened."

"What?" Stone said, his voice sharp with anxiety. "Why?"

Kowinsky shook his head. Fear was written clearly across his face.

"You said valves. How many? More than one?"

"At least three. In Red, White, Maroon."

"That's impossible," Stone went on. "The safety protocols—"

"They've been compromised somehow. That's why it was discovered only now. Fires are breaking out in the crawl spaces beneath the wings, there've been explosions, flames are beginning to reach up into the Station itself. And if they're unable to get to those valves in order to shut them off—"

Stone jerked a thumb in the direction of the tomb exit. "Everyone out, get topside. Now!" He took the radio from Kowinksy, snapped it on. "This is Porter Stone. Who am I speaking to?"

"Menendez, sir, in the Staging Area." In the background, Logan could hear shouting, what sounded like the rushing of a blowtorch. "We're sending a team down to you with emergency ropes now."

"We've got close to a dozen people down here," Stone said. "You're going to need to—"

But he was interrupted by a frantic series of cries on the radio, voices overlapping each other, cutting in and out.

"What's that she's got? Nitroglycerin?"

"Get back! **Get back!**"

"Don't let her near the Maw, she'll—"

And then there was a brilliant light from the direction of the Umbilicus, like the flare of a hundred suns—an explosion that pierced Logan's ears and knocked him to the floor of the tomb—and then all went dark and his world ended.

53

Logan didn't know if he'd been out for an hour—didn't know if he'd been out for a day. But as he opened his eyes and tried to rise to a sitting position, shaking his head to clear it, he realized it could only have been a few seconds. The tomb was full of raised voices and the sound of running feet. A handful of tiny emergency lights had come on, bathing the chamber in a sepulchral crimson glow. Rush was bending over him, massaging his wrists and trying to get him on his feet.

"Come on, Jeremy," he said. "We've got to go."

The tomb was beginning to fill with choking, acrid smoke. There was a strange smell in the air: a combination of burning rubber, ozone, and—ominously—methane.

"What's happening?" one of the roustabouts was shouting, in a ragged, hysterical tone. He had a gash on his temple that was bleeding freely. "What's happening?"

What's happening? The words of Narmer's curse came into Logan's mind. **Any man who dares enter my tomb will meet an end certain and swift. The hand that touches my immortal form will burn with unquenchable fire. Should any in their temerity pass the third gate, then the black god of the deepest pit will seize him, and his limbs will be scattered to the uttermost corners of the earth.**

"It's Narmer's queen," he said. "Niethotep. She's trying to preserve her immortality by burying her tomb—the tomb she stole from her husband—all over again. Killing all who would attempt to despoil it—who might attempt to wield the crown. It's the queen—with a little help from Jennifer Rush."

Logan realized that, in fact, he had only thought these words, not spoken them aloud. Ethan Rush was still at his side, urging him to stand. With an effort, he rose to his feet; the world swayed around him, then slowly righted itself. Rush looked intently into his eyes, grunted, then began leading the way out of the tomb.

They left the ebony nightmare of chamber three, passed through chamber two and into the larger space of chamber one. Here, the entire team was clustered around the Lock and the platform that lay beyond. There were no emergency lights here, and several people had their flashlights out, the yellow beams lancing through the thickening air. Numerous radios were chattering, filling the background with a steady, electronic din. Logan could make out the figure of Stone, standing on the air lock platform, starting to direct people up the sloping tunnel of the Umbilicus. One of the security guards urged Stone to make the climb himself, and after a moment Stone relented and went next in line. He was followed by two of the technicians. Then one of the grunts, the one named Kowinsky, forced himself to the head of the line and began climbing frantically, despite the angry shouts of Valentino, who was standing at the rear, urging everyone else on before him.

And now, shuffling forward with the others, Logan found himself ducking through the heavy door of the Lock, past the dressed granite that made up the entrance to Narmer's tomb, and onto the thick metal grating of the air lock platform. Tina Romero was directly in front of him; she looked back, gave him a wan smile, and started to ascend. And then it was his turn. He grabbed the first handhold, looked up in preparation to climb—and stopped dead.

The yellow length of the Umbilicus tube—normally so orderly—was a shocking mess. The heavy cabling that ran down its length had come loose and was hanging limply across the span, like so much viscera. The wooden framework of skeletal bracing was crushed in several places, the overlapping hexagonal beams now just a labyrinth of lumber, and the climbers above him were being forced to thread their way arduously through the planking. Ropes had been dropped by those in the Staging Area above, but in the ruined jumble of cabling and cracked wood they were of little help. In the distance—at the top of the Umbilicus—Logan thought he could make out the Maw itself; but it looked blackened and distorted, its metal edging strangely petaled, as if from the force of some great explosion. But the distance was too great, and the air too thick with smoke, for him to be certain.

But it was the Umbilicus itself that stopped him in his tracks. Its yellow skin, normally so smooth and regular, was distorted into an ugly mass of runaway wrinkles and bulging concavities. At the points where the wooden bracing had partially collapsed, the Umbilicus walls pressed frighteningly in on the half-dozen people overhead, moving one after another like mountain climbers, heading for the surface. The great weight of the Sudd was squeezing in on them from all sides, probing the damaged tube, searching for a way, **any** way, to . . .

Logan felt a pressure on his shoulder. "Come on,

man!" he heard the voice of Valentino say. "Climb! **Sbrigati!**"

Romero was now several feet above him. Logan forced himself to look only at the hand and footholds, to ignore what was above, and to begin the climb. He resolutely refused to look up again, concentrating on putting one hand above the other, first the left, then the right. Below, at the edges of his vision, he saw another technician mount the lowest step, begin to climb. . . .

And then he felt Romero's foot graze the side of his head. Without thinking, he glanced up to see what had stopped her ascent.

As he did so, he heard gasps—and curses—from the climbers above.

He glanced past Tina—and his heart sank. About twenty feet over his head, near the top of the Umbilicus tube, one of the wooden supports—broken in two, its edges like sharp stakes—was being pressed against an inward bulge in the Umbilicus wall, its material weakened by whatever explosion had caused this devastation. Even as he stared in horrified fascination, the yellow fabric met the sharp edges of the wood. A tear formed; first small, then quickly growing, as the external pressure of the swamp found the weak spot and exploited it.

"No!" the grunt overhead, Kowinsky, screamed. "Jesus, **no!**"

And then, with a strange sound that was half a sigh, half a shriek of rending fabric, the wall of the

Umbilicus gave way. And instantly the Sudd poured in: a vomiting eruption of quicksand. Like water traveling the length of a garden hose it came down toward them. Under its irresistible pressure the Umbilicus began to unravel, from top to bottom, a long seam of black that began tearing itself apart with alarming speed, the foul sludge thrusting inward and downward. Cries and shrieks arose from the climbers above—a cacophony of mingled dismay and terror.

Logan did the only thing that came to mind. Instinctively, without thinking, he reached up, put his hands around Tina Romero's feet, then let go of the ladder, sliding down past the climbing tech and falling heavily onto the floor of the air lock platform.

She struggled against him. "What are you doing?" she cried.

"Tina!" he shouted over her protests. "Close your eyes!"

There was a rushing sound; a strange tremor, like an approaching earthquake; a chill puff of cesspool wind—and then they were enveloped in cloying, suffocating, disorienting blackness.

54

In the sudden dark, there was a confusion of sensations: cries; screams of pain and fear; slippery, struggling limbs; the cold, fetid grip of the vile muck as it began piling up in all directions around them. Logan wasn't sure why he'd dropped back to the floor of the air lock platform, the very base of the Umbilicus. A galvanic burst of self-preservation had told him to run from the onrushing foulness of the Sudd, to keep ahead of it at all costs. But almost as quickly as this thought had come, he realized it was madness: they were forty feet below the surface, there were no air tanks or scuba gear at hand, the irresistible submarine pressure of the swamp would quickly fill the tomb, one chamber after another, like a colostomy bag. . . . He quickly shook away this horrible image, as he also did the image that immediately followed it: running, with a half-dozen other panicked people, back to the rear of the tomb, there to wait as the rotting filth came roiling toward them, rising, rising. . . .

There was a violent movement beneath him; a sharp cry. He realized it was Tina Romero, trying to break free of his grip. He let go of her, shielding his eyes from the down-rushing viscous nightmare, digging into his pocket for his flashlight and snapping it on. From their own position—where the bottom of the Umbilicus was affixed to the granite wall of Narmer's tomb—several of the supporting beams from overhead had collapsed and fallen down around them, forming a crude, jungle-gym riot of wood that rose toward the ceiling of the tomb entrance just overhead.

As he swiveled the flashlight around, he noticed that the black foulness of the Sudd was quickly pouring down the length of the ruined Umbilicus, crushing beams and cabling and people alike under its weight. Somebody overhead—one of the techs—disappeared into a boiling, heaving riot of mud, shafts of wood, coilings of metal; for a minute his hands remained visible, covered in blood; then they, too, disappeared into the black storm. The Umbilicus was shaken by an intense tremor, as if the pressure of the tons of swamp roiling down through its length was twisting it in upon itself.

He looked away, started to yell to Tina. As he did so, a gobbet of flying muck hit his face, filling his mouth. He spat it out, retching at the taste—many thousand years' worth of rot and decay—then he grabbed her hand and managed to shout.

"Tina!" he cried, pulling at her and pointing at the tangle of beams directly above them. "Climb! **Climb!**"

Machine Specialist Frank Kowinsky had been lucky. When the Umbilicus tore apart and the Sudd rushed in, the technician climbing the rungs directly above him had slipped and begun to fall, becoming tangled in the floating entrails of cabling that hung everywhere. Kowinsky had used the man's body as part catwalk, part springboard, and he'd managed to launch himself out through the widening rend in the yellow tubing. He knew he'd never be able to climb up through the remains of the Umbilicus itself—one look at the crush of wood and tangle of bodies and oozing black filth above had told him that—but if he could force himself out into the swamp, he could swim and claw his way to the surface. He'd had to fight hard against the inrushing mud, but by using the technician's body as an unwilling fulcrum, he'd managed to grasp at the torn fabric of the Umbilicus and pull himself out, kicking and struggling, into the swamp.

And now he was free. Free of the screaming, struggling death scene within. But he hadn't counted on just how thick and black the depths of the Sudd were; he hadn't paused to think of how its horrible consistency—thick as tar, yet gritty, like sandpaper—would scratch his skin, hurt his eyes. He quickly closed them, but the sharp grit was in them now and there was no way to rinse it away.

No time to worry about that—he had to get to the surface. He took a moment to orient himself in the blackness, and then he began to struggle upward.

As quickly as he could, Logan climbed up through the welter of ruined beams and supporting spars that rose to the ceiling of the tomb entrance. The wood was black and slippery with mud, and it seemed that for each beam he climbed, he slipped back at least two. Now and then he glanced down to make sure Tina was following him.

There was another dreadful shudder, and the entire ruined tube that had been the Umbilicus seemed to bow away from the tomb interface with a groan of protesting metal. The shouts, the screams, the cries for help had all ceased now—and that, more than anything, filled him with despair: there was only the sloppy, splattery noise of the Sudd as it ran down the remains of the yellow tube, quickly filling the tomb and rising around them.

Flashlight held between his teeth, he pulled himself onto the top spar, his head mere inches below the roof of the interface with the tomb entrance. The ceiling of the Umbilicus—where the tube's lowest section met with the air lock—drooped ominously overhead. At this height, the makeshift structure of wooden beams was precarious and unstable, but the unctuous swamp, rising within the tomb and already creeping up his calves, held it in place like black glue. Stabilizing himself against the uppermost metal pylon of the Lock, he reached down and helped pull Tina onto the spar beside him.

In the dim glow of his flashlight, she was barely recognizable, her face, hair and clothes thickly daubed with ordure, her eyes small white points in an otherwise unbroken carapace of muck.

"Now what?" she screamed. "Wait to drown in this shit?"

"We're not going to drown!" Logan cried back.

As he spoke, there was another, still more violent shudder; the two clung to each other as the entire structure trembled, then sheared to one side.

Logan directed his flashlight up, at the point where the fabric of the Umbilicus met the Lock. "That's going to fail any moment!" he said. "When it does—listen to me carefully—**do not panic**. The swamp will come down around us. Whatever happens, hold on to me. Hold on tight. I'll be gripping this pylon, here—it's anchored to granite and basalt, it's not going anywhere."

He tore off his shirt, then undid his belt and shrugged out of his pants. Reaching over, he grasped Tina's shirt and tore it away as well, buttons flying, exposing her bra.

"What the hell are you doing?" she cried.

"Take off your pants," he said. "Quickly. Your clothes—they'll act like weights. You'll never make it to the surface."

She understood immediately, unzipping her fly and slipping out of her jeans.

"As soon as the pressure's equalized, we'll rise. Keep hold of me. Whatever you do, don't get disoriented. Shut your eyes **before** we start upward—that will help you keep your bearings in the mud." He glanced down at the wooden structure beneath them, made a quick calculation. "We've got thirty-five feet of swamp to rise through. Pace yourself. Pace your oxygen. Got it?"

Tina said nothing. She was looking at the muck that was now up to their waists and still rising, thick as a foul, black milkshake.

"Tina!" he shouted. "**Do you understand?**"

The round circles of white in her otherwise black face turned to him, blinked, then rose up and down—a nod. Logan took tight hold of her hand, squeezed it.

"Don't let go," he said.

Just then there came a final, cataclysmic shudder—a rising squeal of metal, stressed beyond endurance—and then the ceiling above them tore away and the black heart of the Sudd descended on them, enfolding them in its noxious embrace.

Frank Kowinksy fought his way up through the muck and ooze. His eyes stung from the grit, and his ears and nostrils were filled with thick silt. The swamp seemed to pull at him, giant invisible hands that tugged at his clothes, trying to drag him down. And there were **things** here in the muddy blackness: sticks and weeds and softer, more slippery things he didn't care to guess at. Some he could use, like hand and footholds, and he made his way up through a slippery universe of mud.

He'd been in this shit now for—what, maybe sixty seconds?—and already his chest was starting to burn. He should have taken a deeper breath when he launched himself out from the Umbilicus. And then, he'd expended precious oxygen just forcing himself out into the swamp. Had that been a mistake? Should he have tried to make his way up through the ruined hell of the Umbilicus? But no—that would have meant certain death.

Mud trickled down past the nape of his neck, down his back, under his arms. It seemed to seep in everywhere, his belly, even his groin. It was too horrible, this blackness, not knowing where he was, not knowing how much farther he had to go, and all the time slowly running out of air. . . .

Suddenly, he hit his head against something, hard. It brought stars to his closed eyes—but it also snapped him out of incipient panic. At first, he thought—hoped—it might be one of the floating pontoons of the Station. But then as he reached out, probing at it with blind fingers, he realized it was a huge chunk of wood, a tree branch, embedded in the quicksand of the Sudd. He shook his head to clear it—shook it as much as the surrounding ooze would allow—then pushed himself away from the chunk of wood, reoriented himself as best he could, and resumed clawing his way up through the black nightmare.

Logan had been utterly unprepared for one thing: the intense, implacable pressure of the Sudd. It pressed in on him like a cold vise: from above, from behind. It squeezed his chest as if trying to force the air from his lungs. For a moment, he just hung in place, an insect trapped in amber, stunned by the overwhelming, awful, claustrophobic sensation. And then, with a mighty effort, he kicked upward, tugging on Tina's hand as he did so. He felt her hand moving back and forth as she, too, began forcing her way upward. He tightened his grip, interlocking his fingers with hers—somehow, he sensed that, if they were to get separated, it would mean death for them both.

He kept his eyes and mouth tight shut, tried to forget the muck that oozed its way into his ears, and he allowed his body to find its own equilibrium as they struggled up toward the surface. He kept his nose clear by blowing out, gently, every few seconds—it had the effect of clearing the mud from his nostrils and also kept him from retaining too much air in his lungs. Now and again, as he flailed with his free hand, he knocked against branches and twigs, caught in the matrix of the Sudd; whenever possible, he used them as hand- or footholds to help force his way upward, all the while keeping a tight grasp on Tina's hand. Once he almost became entangled in the rotting tendrils of some submerged plant. Fighting down panic, he pushed it away, still careful to maintain his equilibrium.

Their upward struggle together, their combined momentum, seemed to make the ascent easier than it would have been for one person alone. Lack of shirts and pants helped coat their bodies in an oil-like slick that counteracted some of the swamp's treacherous downward pull. And yet, all too soon, Logan began to feel Tina's hand twitch and tremble. She was running out of air.

How far had they risen? Fifteen feet? Twenty? It was impossible to tell in this black oblivion. His hand encountered another branch; he used it to pull himself upward, then felt for it with his foot and forced himself up yet again. Now his own lungs were starting to burn. The twitching of Tina's hand became

more urgent; he had to hold on still tighter to keep her
from letting go. Another few moments and either she
would breathe in or go unconscious. He would not be
able to continue to lift her as a deadweight. Already,
he could feel his strength ebbing. They would both
sink down into the endless blackness, and their bodies would join all those of Narmer's train, who had—

All of a sudden, he felt a strange thing. His free
hand was not struggling as much to force its way
through the thick medium of the swamp. He inter-
locked his fingers with Tina's more tightly still,
pulled her toward him, and then—with the last of his
strength—wriggled upward in a sinuous motion, legs
together, as if swimming a vertical butterfly stroke.
And then his head felt the same freedom his hand
had—it could move more easily, no longer encum-
bered by a surrounding matrix of mud. Sputtering,
coughing, spitting mud, he pulled Tina up until she,
too, broke through. They were encrusted with black
mire—creatures more of the swamp than of the dry
land—but they could once again breathe.

They had reached the surface.

Kowinsky was beyond desperate. It had been over
ninety seconds now, maybe two minutes. He was in
decent shape, he worked out regularly, but even so
every atom in his body was now screaming out for
oxygen. He struggled ever more furiously through
the muck and mire. He must be near the surface—he

must. His eyes were wide open now, heedless of the pain. Surely a little light must penetrate this goddamned hell. Surely, any moment, the intolerable blackness around him would get a little lighter, and then a little lighter still, and then . . . air.

It was all he could do to keep his mouth closed. Air, he had to have air. Every movement sent little stabs of agony shooting through his lungs. He was no longer aware of the muck or the stench or the way the swamp sneaked into every orifice, every crevice, even those he hadn't known he possessed. Air was what he needed. **Air.**

Oh, God, it was too terrible. Where was he? Why was it all so black? Why was he still beneath the surface?

In his frenzied thrashings, his hands encountered something. Eyes wide but sightless, his nose dribbling little oily bubbles out into the mud, he probed along it. A hand—an arm—a head. It was a human body, freshly dead. But in his agony, Kowinsky didn't give it a second thought. He pushed it away and struggled forward.

Now his scrabbling hands hit something else—something hard this time, hard and smooth. **Metal.** This was it—at last, he'd reached the Station! Hope, almost gone, surged in him afresh. Another five seconds, maybe ten, and he'd have been a goner. That's how close it had been. He reached out with his other hand, trying to orient himself in the blackness, preparing to heave himself up and out. . . .

And then he noticed something. The hard, smooth piece of metal dead-ended into another—this one curved, studded with heavy rivets. What part of the Station was this? The pontoons were all smooth, and the crawl spaces beneath the various wings had only . . .

And then he felt something else, something attached to one of the rivets. A heavy piece of fabric, slippery, rough at the edges as if it had been violently ripped away.

Reality came crashing down. This wasn't the Station. This was the Lock. Somehow, maybe when he'd hit that chunk of wood, he'd become disoriented in the blackness. He'd turned himself around—and headed back down to the bottom. To the tomb.

No. **No**. It couldn't be true. He had to be hallucinating. It was panic—panic, and lack of oxygen. He'd ignore this illusion, pull himself up, then take that breath of sweet, sweet air.

He grasped the metal spar, pulled himself upward, until it was touching his chest. His movements were still slow, like a fly caught in gelatin, and his eyes were blind—but it didn't matter. He was on the surface now. He **had** to be. He opened his mouth . . .

And in an instant it was filled with a mixture of mire, and silt, and particulate matter, and foul decay as old as the oldest tomb. And despite this most revolting of violations, Kowinsky—in extremis, as his last mortal act—**breathed it in**.

55

They broke free from the prison of mud only to find themselves in a world of fire. Keeping Tina close, Logan swam along the perimeter of the Station, sucking in air in great heaving gasps. Four of the Station's wings—Red, Maroon, White, and apparently Yellow—were ablaze, gouts of flame licking out from below the heavy canvas tarps, eating away the mosquito netting covering the pontoon bridges as if it were strands of silk. The labs and medical facilities of

Red seemed to be burning with special ferocity—the inflatable dome surrounding that wing was strangely aglow, lit from inside a hellish orange-red. As he watched, a huge fireball erupted from its dome, peeling back the canvas covering and rising in boiling clouds of black and crimson to engulf the Crow's Nest. At least a half-dozen boats—tenders, one of the large airboats, other craft—were circling the Station, throwing tall arcs of water toward the flames. But the fire was too intense and the supply of water too limited—the Sudd itself was far too viscous to pulse through the pressurized jets. Logan felt the heat of the blaze hot on his face, baking the already-drying muck of the Sudd, and he turned away.

Now he could make out other figures, half swimming, half crawling through the swamp toward the burning Station. They were encrusted with the same brownish-black mud and impossible to distinguish, but Logan thought that one of them was Stone, another maybe Ethan Rush. They seemed to be making for Green, where Maintenance and the boat basin were located—the roaring inferno had not yet reached that wing. Still helping the exhausted Tina, Logan began to follow in their wake. A Jet Ski, circling the conflagration, spotted them and came over. The rider pulled first Tina, then Logan, onto the rear of his craft, turned, and headed back toward Green, under the protective tarp and into the shelter of the marina. Logan thanked the rider, then helped Tina off the Jet Ski and onto a jetty. He was clad only in his underwear, but with the coating of muck covering his body he could just as well have been dressed in a space suit.

The marina was a scene of barely controlled chaos. The din of shouted commands, shrieking alarms, and grinding engines was intolerable. The air was dense with acrid smoke. Technicians, lab assistants, roustabouts, and even cooks were rushing in from other areas of the Station, many with smoke-covered clothes and faces, carrying documents, foodstuffs, and as many of the precious artifacts from the tomb as could be salvaged. Logan saw at least a dozen evidence containers, piled willy-nilly against one wall. Even the coffinlike locker that held Narmer's mummy—**Niethotep's** mummy, he reminded himself—stood in a corner, listing slightly to one side. Other people were hurriedly carting objects onto the large airboat tied up to a nearby quay. Plowright, the senior pilot, stood beside the boat's forward gangplank, barking orders.

Meanwhile, a few men and women in emergency gear were running out of the marina, back into the deeper sections of the Station, apparently in search of stragglers. A man in a lab coat carrying a blue evidence container in his hands tripped over a coil of rope and fell to his knees, dropping the container. Its lid sprang open and countless gemstones, rings, trinkets, and tiny golden statuettes spilled out, each in a sealed baggie with a printed label attached. Out of nowhere, Porter Stone rushed forward, knelt, and began stuffing the baggies back into the container with fumbling, clumsy movements. He was still completely covered in mud. Sweat—or, more likely, tears—were coursing down his cheeks, leaving thin trails of white in an otherwise unbroken mask of black.

Glancing around, Logan made out Valentino. He was speaking animatedly to a knot of security guards. Instinctively, Logan stepped toward the group. Out of the corner of his eye, he saw Ethan Rush approaching as well. Rush, Stone, Valentino—at least three of the others had escaped the tomb.

"How many casualties?" Logan and Rush asked in unison as they came up to Valentino.

The chief engineer looked at them, mud dripping from his meaty face. "They can't give me exact numbers. Fifteen, maybe twenty, trapped in the flames."

Someone tossed a lab coat at Logan; he shrugged into it, tied it into place around his waist.

"The explosions happened so fast," one of Valentino's men was saying. "The methane built up in the crawl spaces beneath the wings—then it just combusted."

"What happened to the methane system, exactly?" Logan asked.

"Compromised," the man replied.

"Can't the emergency vents be sealed?" Rush asked.

Valentino shook his head. "It's past the point of no return. The only way to the manual overrides is through either Red or White—and they're both infernos. **Impossible.** The firewall's approaching the central converter and storage tank. We have four, maybe five minutes. Then we'd all better be the hell away from here."

"How did this happen?" Logan asked—but even as he asked, he was afraid he already knew the answer.

"We don't know for sure," Valentino's man said. "But we think it was Mrs. Rush."

"Jennifer?" Rush said, going pale beneath his mud-streaked face.

"She showed up at the Staging Area while you all were in chamber three. Had two canisters of nitro. She threw one of them at the Umbilicus. She's still got the other."

"You mean, she's still in there?" Logan asked. "At the Maw?"

"She's been holding everyone at bay with the second canister of nitro," the man said.

"That does it," said Valentino. "I'm giving my last team an order to retreat now—we have to evacuate immediately. Crazy, crazy woman." He turned toward Rush. **"Scusi!"**

But Rush was no longer standing there. He had taken off down the gangway, heading in the direction of Yellow.

"Ethan!" Logan called after him. The doctor, forcing his way through the crowds streaming into the marina, did not look back.

Now the second huge airboat—as if admitting defeat in its fight against the firestorm—was approaching the marina, announcing its arrival with an ear-splitting blast of its horn. Knots of people began lining up along the quay, carrying as many of the priceless antiquities as they could hold. Some of the smaller watercraft had already begun to evacuate the Station, heading north, not even waiting for the big airboats to cut them a path, riding low in the water and mud, overburdened with people and artifacts. Logan turned back, found Tina standing at his side. She, too, had covered herself in a lab coat.

"I'll be right back," he said, then wheeled away again—only to feel her seize his hand desperately.

"**No!**" she cried, wide-eyed.

He took her shoulders in his hands. The shock of the ordeal was just now beginning to take hold of her. "Get in one of the airboats," he said. "I'll be back in a minute." Then he turned, grabbed the radio from Valentino's man, and raced up the gangway in the direction Rush had gone.

56

He tore past the deserted offices, cubicles, and equipment bays of Green. Most of the evacuation seemed to be wrapping up; the labyrinth of hallways was almost completely deserted. It was a matter of two minutes to get through the wing to the barrier at the far end. Ducking through the strips of plastic sheeting, he ran across the covered pontoon bridge to Yellow. The air was worse here, the heat growing increasingly intense.

Another moment and he was through the far barrier and at the Staging Area.

He stopped. The vast space looked as if it had been struck by a tornado. Racks of instrumentation had been overturned, spewing high-tech equipment across the concrete. The leads and power cables that snaked across the floor were blackened and charred, several spitting and arcing sparks. The rows of monitoring equipment were all dark. And the Maw itself, the centerpiece of the room, was a smoking ruin, huge curls of metal peeled back upon themselves, the torn and blackened shreds of the top ring of the Umbilicus testament to the explosion that had doomed the final expedition into chamber three.

And there—before the Maw—was Jennifer Rush. Her hospital gown was torn, and her normally perfectly coiffed hair wild. In one hand, she held up a small red canister that, Logan realized, must contain nitroglycerin.

Ethan Rush was standing about five feet away from her. His hands were reaching out in supplication. "Jennifer," he was saying. "Please. It's Ethan."

Jennifer Rush looked at him, red-rimmed eyes cloudy.

Logan came up behind him, but Rush gave him a signal to keep back. "Jennifer, it's okay. Put down the container and come with me."

She blinked. "Infidel," she said.

As he stood there, Logan felt a chill course through him. He recognized the voice—it was the gravelly, dry, distant voice he'd heard in the two crossings he had witnessed. His impression of a malign presence—which he had first felt at the accident by the generator, and sensed all too frequently since—spiked sharply, and he felt his heart start to hammer in his chest.

"Honey," Rush was saying, "just come with me. Please. Everything's going to be all right." He took another step forward, then stopped again as Jennifer raised the container threateningly.

"Thou hast passed the third gate," she said in that same terrible voice. "Now thou shalt burn in unquenchable fire. And my tomb will be sealed anew—**and for all time**." She retreated toward the Maw, hand outstretched, as if to drop the canister into its depths.

The radio in Logan's hand squawked. He retreated toward the doorway, lifted the radio to his lips. "Logan here."

"Logan!" came the thin, scratchy voice of Valentino. "Get back here. Get back here **now**! I've recalled all search and rescue teams. The fires have reached the central converter, the main storage tank is about to blow!"

Logan put down the radio. "Ethan," he said in as calm a voice as he could manage. "Ethan, we have to go."

"No!" the doctor said, not turning to look at him. "I'm not leaving her. I'm **not** going to let her die—not a second time!"

"Logan!" came Valentino's urgent voice. "That

tank won't last another sixty seconds! The final boats are leaving—!"

Logan snapped off the radio. Now he turned toward Jennifer Rush.

"Your highness," he said. "Come with us."

She turned, red-rimmed eyes swiveling his way as if seeing him for the first time.

"You can leave this place now," Logan said. "You're free. You've won."

For a moment, she swayed, as if from great weariness. A new expression came over her face—one of uncertainty and doubt. She blinked, staring at Logan.

"Jen," Rush said, "he's right. Let's go. Step away from the pit." And he walked to her, arms once again outstretched.

Suddenly, Jennifer swiveled back toward her husband. As she looked at him, her eyes glazed over once again—and a strange smile formed on her lips.

"The pit!" she cried in a great, ringing voice. "The black god of the deepest pit will seize him! **And his limbs will be scattered to the uttermost corners of the earth!**" And then—with a sound that could either have been a bark of victory or a sob of despair, or perhaps a combination of both—she hurled the canister of nitroglycerin toward the concrete floor between her feet and those of her husband.

Instantly, Logan turned away but was knocked to his knees by the force of the explosion. He felt a spray of wet matter stripe its way up the small of his back.

"No," he murmured.

Staggering to his feet, not looking back, he made his way as quickly as he could across the pontoon bridge and through the ruined corridors of Green, the smoke now so thick he could barely see.

The marina was, miraculously, as empty now as it had been jammed with people just ten minutes before. All the vessels were gone. A riot of papyri, scarabs, statuettes, evidence bags, gold figurines, coins, gems, printouts, broken crates, and countless other jetsam—much of it invaluable—lay scattered around the flooring, catwalks, and jetties.

Above the ever-increasing roar of the flames, he heard the honk of a nautical horn. A small tender had just left the dock, the last to depart the Station. Beyond it, Logan could make out a long line of other craft, some large, like the two airboats, others tiny, all stretched out across the Sudd, heading away as quickly as the foul swamp would permit.

The tender honked again, turned around, and approached the farthest jetty of the marina. On impulse, Logan reached down, scooped up a handful from the treasure strewn at his feet, pushed it into the pocket of the lab coat. Then he raced along the catwalk, tore down the jetty, and leaped from its end into the rear of the tender. The little craft banked around and resumed its course, following the caravan of retreating vessels.

"Thanks," Logan said, gasping for breath.

"Better keep your head down," the pilot said in return.

Logan ducked into what served as the vessel's hold: a small space barely large enough for a few life jackets and a spare can of gasoline. And then—with a violence he thought would have been reserved for Armageddon, and Armageddon alone—the Station tore itself apart behind them with a roar that seemed to rend the universe and that turned the sky, and the surrounding earth, as black as night.

57

The motley procession of vessels steamed north in the fading light of afternoon. They had at last left the swampy hell of the Sudd behind and were headed for the upper cataracts of the Nile.

Whether the craft were going to attempt to pass the cataracts and head into Egypt proper, or whether they would land at some intermediate point and relocate the expedition to trucks or aircraft, Logan didn't know—and he didn't much care. After transferring from the tender to one of the large airboats, he had spent the journey staring moodily out of a porthole, watching the passing landscape but seeing nothing, wrapped in a coarse ship's blanket. The overall mood of the ship seemed to match his own: shock, grief, uncertainty. People huddled in small groups, talking in low tones or comforting one another.

As the sun began to set, Logan stirred. He stood up, put the blanket aside, and walked out onto the deck. Not once during the journey had he looked back at the destruction and burning ruin they'd left behind; he did not look back now. Instead, he walked forward in search of coffee. He found some in a cramped galley near the bow. Within were Valentino and a few of his men, standing in a half circle around an espresso machine. Valentino nodded to him and wordlessly passed him a demitasse.

Cradling the cup, Logan walked sternward, then climbed the stairs to the vessel's upper deck. Here he found Tina Romero, sitting on a deck chair, wrapped in her own blanket. She had managed to clean herself up, but in spots her hair was still sprinkled with flecks of dried mud.

He sat down beside her, passed her the espresso. She smiled wanly, took a sip.

As he settled into position in the deck chair, he felt something prick his side. He reached down, felt in the pocket of the lab coat, and drew out a small handful of items. In his palm, carnelians and rubies glowed richly in the light of the setting sun. He had completely forgotten snatching them up in his desperate run for safety. Now, looking down at them, he couldn't imagine why he had done so. Was it some desire—some need—to salvage something from the ruin of the ill-fated expedition? Or something deeper, more atavistic—something to do with the loss of Ethan and Jennifer Rush?

Tina looked over. Her eyes, which had been dull and faraway, brightened somewhat. She reached down, her fingers rifling gently through the artifacts, and picked up a small faience amulet. She held it up to the fading light. It was an eye—seen, as in all ancient Egyptian art, in full face rather than in profile—surrounded above and below by decorative sculpted curls.

"A wadjet," she said over the cry of the waterbirds.

"Wadjet?"

"The story goes that one day, while Horus was asleep, Seth—his great enemy at the time—crept up and stole one of his eyes. When Horus awoke, he went to Isis, his mother, and asked her for another. This was the replacement she made: the wadjet, or healed, eye. It supposedly holds great magical power." She stared at it. "This must have come from Niethotep's mummy."

"How do you know that?"

"Priests wrapped wadjet eyes into the bandages of mummies as a form of magical protection." She turned it on its side, pointing at something.

Logan peered closer. There, engraved, were two images: a catfish and a chisel.

"Narmer," he murmured.

"She appropriated even this," Tina said. She sighed, shook her head, and passed it back.

"Keep it," Logan said.

For a long time, they just sat there, in the slow, healing silence, as the vessel moved north.

"What do you think Stone's going to do?" Logan asked at last. He hadn't seen the expedition's leader since the voyage north began.

Tina glanced at him. "About all this? He'll come out smelling like a rose. He always does. He'll have an interesting story to tell—assuming anyone believes it. But from what I can tell, it appears we managed to salvage a large number of the more important grave goods."

"Salvage? I thought that word was anathema to you."

She smiled mirthlessly. "Normally, it is. But here, we had no choice. The discovery was simply too important to leave to the flames—especially the large number of papyri we recovered. They hold priceless information—even if they do raise more questions than they answer."

"You mean, why Narmer was so far ahead of his time."

"Yes. Why did so many ceremonies, so much art, so many beliefs that we thought didn't develop until many centuries after his time actually originate with him? And what happened to them? Why were they lost for so long?"

"I can guess the answer to that last question," Logan said. And he pointed at the wadjet eye that was still clasped in her hand.

Tina nodded slowly, closing her fingers over the artifact. "At least I won't have to worry about my job. I've got years of research ahead of me."

Another, longer silence settled over them. The sun crept lower, then sank, behind the horizon.

"Why did she do it?" Tina asked at last, in a very low voice.

He turned toward her in the gathering dark.

"What happened to Jennifer Rush?" she asked.

For a moment, Logan said nothing. And then he began to answer—an answer that, he realized, he had been unconsciously rehearsing the entire time they'd been traveling downriver. The comfortable, the orthodox, answer. "Jennifer had certain—psychological issues," he said. "Rush told no one about them. He felt that her unique gifts, the length of her own near-death experience, made her valuable enough to the expedition that it outweighed those issues."

"Valuable to his precious Center, you mean," Tina said bitterly. "Think of the publicity value it would have meant for him."

"No," Logan replied. "I don't think he ever thought about it in those terms. He cared for her—cared for her deeply. But I think his attachment to his research blinded him somewhat. He didn't see, or refused to see, the toll that the crossings were taking on Jennifer."

"In that case, he was blind. I could see it. I **did** see it, that time I witnessed her going over. If Ethan knew she was emotionally unbalanced, he shouldn't have forced her to undergo that. Not once, and certainly not again and again. Especially after her own personal trauma—clinically dead for fourteen minutes. It's no wonder she ultimately came to believe herself possessed by a spirit from the dead."

When Logan didn't answer, Tina fetched a deep sigh. "That time we watched Ethan induce the hypnotic state, ask her all those questions . . . I couldn't help but wonder: What did it feel like for her? I mean, when she came back out of it? Poor Jennifer."

Still, Logan said nothing. He was remembering an earlier conversation he'd had—a very different conversation—with Ethan Rush. **I've been thinking about what you said,** the doctor had told him. **That Jen was brain-dead for so long—that her NDE was so protracted—that, in essence, she might have lost her soul.**

Fourteen minutes . . .

"Came back?" he said at last. "We don't know what came back." But his voice was so soft that Tina did not hear it over the thrum of the engine and the lapping of the waves.

AUTHOR'S NOTE

While research for **The Third Gate** drew on many factual sources, Egyptologists will note that I have not hesitated to alter numerous relative dates, rites, beliefs, and many other facets of ancient Egyptian history—both general and specific—in the service of this novel. And while the Sudd is most certainly a real place, I have also altered various geographic, political, and temporal aspects of the swamp, returning it to the kind of unearthly place described so vividly in Alan Moorehead's **The White Nile.**

Be that as it may, **The Third Gate** is a work of fiction, and all characters, events, and particulars in the novel are entirely imaginary.

Many people helped see this book to its conclusion. In particular, I want to thank the endlessly patient and enthusiastic Jason Kaufman, as well as Rob Bloom, Douglas Preston, Greg Tear, and Eric Simonoff.

ABOUT THE AUTHOR

Lincoln Child is the **New York Times** bestselling author of **Terminal Freeze, Deep Storm, Death Match,** and **Utopia,** as well as coauthor, with Douglas Preston, of numerous **New York Times** bestsellers, most recently **Cold Vengeance** and **Gideon's Corpse**. He lives with his wife and daughter in Morristown, New Jersey.

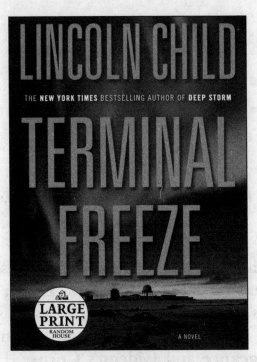